COLD WAR TWO

Ed Bowie

solus

COLD WAR TWO by Ed Bowie

First published in Great Britain in 2017 by Solus

Copyright © Ed Bowie, 2017

Ed Bowie has asserted his right under the Copyright, Designs and Patents act 1988 to be identified as the author of this work. This book is a work of fiction and, except in the case of historical fact, any resemblance to actual persons, living or dead, is purely coincidental.

ISBN: 9781973247890

solus

For
Will

Humboldt Glacier, Greenland

Christmas Day

The walls of the cabin warped and buckled as they were buffeted by the relentless storm. Outside, in the soul-crushing darkness of the Arctic winter it was midday – but it might as well be midnight.

Inside, four men stared intently at a faint, flickering screen: a long wavelength image, sent down from a drone hovering precariously in a layer of calm air, thirteen miles above them; its signal deliberately weakened – so weak it barely reached the receiver.

Every thirty seconds Warren pressed "zero" on his keyboard, then "enter". No contact. He'd been doing the same thing for the last three hours:

Zero – Enter ... No contact.

His control, sitting in a command centre three thousand miles away, was receiving a string of zeros – nothing more. Transmitted in a trillionth of a second – too fleeting to be traced. Low technology: no codes, no encryption, no scrambling – nothing for the Enemy to work on. One single bit of information – meaningless without context. Only his control knew what the basic commands "one" and "zero" meant.

Zero – Enter ... No contact.

From time to time the other men shot furtive glances in his direction. Warren had got it wrong. Everyone had trusted him, everyone had believed in him – and he'd got it wrong. The consequences could be catastrophic.

No, there was no "could" about it – they were staring at a disaster.

Warren went over the timings in his head: he'd allowed the first sixty minutes in case the target was ahead of time; the second sixty was when he expected it to get here; the third was a contingency in case it had been delayed.

The third sixty was up ten minutes ago.

Zero – Enter ... No contact.

Peary looked up from the screen: 'Shall we call it, sir?'

Warren shook his head: 'Not yet,' he replied calmly, even though his mind was racing – what the Hell had happened? Had they been spotted? That was unlikely – they'd set up their base under the wreckage of an old, burned-out B17 bomber that had made a forced landing on the glacier during World War Two. From above everything looked exactly the same as it had for decades.

What if they'd spotted them while they'd been out on the ice? It was a possibility – the Russian satellites were set in high trajectory *Molinya* orbits, which meant they had more than eight hours over the Arctic Circle in any twelve hour period. But that came at a severe cost in resolution: they couldn't detect anything as small as a human being on the ground. But, just to be on the safe side, Warren had arranged their work details to coincide with the two-hour blind spots that occurred twice every thirty-six hours. They were never out in the open when the satellites passed over.

And, anyhow, they'd have known if they'd been spotted – they were getting the satellites' transmissions, just the same as the Russians were.

Zero – Enter ... No contact.

Where was it?

The target had left its base on Ara Bay, in the Murmansk Oblast, forty-five hours ago. It was tracked as it passed north east of Svalbard, moving at thirty knots and turning due west. Then it'd disappeared under the ice. That was twenty-four hours ago.

Zero – Enter ... No contact.

It should be here by now.

What if it'd carried on west under the magnetic pole and down to the Queen Elizabeth Islands – or made a run straight for the Bering Strait? No. That was ridiculous. The ice that way was unpredictable: the northern channels would be completely frozen-up – and the strait was so closely watched you couldn't get a rowing boat south of the 66th parallel without it being blasted into matchwood.

So, where was it?

Another thirty seconds passed. Warren was beginning to doubt himself.

Zero...

A dark, fuzzy smudge insinuated itself into the top right corner of the screen. Slowly it resolved into an indistinct, cigar-shaped object. After a few seconds it detached itself from the screen edge, then started creeping diagonally down, making for the bottom left corner.

It was coming.

'Bloody Hell...' Peary whispered under his breath.

Backspace – One – Enter. Contact.

It was like the worst sort of computer game: if the cigar-shape made it all the way down to the bottom of the screen it was game over – you lose.

But this wasn't a computer game: the cigar-shape was a planter – a Borei-class submarine – moving fast under the ice on the strong underwater current that ran down the Kennedy Channel between Greenland and Ellesmere Island, making for the Kane Basin and the open sea beyond.

The Borei-class was still the last word in Russian submarine technology. At 170 metres long and weighing in at 24,000 tonnes, they were slightly smaller than the Typhoon class they'd replaced. But they were fast. Borei had been tracked at fifty knots underwater, which was unheard-of for a submarine. When they were first built they'd been fitted with a D-19M missile complex and a rack of twelve R-30 Bulava ICBMs – but nowadays they carried a smaller, dirtier, far nastier payload.

If this one broke out into Baffin Bay it could hug the Labrador coast, go round Newfoundland and run right down the Eastern Seaboard, leaving a trail of lurking destruction in its path. Or it could steer west through Lancaster Sound and lose itself in the myriad archipelago of islands above northern Canada, hiding out for months until the time was ripe to make its move: skulking, biding its time – holding the whole North American continent to ransom.

Warren watched as the cigar-shape crept down the screen. It was just clear of the channel now, moving out into the Kane Basin.

Dern, the weapons specialist, swung his seat round to take up his station at another screen.

'All OK and ready to go, sir,' he said, checking his instruments.

Warren nodded in acknowledgement, but said nothing.

'Sir?' Dern persisted.

'Wait.'

It was too early. If they tried to take it now, there was a chance the target could escape back up the Kennedy Channel – back under the polar ice cap – and they'd never see it again.

He had to be patient – he had to wait.

But what if the primary system failed? What then? Would there be enough time to deploy the secondary? It was a gamble. The target had to be destroyed – that went without question. The problem was, the primary system had never been tested – there was no guarantee it would even work.

But if they deployed the secondary, the Russians could interpret that as an act of war...

Suddenly the screen went blank – they'd lost the signal from the drone.

All faces turned to Warren – what should they do now?

Warren closed his eyes and tried to visualise the cigar shape as it moved down the screen, roughly one mile every seventy seconds. He checked his wristwatch, feeling his heartbeat synch with each movement of the second hand as it crawled round the dial.

Tick... tick... tick: one minute... two minutes... three...

The sub was approaching the middle of the Kane Basin – he knew it – he could feel it.

It was time.

Warren nodded.

Dern engaged the primary system. Sonic disrupters, located all along a seventy-mile fault in the Humboldt Glacier, started to vibrate – slowly increasing in intensity, until a single standing wave resonated all along the fault. They could feel the ice moving underneath them, even though they were more than ten miles away.

Warren felt the pressure building in his ears as the air in the cabin was compressed by a solid wall of sound.

Then, suddenly, it was gone. Moments later everything was thrown into confusion by the whiplash force of an icequake, running all the way up the glacier. The wreckage of the bomber above them groaned and shrieked as it was tossed about like a tin can in a fountain. Inside the cabin the four men thrashed and crashed around their little wooden box, desperately clinging onto their equipment.

Stewart, the youngest and smallest man in the team was thrown right up into the air, spread-eagling him against the ceiling, before he fell in a tangled bundle of legs and arms – right on top of Warren.

'Oh, my word,' Stewart muttered, apologetically, his mop of blond hair flopping over his eyes. 'I'm awfully sorry, sir – are you alright?'

'I'm fine,' Warren replied, half-smiling. Stewart was always ridiculously polite.

A minute later, just as they were recovering themselves and putting stuff back into place, a deafening, screeching, rumbling roar tore through the air.

In his mind's eye, Warren tried to imagine the spectacle as an iceberg the size of Long Island detached itself from the glacier and fell crashing into the sea: billions of tons of ice sweeping all before it, triggering a tsunami of such force and violence that it would crush everything in the enclosed waters of the Kane Basin.

Locked beneath metres of winter ice, with nowhere to escape to, the underwater pressure would build instantly to intolerable levels. He tried to conceive of the horror inside the submarine as its twin-skinned titanium hull buckled and crumpled under the irresistible pressure bearing in on it from all sides.

But of course there wouldn't have been any horror. The crew would have perished instantly – crushed like insects – a hundred lives snuffed out in the space of a heartbeat: fathers, sons, brothers – all gone.

Warren felt sorry for their passing – but their deaths meant that millions of lives would be safe.

The screen flickered back into life – they'd reacquired the signal from the drone. The image showed what looked like three separate dark smudges, slowly drifting away from eachother. The submarine had broken up.

Warren reached across to the keyboard, and pressed:

Zero – Enter...

No contact.

*

'We've got to work fast,' Warren said, shrugging his heavy down-filled parka over his shoulders. 'Pretty soon this whole area's going to be crawling with TV environmentalists, eager to denounce man's latest outrage against the planet.'

Peary grinned: 'I can see the headline now: "Humboldt Glacier — latest victim of global warming"...'

'That'll get them another decade's worth of funding for their projects,' Stewart added, jamming on his crash helmet.

Warren pulled his gauntlets over his mittens: 'We've got two hours 'til the next satellite passes over. The Russians are going to be watching this area like hawks, scouring every little bit of detail to find out what's happened to their missing sub.'

Peary and Dern sped off south on their snowmobiles, Warren and Stewart went north. They had to account for every single disruptor – either bring them in, or make sure they'd been lost or destroyed when the ice sheet had broken away.

No evidence – nothing to see. Plausible deniability.

Warren knew it wasn't going to be easy, working in the dark with temperatures hitting minus thirty-five. At least the storm had passed – a fifty knot wind would have added another fifteen degrees of wind chill, and that would've made staying out in the open for two hours impossible.

But he hadn't reckoned on the destructive force of the quake. It had thrown up new ice cliffs, opened new faults and awning chasms that threatened to swallow up their snowmobiles in the blink of an eye. All their familiar routes down to the fault had just disappeared.

He glanced down at the distance/time display on his visor. They'd been out half an hour and they were still two miles from the location of the first disruptor. He slowed down to a stop and checked to see that Stewart was doing likewise.

'We're not going to do it,' he said, speaking into his short-range communicator. 'Not in one go, anyway. You take seven and eight – I'll get nine and ten.'

'Aye-aye, skipper,' Stewart replied, cheerily.

'Stewart,' Warren warned him. 'Don't do anything stupid...'

'What, me sir?'

'Yes, you. Keep an eye on the time. Getting back to base before the next satellite is more important than bringing in another disruptor. Got that?'

'Loud and clear, sir!' Stewart saluted, bringing his huge-mittened hand up to his crash helmet – then tore off into the darkness.

Warren watched him go. He didn't like splitting up. Being out here alone was courting disaster. He'd already lost one man: Tanner, the team's artificer. He'd been out surveying the fault with Stewart and the ice just opened up under him. By the time Stewart got to the chasm there was no sign of Tanner or his snowmobile — he'd just disappeared.

It was dangerous, foolhardy, even – but he didn't have any choice. They had to get the disruptors. There'd be another window in sixteen hours time. If he could get nine and ten now – maybe even eleven and twelve if he pushed himself – and the others had done the same, they might be able to retrieve the last ones in the next window.

And, with a bit of luck the storm would close in again – and that would keep the dratted environmentalists at bay for a while.

*

One hour forty-five. Warren was nearly back at base. He was feeling pretty pleased with himself – he had nine and ten in the panniers of his snowmobile and twelve was strapped over the top. Eleven had completely disappeared. In fact, not only had the disruptor disappeared, everything around it for a radius of about half a mile was just open water now.

He hoped it'd fallen, crushed and shattered, into the sea – but he couldn't help wondering if it was just sitting out there, somewhere in the darkness, bobbing around on an ice floe in the Kane Basin. But there was nothing he could do about that. Warren reminded himself that even if it was sitting on a whole island of ice there was precious little chance of it ever being found.

His communicator crackled into life: 'I say, skipper – that was fun!'

'That you Stewart?'

'Certainly is!'

'How did you get on?

'Eight and six. No sign of seven. I had time to go for five, but I thought I'd be treading on the other chaps' toes.'

'Have you heard anything from them?'

'Not a dickey-bird, skip. Thought I might come within range of them, but they must've gone further south... Whoa!'

Warren's communicator fell silent.

'Stewart?'

Silence.

'Stewart? Are you OK?'

'Phew! That was a close one! We've got a new crevasse – about half a mile West-North-West of the base.'

'I'll look out for it. Sounds like you're just ahead of me.'

'I'll wait for you, sir. It's a bit tricky to spot. See you in a sec. Out.'

He could already see the red tail light of Stewart's snowmobile. He was pressing his brake pedal up and down, so it flashed like a beacon.

But further ahead Warren could see another light – a searchlight.

It was coming from the base.

The base didn't have a searchlight.

Warren pulled up next to Stewart and pointed at it. Stewart nodded: he'd seen it too. The two men picked their way forward slowly, in low gear, cursing each time the Kevlar tracks of their snowmobiles span on the ice, sending their engines racing – even though the noise was swept downwind, away from the base by the strengthening storm.

When they were only a couple of hundred yards from the base they dismounted and crept closer. The light was coming from the nose-cone of a ski plane, which was pulled-up right next to the wreckage of the old bomber. Its twin engines were still running, throwing up flurries of ice that sparkled in the searchlight beam. There was no sign of any other movement. Whoever they were, they were either in the plane, or else they'd found the concealed entrance to the cabin.

They crouched behind a wind-sculpted ice-hummock, just beyond the range of the searchlight.

'What do we do now, sir?' Stewart asked over the communicator.

'Warn the others,' Warren replied, thoughtfully, weighing up his options – none of which seemed particularly attractive. 'They can't be far away...'

A strange voice cut in on him:

'Commander Warren – is that you?'

'Who's that?'

'Myers, sir. Lieutenant Myers, USAF. I've come to bring you in.'

*

Warren was furious: he practically dragged the pilot out of the cockpit.

'What the Hell do you think you're doing here?' he yelled over the drone of the engines. 'Don't you know there's a satellite coming over!'

'S-sorry, sir,' Myers stammered. 'B-but I've got orders to take you back to Thule – there's a flight waiting to take you directly to the JWC.'

'What – *now*?' Warren was dumbfounded – what did the Joint Warfare Centre want him so urgently for?

'Yes, sir.' Myers glanced at the plane's chronometer. 'In fact in the next five minutes – before the satellite...'

'But we can't leave. We haven't got all the disruptors in. Two of my men aren't even back...'

'My orders are for you only, sir – your team stays put.'

'Don't worry,' Stewart chipped-in, cheerfully. 'We'll get the rest of them. Shouldn't take more than a couple of sorties, maybe just the one. We'll all be back home in time for Hogmanay.'

The pilot glanced anxiously at the chronometer: 'We've got to go, sir – now.'

'What about my kit?'

'We'll look after it for you,' Stewart reassured him. 'Now off you go – it'll be nice not to have to put up with your snoring for a few nights.'

There was nothing else for it. Warren clambered into the plane, then turned and rapped his knuckles on Stewart's crash helmet.'

'Sir?'

'I got you Christmas presents. They're in my locker – the combination is...'

'Don't worry, sir – we all know it. Merry Christmas.'

'Merry Christmas.'

The pitch of C41-A's twin engines picked up as it slithered forward on the ice, gathering speed as it went. Myers pointed his aircraft straight into the eye of the strengthening storm and glanced at the chronometer.

'One minute...' he muttered through gritted teeth, as he pushed the engine controls to full power. '...Better get this heap of junk airborne.'

The plane rumbled into the darkness. Its engines snarled and resonated, the wings vibrated alarmingly as they took the force of the driving wind. Then, with a sick-inducing lurch that nearly flipped them over, the storm swept them up into the sky.

Warren gazed down into the darkness below. There was no sign of the base – no sign of anything at all. He flipped his visor to night vision. Stewart was still there, glowing a dull green – barely warm – the only thing that registered down there.

He was waving.

*

NATO Joint Warfare Centre
Stavanger, Norway

After spending so long in the seemingly endless Arctic night, it felt weird to see the sun rise again, shining through the windscreen, straight into his eyes, dazzling him – a great, glorious, golden ball. It wouldn't rise over the Humboldt Glacier until mid-February, and even then it would only just clear the horizon before it sank again, plunging the frozen world back into darkness.

Warren glanced at his wristwatch – he was keeping it on Greenland time. He'd been travelling for sixteen hours — the next window was just about to start. He imagined his men struggling into their cumbersome polar gear, going through their pre-sortie checks, the familiar routine. Soon they'd be setting out on their snowmobiles to bring in the last of the disruptors. Out into the dark. He wished them luck.

But they'd all be seeing the sunrise again, pretty soon.

*

To the outside world, the NATO Joint Warfare Centre looked like a medium-sized office development, its sports courts suggested maybe a small college campus. It was only when you realised it was built into the looming, wooded mass of Mount Jåttå, towering behind it, that you began to guess at its real function.

Mount Jåttå had always been a fortress, ever since Viking times. It was the highest point for miles around and had a commanding view over Stavanger and the fjord that surrounded it. The Nazis had appreciated its significance and employed an army of slave labourers to excavate a complex system of tunnels and bunkers, right into the very heart of the mountain. It was the headquarters of the Norwegian military for about forty years, then they handed it over to NATO back in the 1990s. During the next thirty years or so its function had gradually metamorphosed into something like its current role.

In happier times the JWC had indeed been a campus. In fact it was still listed as a NATO training facility. In the most basic terms, it taught the military leaders of the different NATO countries how to work together – which, in itself, was no mean achievement.

But there was one small part of its remit that just kept on growing and growing, so much so that it was gradually taking over the whole place. From its inception, the JWC had been identified as the NATO centre for all: "developmental and experimental work on new concepts and technologies" – and that was why Warren had been ordered to report here.

He'd done an eighteen-month assignment at the JWC, about five years ago. As his driver turned left, off the familiar suburban street he used to travel along every day, he was surprised to see that the flimsy low-key barrier they all used to joke about, had been replaced by a formidable gatehouse complex – more in keeping with a middle-eastern embassy than sleepy-town, south Stavanger.

His driver pulled right into the visitor processing bay. Warren got out and approached the trooper who was beckoning him forward. He handed her his ID, which she scrutinised carefully.

'No baggage, sir?' she asked.

'I'm travelling light,' Warren replied. At Thule they'd exchanged his polar gear for a set of fatigues and a parka. Apart from his ID the only thing he was carrying was a single-use toothbrush – which he'd used twice already.

'OK,' the trooper said, pointing to a frosted glass door that clicked open. 'You go through there.'

And so began the tedium of fingerprints, facial and retinal scans, DNA swabs – and having his ID chip read. He always hated that last one: it reminded him of when he was a kid – when only pets had ID chips. Finally, when they were satisfied he was who he said he was, they allowed him to get back into the waiting car, which took him on up to the main complex.

At least the civilian staff at the reception area hadn't changed – they were still as inefficient as ever. No, they didn't have a pass for him. And no, his own pass wasn't valid here – even though they'd issued it from this very desk, five years before. Yes, they could see he had orders to report to JWC. But no: no-one had told them he was coming – and, no, they hadn't arranged any accommodation for him.

When he asked them to call and get someone down here, they stared at him blankly: didn't he know it was Christmas?

It was impossible. He was just about to give up and get the driver to take him back into Stavanger, when he felt the weight of a heavy hand on his shoulder.

'You're early, Warren. I thought I'd be here before you.'

He recognised the voice immediately, and turned to greet his old friend and mentor:

'Leo...' His face must have registered his surprise: he'd never seen General Morgan in civilian clothes before.

The general looked down at himself and laughed: 'I'm supposed to be on vacation 'til New Year – Agatha's sent everything to the cleaners.' He shrugged and held out his hands in a gesture of hopelessness: 'So ...'

'It's good to see you,' Warren said, shaking the general's huge paw and allowing himself to be enveloped in the big man's familiar bear hug.

Brigadier General Leonidas S Morgan was a man with fire and iron running through his veins. A direct descendant of General Daniel Morgan, one of George Washington's most successful commanders – who was himself a descendant of the privateer Henry Morgan – every generation of his family had served in the armed forces of the United States of America. Even now, his daughter Amy was a cadet at West Point.

His father had insisted on naming him Leonidas, after the Spartan king who died with three hundred of his followers, fighting the Persians at Thermopylae. Leo himself had adopted the "S" in his name, in honour of his heroes and role-models: George S Patton, Ulysses S Grant and Winston S Churchill.

He shared many of their best characteristics: he was tough, resourceful, uncompromising and clear-sighted – but, like them, he was also irascible and intolerant of time-wasters. For all these reasons Morgan was unpopular with his peers in the general staff, and had often been passed over for promotion in favour of officers who were easier to work with. But

Morgan didn't mind one bit. He was head of NATO New Concepts and Technologies – NCAT – and that suited him just fine.

'What's all the urgency for, Leo?' Warren asked as the general led him past the reception desk. 'We were just finishing up on the glacier. Another day and we'd...'

'I know, and I'm sorry. I don't like leaving a job half done any more than you do...' He paused as he placed his palm up to a biometric reader on a door: 'Morgan – plus one,' he recited into a microphone. 'Put your hand up to it. It's the last bit of security...' He chuckled: 'until you try and get out, that is.'

Daylight disappeared on the other side of the door. Warren remembered this part of the building well. An internal atrium, its revolutionary design incorporated slate-grey translucent walls, that emanated a slate-grey light. The overall effect – which was designed to be both serene and calming – radiated only gloom and despondency.

'I'd almost forgotten how crap this place was,' he muttered.

'Yeah,' Morgan agreed. 'They say the architect was a communist...'

Warren smiled: the same old joke – at least that hadn't changed. It was a possibility, he supposed: there must have been a few die-hard communists around in those days. But the term didn't have any meaning now. The world had moved on. The fault lines of their present-day conflicts had nothing to do with ideology.

Morgan ushered him through the atrium and up a long staircase that Warren didn't remember. He tried to think what had been here before. He was pretty sure it'd just been a blank, slate-grey wall – obviously they'd been doing some more burrowing while he'd been away.

At the top of the staircase a pair of steel doors slid open to reveal a vast conical-shaped room that he realised must have been excavated right up into the peak of the mountain.

The general turned as if to speak to him. Warren stared at him – his lips were moving, but no sound was coming out of his mouth. Morgan grinned and handed him a short-range communicator.

'...Good, isn't it?' he said, his booming voice reduced to an almost comical squeak by the earpiece. '100% soundproof – had it designed myself.'

'Very impressive. No security to get in?'

'Oh, yeah – plenty. We were scanned six times as we came up the stairs. If we'd failed, the stairs would've opened up and dropped us both into a bath of concentrated sulfuric acid.'

'Sounds a bit extreme.'

Morgan shrugged: 'Only joking. I tried to get it incorporated into the design – but there were a few health and safety considerations...'

Warren looked around. The room was completely empty except for what looked like a large matt black igloo in its very centre. 'So what is this place?' he asked.

The general didn't reply, he just motioned for Warren to follow him into the igloo.

Inside there were six immersion seats, ranged around a circular table.

'You don't need a communicator in here,' Morgan said, sitting down and taking his off — and indicating that his friend should do likewise. 'This is the only place that's safe to talk...'

The general placed his palms flat down on the table and stared at them for a long moment. When he finally raised his eyes, Warren was surprised: for the first time in all the years he'd known him, Brigadier General Leonidas S Morgan actually looked scared:

'I'm sorry to have to tell you this, Warren – but I think we could have one Hell of a problem.'

*

Five hundred feet beneath them, in the subterranean chambers at the base of the mountain, Siv Jagland was just starting her shift in the surveillance centre. She wished she hadn't signed up for this roster, but it always fell to the child-free members of the team to cover Christmas – they got their time-off to celebrate at New Year.

But being child-free didn't mean Siv didn't have a family – in fact she had an enormous, raucous, totally ridiculous family. Her father was one of seven brothers and every year they all got together at one of their houses. This year it'd been her parents' turn to host the Jagland horde. The other six families, plus her grandparents, had descended on them on Christmas Eve – and each family had brought their own supply of powerful, home-made *akvavit*.

Their Christmas tradition of sampling each family's offering – and deciding on a winner – was the main reason why Siv hadn't wanted to do this shift. Twelve hours in the darkness, staring at a wall of images from twenty satellites – while nursing a pounding hangover – was something she could really do without.

'Morning Per,' she said, dumping her bag and parka on her desk. 'Good Christmas?'

'Very funny,' Per Eisenträger grunted. 'I've been on duty since 2100hrs yesterday – what sort of Christmas do you think I've had?' He glanced up at his co-worker: 'Christ, Siv – you look like shit.'

'Yeah, I know. I had to stop the car on the way here to throw up.' She went to pour herself some coffee. 'Anything interesting?' she asked, expecting the usual reply.

'Yep. Plenty.'

'What?' Siv stopped pouring and stared at Eisenträger in amazement.

'Lot of action round Northwest Greenland. Big chunk of glacier broke off and wrecked some Russian boat...'

'What's a Russian doing there?' she asked, focussing all her attention on the bank of screens – her hangover forgotten.

'Search me. But they've got planes flying all over – ships coming in from every direction – and not just Russians, I'm thinking.'

'OK,' she replied, thoughtfully. 'What are the orders of the day?'

'Just keep looking at this, going through all the wavelengths. That's it. There's a big storm over there right now. Met says it's going to last twenty-four hours at least, so I'm right down in the long wave and using all the enhancement I can get. It's not very good...' he pointed to the central screen. 'This is what we're looking at. It's called the Kane Basin...'

'What? You mean it's the Humboldt Glacier that's calved? That's ridiculous – it's midwinter!'

'Oh yeah, I forgot – glaciers are your thing, aren't they...' Per Eisenträger shrugged. 'Well, anyhow – if you get anything interesting, anything at all – you've got to let General Morgan know straight away. That's orders straight from the top. OK?'

'Yeah, I got it...' Siv replied, distractedly, waving him away. 'You get off now. You've had a long shift...'

Already she was totally engrossed in her work: her eyes flicking between the images that flashed up in front of her, cross-referencing satellite feeds, modulating frequencies, tweaking resolutions, trying different enhancements.

Per picked up his things and bade her goodbye as he left.

Siv didn't even notice.

*

Morgan tapped the circular table and immediately it lit up.

'Load latest,' he said, as if he was speaking into the table itself. An image flashed onto a circular screen that occupied the whole table. Warren recognised it straight away. It was the Kane Basin, with the submarine just about to reach the point where they'd deployed the primary system – except this image was infinitely brighter, clearer and crisply-defined.

'Run sequence,' Morgan muttered, staring, as though he was almost hypnotised by it.

'So, this is your attack sequence from yesterday...'

Warren marvelled at the images as they unfolded before him. The interval between each one looked to be about fifteen or twenty seconds, so it appeared to take on an almost animated feel.

'You left it pretty late...' Morgan observed as the fault began to open up and the end of the glacier started grinding down into the sea.

'We were running blind.'

'You were ...What?' Morgan demanded, angrily.

'We'd lost the signal from the drone. I had to estimate its position...'

'Who the Hell was your eyes-in-the-sky?'

'Stewart.'

'Never heard of him.'

'He's new. Just a kid. It wasn't his fault – there was a storm raging...'

'There's always a storm – and there'll be one Hell of a storm when he gets back...'

Morgan's anger passed as quickly as it'd erupted. Right now he had more important things to think about: 'OK. Watch closely. Here comes the break-up.'

Warren watched in rapt fascination as the submarine seemed to crumple and then rupture – like a rotten banana splitting apart. He was amazed to see that the ice wall hadn't even touched it – so intense was the pressure that'd built up as it crashed into the sea.

'Pause sequence,' Morgan pointed at the wreckage. 'There – what do you see?'

Warren stared at the point where the general was pointing. Two thin cylinders, shaped like party candles, had been forced out from the waist of the dying sub.

'Any ideas?'

'They look like ICBMs.'

'That's my interpretation also.'

'But I thought they didn't have any...'

'That's what we all thought. But there they are, large as life – and a million times more deadly.'

*

Siv was flipping back and forth between images immediately before and after the catastrophe. She wanted to know why the Humboldt had suffered such a spectacular fracture. Glaciers generally tended to advance in the winter, then start calving-off icebergs as they retreated in the Arctic summer.

Just the scale of the thing was almost incomprehensible. The broken-off sheet was fifteen kilometres wide and over a hundred kilometres long. If it turned up on the Norwegian coast, the thing would stretch all the way from Stavanger to Bergen.

It couldn't be right... Something else must have caused it. Maybe it wasn't the glacier that destroyed the ship: what if something had happened to the ship – and that'd triggered the breakup of the glacier?

She switched over to the alpha-gamma range.

'Whoa!' she exclaimed, nearly falling off her seat. The whole western shore of the basin was lit up like it was decorated with fairy lights. It was riddled with radioactive sources – really concentrated – but nothing on the glacier, or the gigantic ice island that was slowly making its way toward the open waters of Baffin Bay.

She flipped back to the pre-breakup images and ran them through the alpha-gamma. Nothing on the shore. She zoomed in on the boat. The range didn't give a good image. But there they were: thirteen glowing sources, all in a line, all on the Russian ship that was just about to be annihilated by the largest tsunami ever witnessed in the Arctic Ocean.

The ship was carrying a radioactive cargo – but it wasn't the ship that caused the disaster, it'd just got caught up in it.

Siv turned her attention back to the glacier itself. Could there be a new geothermal feature –hydrothermal vents, or maybe even a new volcano? She switched to infra-red and started flipping between the before and after sequences. Nothing … a build-up of heat along the fault line just before the break, but now...

Siv's eyes widened – she couldn't believe what she was seeing. In the three years she'd been working in the surveillance centre, this was exactly what she'd been taught to look out for. And now that she was witnessing it – she couldn't believe it was actually happening.

*

'So now we come to the heart of the problem,' Morgan said, tapping the table with his fingertip. 'We have a Borei-class submarine, armed with ICBMs, trying to sneak round behind our North Atlantic patrols – but why?'

'We just assumed it was another planter, trying to lay unstable old warheads near the cities of the Eastern Seaboard, that would lie there waiting until they sent a signal to detonate them.'

'A plan which we've managed to thwart every time they've tried it. But now this Borei turns up with a full rack of missiles.'

'Which they know we can knock out before they even reach the stratosphere.'

'Precisely. So, if they're suddenly starting to deploy – what does that tell you?'

Warren shook his head.

'Oh, come on,' Morgan pressed him. 'You were my best student – the brightest young officer I've ever known. Think logically.'

Warren smiled. He was back in Morgan's classroom again: *Philosophy of War #101 – logical analysis of evidence.*

'The Russians are deploying because they think they can get their missiles past our defences.'

'Exactly. But I checked – and all our defence platforms are registering A-OK. So I dug a little deeper – I extrapolated the trajectories of a series of hypothetical missile launches from Baffin Bay and the Canadian islands, to see which platform would have to be deployed to intercept those trajectories.

'And, guess what? It all came down to the same platform – BNW-55. I had it checked-out again — and once again I got the message back that everything was just fine. So I asked them for a visual. That shocked the

Hell out of them – they'd never been asked for that before. They had to commandeer one of the big civilian telescopes...'

'And?' Warren asked. 'What did they find?'

Morgan touched a panel on the screen. Immediately, the Kane Basin disappeared.

'Hologram: BNW-55 – latest,' he said, staring into mid space. Slowly, a three-dimensional image started to manifest itself before their eyes: a silver ellipse hovering in space with what looked like cables and electrical components floating from it. A whole range of military-looking hardware circled round it like asteroids.

'I don't understand,' Warren muttered. 'What is it?'

'That, my friend, is bravo-november-whiskey-five-five – a second tier defensive weapons platform.'

'But it's just a piece of space junk.'

'On the contrary, it's still sending out signals confirming all its systems are working perfectly. Until twenty hours ago, we still believed this was a fully-functional component in our first-strike defensive shield. And that, I'm afraid, is our problem. We don't know if this is the only one – or if there are others like this. To be frank, we don't even know if our ICBM shield actually exists anymore...'

Warren stared at Morgan dumbfounded as he tried to come to terms with what he was being told. The shield was the basis of everything. The whole balance of power, that had existed since the collapse of the Soviet Union at the end of the last century, was predicated on NATO's ability to intercept any first strike.

'So, that's why you've got me here, I understand that,' Warren said, thinking aloud. 'But what do you want me to do about it?'

Morgan sighed and rubbed his forehead with his fingertips. 'I need you to think – think about what's happening here. Christ knows, I've been coming at it from all angles – and I'm hitting a brick wall every time.' He pointed to the revolving image, hovering in front of them: 'Nothing has come near it. If it had we'd have known about it. And it's definitely not asteroid damage. BNW-55 has been expertly carved up – almost like it's been surgically dissected – and we haven't the slightest idea how they did it...'

*

Siv was working as fast as she could. She'd resolved the twenty screens into four banks of five feeds, all working on the same location in different timeframes and wavelengths. Her eyes flicked between images, aggregating digital information in her mind, using her intelligence to compress the sort of work that would normally take days and weeks – into a few brief minutes.

She ran the composite feed – it looked like shit.

'Come on, Siv – think!' she whispered to herself. 'What's wrong, what's wrong...' She stared at the image: it hadn't resolved the way she'd expected it to – everything was distorted – but why?

'...Yes! That's it!' she cried triumphantly as she slotted the satellites' trajectories into the matrix. One by one, the layers started to resolve, falling into line with the base data. She ran the sequence from the start, her eyes widening as she refined the resolution.

'Oh, my God...' she muttered, as she realised what she was seeing.

The composite took a few seconds to save. Siv used the time to call General Morgan. He'd want to see this straight away. She dialled his office: her brow furrowed with confusion as a woman answered. She glanced down at her phone – she'd been bounced to the switchboard.

'Where's Morgan?' Siv snapped.

'He's indisposed,' the female voice replied, primly.

'Where is he? This is urgent!'

The voice at the other end fell silent.

'Dammit!' Siv barked. 'Where is he?'

'... He's up in the *Kjegle*.'

'Fine. Can you patch me in?'

'I'm sorry, there are no telecommunications in the *Kjegle*... Hello? Hello?'

But Siv was gone. She'd already sprinted out of the surveillance centre – and was nearly up at ground level before the switchboard operator even realised she wasn't there anymore.

*

Warren stared at the 3D hologram floating before his eyes.

'This isn't doing us any good,' he said, thinking aloud.

'What do you mean?' Morgan asked.

'We don't know when this happened – and we don't know if it's the only one.'

'I know. That's why I've got people commandeering telescopes all over the Northern Hemisphere – to get visuals on every single platform.'

'We need to find a work in progress – a platform they're still dismembering.'

'If they aren't all like this...'

Warren shook his head, still staring at the hologram.

'If they'd knocked out the first tier platforms they wouldn't have sent the Borei down through the Kane Basin – they'd be popping up missiles from their home bases...'

A red light above them started to flash. Immediately, the hologram disintegrated as the system went into shutdown.

'What's going on?' Warren said, staring up at the light.

'Security alert,' Morgan replied. 'Someone's trying to break in.'

*

The steel doors slid open. The ear-piercing screech of the alarm reverberated around the atrium. Warren and Morgan peered down the stairs in astonishment: four armed troopers were struggling to restrain a young soldier with short, spiky, blond hair, as she tried to kick and squirm herself free from their clutches:

'Let me go – you idiots!' she yelled at them, yanking her right hand free and delivering a short arm uppercut with the heel of her palm – right on the chin-guard of a trooper – who slumped to the floor, unconscious.

Morgan keyed a code into a panel on the wall beside him. Immediately the screeching stopped.

'Corporal Jagland?' he thundered. 'What's the meaning of this?'

Siv was hanging, half-standing, half-suspended in the arms of her captors. She writhed around and saluted the general with her still-free hand: 'General Morgan – sir!'

Straight away the troopers stood to attention and did likewise, releasing Siv and allowing her to fall sprawling on the stairs.

'Well, Jagland?' Morgan snarled. 'I'm waiting...'

'My orders were to bring anything new straight to you...' Siv explained, getting to her feet and massaging her twisted neck. 'They told me you were up here – they didn't tell me about the extra security... Sir.'

'OK,' the general replied, still bristling. 'What have you got?'

Siv stared at him incredulously: 'What – you want me to show you ... out here?'

Morgan thought for a moment: 'No. You're right,' he said, beckoning to her: 'You'd better come up.'

Siv shot the troopers a withering glance as she scampered up the staircase. At the top of the stairs she paused at the entrance to the *Kjegle* – the cone. She'd never been up here – she didn't know anyone who had. 'Wow, this is impress...' she muttered as she crossed the threshold – then she held her hand up to her mouth.

A younger man tapped her on the shoulder. He was in his thirties maybe, unshaven with dark unkempt hair, wearing US Air Force fatigues that were a couple of sizes too big for him. She stared at him idiotically, her mouth flapping. He pointed to his lips and shook his head – then smiled and motioned for her to follow him into a large black dome in the middle of the room.

Inside, General Morgan was waiting impatiently for her: 'Alright, Jagland,' he growled. What's going on?'

Undeterred, Siv stepped up to the black glass-topped table. She'd seen a device like this in a tech store in Berlin a few months ago. She kind of got how it worked – but anyway she wasn't going to let on to these guys that she didn't.

'Jagland S,' she muttered, 'Composite Four – latest...' the screen sprang magically into life.

A three-dimensional map started to appear on the table. She raised her eyebrow – it looked pretty impressive.

'Angle: ten degrees, elevation: one hundred fifty metres...'

As if they were on a helicopter, the image swooped down – and now they appeared to be hovering over a massive wall of ice.

'I wish I knew how she did that,' Morgan whispered. 'I want to be able to do that...'

'Ssh...' Siv hissed, imperiously, as she manipulated the image.

The general grinned at Warren, his eyes twinkling mischievously – he liked this girl. Morgan liked people who weren't frightened of him.

'OK,' Siv began, still staring at the image on the table. 'This is the new terminus of the Humboldt Glacier, halfway down, running roughly northeast to southwest... rotate one-eighty ...'

The image span round to show the vast island of ice, floating south toward Baffin Bay.

'...And this is the disarticulation. On the far side of the disarticulation is the heavily-irradiated west shoreline, where most of the debris from the Russian ship has washed-up. ...revert...'

The image span back to the main glacier. 'Advance – twenty per second...' It now seemed as though they were flying over the ice. 'I was going over surface of the Humboldt the to see if I could figure out why it'd broken up...'

'That wasn't part of your orders...' Morgan observed, testily.

Siv shrugged, still staring down at the image: 'It amounts to the same thing – and if I hadn't, I wouldn't have found what I came up here to show you.'

'How are you getting this image?' Warren asked.

'It's a composite from five satellites: four of ours – and one of theirs that had just come on line when the sequence started. Then I adjusted the images for the different times and trajectories of their orbits. I brought the virtual altitude down to fifty metres. Any lower and the image starts to break up.'

'So, what do you want to show us?' the general asked, totally engrossed.

She glanced across at him, her eyes luminous, her face underlit by the image of the glacier beneath her: 'Advance – one thousand per second.'

Everything speeded up. 'We're going up the glacier at a kilometre a second now. It won't take too long...'

Warren watched with increasing unease. If her start point was halfway down the glacier's sea wall, and they were moving inland...

'There...' she said, pointing at a static, swirling white corkscrew, raking off to the south at an erratic angle. With all the movement of traversing the glacier, Warren had forgotten they'd been looking at a static image all this time. Siv pointed at the corkscrew:

'...That's heat. Intense heat, dissipating in the high winds of an Arctic storm.

Warren realised there was only one thing it could be. 'When was this taken?' he asked, anxiously.

Siv held her watch down to the light: 'Twenty minutes ago.'

'Do you have anything else?'

Siv nodded, picking up on the fear in his voice. 'I managed to retrieve about an hour's worth...'

'OK... Let's see it.'

'...Run from start...' The spiral disappeared. Warren thought he could make out the outline of the burned-out bomber on the ice.

Siv breathed in deeply as she composed her thoughts: 'Right. The sequence is about an hour, at ten second intervals – anything less and the data load goes ... like, crazy,' she said, shaking her head as she stared intently at the icescape spread out before them. 'Remember, this is all happening in a storm. Winds gusting over one-twenty, one-fifty...'

'She's talking in kilometres,' Morgan whispered to his friend.

Siv took no notice: 'Now look – you can see three heat sources, coming from the west – from the glacier's terminus. They're moving fast – I'm guessing they're snowmobiles.'

Warren nodded. She was right. It was his team – it had to be. But why were they still out on the ice when there was a Russian satellite overhead?

'OK,' she continued. 'The three sources stop at this point and start cooling straight away, so...'

'They've switched off their engines,' the general muttered.

'Precisely. If you look closely, you can just make out dim objects detaching from the brighter ones. That could be men dismounting. Now look...'

Siv pointed up, toward the top of the dome. A dark shadow was hovering above the centre of the table. As each image refreshed, it descended, nearer and nearer to the cooling snowmobiles.

'What is that?' Morgan asked.

'It's not a helicopter,' Siv replied. 'In this wind it has to be a fixed wing – and even then you'd have to be crazy to try and land it in this storm. But look – we can only see it because it's blotting out our surveillance — there's no heat signature, just a shadow. But as to what it is? I'm thinking a VTOL, maybe. But big – really big.'

Siv leant forward, so that she was nearly touching the table.

'Look here,' she said, stretching over the table to point at the shadow as it came to rest on the surface of the glacier, a short distance south of the other sources. Almost immediately, lights — more heat sources — seemed to issue from it. 'See – they look like vehicles. Some the same as the others: they're snowmobiles, maybe. And another one, much bigger. Could be a Sno-Cat or an all-terrain vehicle.'

Every time the image refreshed, the heat sources had moved a further north. In his mind's eye, Warren imagined them converging on his isolated, defenceless base.

Siv placed her thumb and forefinger over them and zoomed the image. 'Sorry,' she muttered, as it disintegrated into incomprehensible cubes of light. 'Yeah, anything below fifty metres is useless.' She brought the view back up again. 'Now look: things start getting pretty confused ...right about now.'

A hazy light appeared, then another. 'This is in long infra-red. I think what we're seeing are the heat signatures from the aftermath of explosions. We get a flash...' Suddenly the whole area was consumed by light. '...Yeah, there.'

Warren thought he could make out the tracks of tracer bullets, pouring into the carcass of the bomber and the concealed cabin beneath. There was another flash, then the firing stopped. Faint images of what might be men converged on their target.

'Nothing much happens for a few minutes,' Siv said, looking up into Warren's eyes. 'Shall I fast-forward?'

Warren nodded. Siv glanced at the time display, hovering next to her.

She ran it forward fifteen minutes. At first everything looked just the same. Then brighter figures started swarming onto the ice.

'We can see them better because they've just come from a warm place.'

Warren nodded. He knew where they'd come from.

'I tried to do a head count,' she said, softly – as though she was breaking the news of a bereavement. 'I think there are two or maybe three more...'

'Three,' Warren muttered.

'They're going back to the VTOL.' They watched in silence.

'Just now they stop.' Siv realised it was a stupid thing to say: everyone could see they'd stopped.

'They leave behind three cooling sources...'

Warren closed his eyes.

'They could just be snowmobiles,' Siv added, trying to sound upbeat. 'If they were human...'

Suddenly, the whole scene was engulfed in a dazzling white light, then another – and another. The shadow hovered in the air for a few moments – then disappeared. Slowly the heat signature from the explosions dimmed and the image reverted to the raking corkscrew of heat, swirling in the Arctic storm.

'That's it,' she said, simply. 'I tried to track the shadow. It travelled due north. I tracked it for a hundred, a hundred and fifty kilometres, then it came to rest. After that I lost it. I'm guessing it waited for our fifteen minute surveillance window, as our satellites' trajectories diverged. Then it got itself lost in the cross-polar air traffic. It was gone when the window closed.'

'Why didn't you alert us earlier?' Morgan demanded.

Siv pointed at the corkscrew heat signature: 'This is what I found when I came in,' she replied, unabashed, staring the general in the eye. 'The rest came from the alpha-layer memory – all this had happened before I even came on shift.'

She turned to Warren: 'You know this place, don't you?'

He nodded, still staring at the scene. There was still a faint glimmer of warmth coming from one of the three heat sources.

The image froze as the sequence came to an end.

*

'I've got to get back there,' Warren muttered to the general, as they stepped out of the *Kjegle*.

Siv's heart leapt – *he's going back to the glacier. Perhaps he could...*

'No, no. It's out of the question,' Morgan replied. 'You're needed here – I need you here.'

'With all due respect sir, I'm no use until those visuals start coming in – and even then...'

Go on, she thought – *don't give in. Then, maybe I...*

Morgan held up his hand for Warren to stop, as he realised the corporal was listening to their conversation:

'Jagland – that was a really impressive piece of work.'

'Thank you sir.'

'I want you to get back to the surveillance centre now...'

'The surveillance centre...' she echoed, the words sounding hollow in her ears.

'That's right – if anything happens in and around the basin, anything at all, you let me know – straight away – got that?'

'Loud and clear, sir,' Siv replied, saluting.

Morgan returned her salute, even though he was out of uniform: 'Very good, corporal. Dismissed.'

Dismissed... That was exactly how she felt as she stepped sadly down the stairs. Back down to the dungeons. The first interesting thing that'd happened to her in three long years. Now she was banished back to the screens – back into the darkness.

Warren watched her go. He'd seen the disappointment in her eyes, sensed her frustration – he felt just the same.

*

Stavanger waterfront

New Year's Eve

The knots of happy revellers, merrily milling around the harbourside, wishing one another *Godt Nyttår*, only served to remind Warren how miserable he felt.

A midwinter storm of epic proportions had closed in around northern Greenland. Thule was completely closed down. Even if he'd managed to browbeat Morgan into letting him go, he couldn't have got to the Humboldt Glacier – and they still hadn't managed to get a search party up there to investigate what had happened.

But Morgan wouldn't have released him anyway. The visuals of the platforms were coming in — painfully slowly. Although there were dozens of observatories dotted around the Northern Hemisphere, it turned out that only very few of them were able to observe near-Earth objects – and even then they could only get a shot of them when the fast-moving platforms traversed their precise locations. So far, from the images they'd got, there was no sign that any of them had been dismembered like BNW-55.

Things round the harbour area had changed quite a bit since he was last here. He was looking for an Irish bar he used to go to. It wasn't that he had anything against Norwegian bars, but the English and Irish bars tended to be cheaper and scruffier. Norwegian bars were more upmarket – and much more expensive.

But when he found the place it had been converted into a vegetarian bistro.

Being New Year, most of the bars he went past were either ticket-only, or they had fierce-looking bouncers on the doors. Warren made a point of never going to those sort of places – if there was a bouncer on the outside, it usually meant it was pretty lousy on the inside.

He was just about to give up on New Year in Stavanger, and make his way back to his hotel, when he came across a place that looked OK. It was dark inside, busy – but not too busy. He sat at the bar and was served straight away. Within thirty seconds he had a tall beer in front of him –

and an eye-wateringly vast sum of money had been debited from his bank account. He'd forgotten how expensive beer was in Norway. He'd go back to the hotel after this – at least he could drink at the expense of the North Atlantic Treaty Organisation.

A DJ started up somewhere in the bar and the whole place was lit up by a flickering ultraviolet strobe. Warren was just about to finish his expensive beer and make his way back to his hotel, when he glanced in the mirror behind the bar and noticed a woman with a spiky halo of bright blond hair, sitting in a booth over in the far corner. Warren recognised her – it was Jagland, the corporal from the surveillance centre. She was with two biker-types. ... What the hell, he thought — he'd stick around 'til she came up to buy a drink, and wish her a happy new year. He might as well wish it to someone.

But she didn't come to the bar. A couple of minutes later one of the bikers came up and ordered three beers. He whispered something to the barman, who took one of the beers back and poured some of it away – then refilled it from a bottle under the counter. Warren had seen this sort of thing before. The barman was spiking one of the drinks with *akvavit* – and it didn't take much imagination to guess whose drink they were spiking. Warren followed the biker back to the booth, and sure enough he placed the spiked beer in front of the girl.

'I wouldn't drink that if I were you, Corporal Jagland,' Warren said.

It took a while for Siv to focus on the interloper – it was the stranger who'd been at the *Kjegle*.

'*Sergeant* Jagland,' she muttered, surprised at how hard it was to speak coherently. 'General Morgan got me promoted... So I'm ...ss... ss.. celebrating.'

'Yeah, she's with us, Anglo,' one of the bikers snarled. 'So fuck off.'

'They've been spiking your beer, Jagland.'

Siv chuckled: 'I thought I was pretty pissed...'

'See, she likes it,' the other biker scoffed, laying his arm possessively over her shoulder. 'We're going back to my place. We're gonna have our own New Year's party – just the three of us.'

Siv's brow furrowed, as she slowly realised what he'd just said:

'In your dreams, *drittsek*.'

'Hey, that's no way to talk, we've spent a lot of money on you...'

'Yeah,' the guy with his arm over her agreed. 'We could've got a real whore for less.'

Siv's eyes narrowed as she considered her options. The guy next to her had made a big mistake leaving his arm there. He was wide open...

Moments later she brought the heel of her palm sharp up into his jaw. It was the same blow she'd delivered to the trooper – only the trooper had had a chin guard to cushion the impact. Warren winced as the biker slithered under the table, unconscious.

Siv confronted the other biker: 'You want some?' she demanded, her eyes blazing.

'Uh, n-no...' he stammered.

'Well fuck off then, *runknisse*.'

He was just about to get up and leave his buddy under the table, when Warren stopped him.

'Just one minute,' he said, handing him the spiked beer. 'You were going to make my friend drink this – now you drink it.'

'But...'

'Drink it – or we'll both beat the crap out of you.'

He took the drink – like it was a poison chalice.

'In one...' Siv said, standing over him, menacingly.

They both watched as he did what he was told. He got about three-quarters through it before he started to sway. He was still drinking as he slipped under the table, unconscious.

'Well, that was fun,' Warren said.

'Yeah – and we get two free beers,' she said picking up the bikers' untouched glasses and passing him one.

He looked at her disapprovingly: 'Don't you think you should...'

'Drink up... this stuff isn't cheap, you know,' she said, staring at him through narrowed eyes – just the same way she'd looked at the biker. Warren got ready to deflect a sudden blow.

Siv grinned mischievously and clinked her glass on his — then downed her beer in a single draught.

*

They were sitting on a huge dock bollard, staring out across the harbour at the northern lights flickering on the far horizon. The only sound they could hear was the sloshing of the tide on great lumps of dirty ice, bumping against the jetty.

'Happy New Year, Corp... Sergeant Jagland,' Warren said, clinking his bottle on hers.

'Siv.'

'That's your name?'

'Sure is – what's yours?'

'Just Warren – everyone calls me Warren.'

'OK...' She thought for a moment, then shrugged and clinked her bottle on his. '*Godt Nyttår* – Warren.'

They sat in silence for a while, staring out across the water.

'Look,' Siv said, breaking the silence. 'This is all very pretty. But can we go someplace else – I'm freezing my ass off here.

*

Hotel Scandia, Stavanger

New Year's Day

Siv opened her eyes – where was she?

There was someone lying next to her – that was bad.

She checked round her body: she was still wearing her t-shirt – that was OK, but in itself it didn't mean much. She had her brassiere on – that was definitely a good sign. Panties still on: even better. She felt between her legs and rolled her tongue round inside her mouth – all clear. So...

The phone rang. The body next to her shifted.

'Warren...'

Shit – Warren – the guy from the Kjegle.

'...Yes…'

She could feel him sitting up.

'OK... Yes, definitely. Can you hold just one second?'

He nudged her in the ribs: 'Have you got your pass?' he whispered, holding his hand over the phone. 'Your jacket's on the chair next to you.'

Siv rummaged in her pocket: 'Uh-huh.'

'Right,' Warren said, resuming his phone call. 'I'm going to need Jagland – is she on duty? No?'

Siv chuckled quietly. Warren shoved her away.

'OK. I'll be... Give me half an hour. Can you contact Jagland and tell her to come in? Directly.'

He hung up. Moments later, the mobile in Siv's jacket started ringing.

'Uh, yeah?' she mumbled.

'*Siv – it's Clara... General Morgan's assistant.*'

'Oh, yeah. Hi, Clara – what can I...?'

'*Can you get here in half an hour? It's urgent.*'

'Uh, yeah – I guess so. What's so important?'

'*Commander Warren will brief you when you get in. Thank you, Siv.*'

She hung up.

Warren was already in the shower. Siv followed him into the bathroom.

'Can I use your toothbrush?' she yelled.

'That's fine,' he yelled back. 'What's your security clearance?'

'Don't show me anything COSMIC – otherwise I'm OK.'

Warren grabbed a towel and stepped out of the cubicle, leaving the shower running.

Siv rinsed off the toothbrush and handed it to him, then stripped off and got into the shower. She didn't feel embarrassed – it was just like being back in barracks.

Like being a proper soldier again.

*

'I'm guessing you haven't always worked in the surveillance centre,' Warren said as he eased his hire car out onto the *Diagonalen* and joined the early morning traffic.

'No way,' Siv replied, swallowing back a lump of bread and *brunost* she'd grabbed off the hotel's breakfast table as they'd swept past. 'I come from the glacier country – practically grew up on the *Jostedalsbreen*. So, when I joined the army I volunteered for the *Jegerkompani*, the Northern Rangers. We were just about to go do our final training – twenty days out on the polar ice without logistic support – but our transport got requisitioned by some NATO tin-hat who wanted to go investigate something.

'The weather closed in after that. We returned to base to wait for the next transport – but the transport never came. Then the recession kicked in: they put *Jeger* recruitment on hold....' she shrugged. 'I got transferred to the *Etterretnings* – surveillance and electronic warfare. I've been at Jåttå for the last three years.'

'You're good at your job,' Warren probed. 'But I get the impression you don't really enjoy it.'

'You could say that...' Siv glowered at the brooding mass of Mount Jåttå, dominating the southern horizon, looming ever larger as they approached it. She hated the fucking place.

Warren drove on in silence. About three years ago he'd requisitioned a transport, bumped a training exercise. He remembered the weather had turned pretty bad after that. There was a good chance he was the reason why Jagland had been stuck down in the bowels of the JWC all this time...

'So?' Siv said, breaking his train of thought.

'So – what?'

'Well it's a pretty dumb thing to say – "I guess you hate your job" – if you're not going to say anything after that. It's like saying "I guess you hate having two heads" – and just leaving it there.'

'I guess it is.'

'So?'

'It's nothing,' Warren replied. 'Sorry – stupid thing to say.' A plan was beginning to form in his mind – a plan to get him back to the Humboldt, to find out what had happened to his men. Jagland figured in his plan: she was tough and clever – and knowing that she'd grown up on the ice made her even more useful. She wanted to get out of the surveillance centre, that much was obvious. But there was no point getting her hopes up, not yet. He'd have to talk Leo round first.

'Damn straight it was.' she muttered under her breath, burying her curiosity. He was a strange fish this: "Just Warren". Clara had called him "Commander Warren" — that was a navy rank. OF-4 at least. It meant he was six ranks above her, even after her recent promotion. So, he was an important guy.

'What are we going in for?' Siv asked, noncommittally. She was still on leave 'til next Wednesday, and there were many, far better surveillance technicians at the JWC – so why did he want her in particular? Was he keen on her? She couldn't tell – but if he'd just wanted to fuck her he could've done that last night. She'd been drunk enough, and he was a pretty good looking guy...

'Wind down your window,' he said, still staring at the road ahead.

'What?' she exclaimed. 'It's fifteen below out there!'

'Just a couple of centimetres. You can turn the heater up.'

Siv did as she was told. The air in the car started to reverberate, thrumming in her ears.

'Sorry,' he said. 'Just a precaution. If there's a directional microphone on us, the fluctuating air pressure acts like a scrambler.' He glanced across at her: 'We're going in so that we can work on an image we've just received. I can't tell you what it is – not yet, not 'til we get into the *Kjegle*.'

*

Back in the igloo Warren placed his fingertips on the circular table and stared down into its jet-black surface.

'Warren,' he muttered. 'Warren: verify.'

Ten tiny lights flickered under his fingertips. Scanners probed his eyes and a magnetic decoder read the security chip in the side of his neck.

'Warren: verified,' a female voice intoned.

'Now you,' he said, indicating that Siv should do likewise.

'But we did all this when we came in,' she protested.

'It needs to re-confirm you before it'll release the image.'

'OK,' she said, slapping her hands on the table and staring down at it: 'Jagland, Siv: verify.' She felt the lights probing, tickling her.

'Jagland: verified.'

Warren stepped forward: 'Now before I open this file you need to know that as soon as it's opened, everything we say and do is being recorded. OK?'

'I'll watch my language,' Siv smirked.

'OK. Display INTASSIS.'

A sequence of fuzzy two-dimensional images flashed onto the screen. Siv stared at them, confused.

'I don't understand. What are they? I need to get some idea of what I'm supposed to be looking at.'

Warren nodded: 'Display A-N-P-one-two; level one — redacted.'

An old-fashioned flat CGI drawing, with all the text around it blanked-out, flashed onto the screen.

'Hmm. Looks like a harmonica stuck to a rugby ball.'

'Not a bad estimation,' Warren conceded. 'In reality, the rugby ball is more-or-less two dimensional. It's a reflector, channelling the sun's rays into a solar panel, which is on the other side of the ...harmonica.'

'And do I get to know what the "harmonica" is?'

Warren shook his head: 'Now that is COSMIC. Can you work with what you've got?'

Siv stared at the fuzzy images: 'The haziness – that's atmospheric pollution – right?'

Warren nodded.

'And this is an image in the visible light range?'

'It's from an optical telescope.'

'On the surface – looking up?'

'Yes – and that's as much as I can tell you...'

'...Without shooting me afterwards?'

'That's about it.'

She turned her attention back to the screen, her eyes flicking back and forth between the images. 'OK, we haven't got much to go on... Automatic: off. Adjustment: manual – all.'

She started manipulating the images. At first it felt strange doing everything on the table screen, but after a few minutes she realised that she could do far more – and work much more quickly – than she ever could with the vertical screens down in the dungeon.

'Alright,' she murmured, thoughtfully. 'What we've got is basically the reverse of what I'm used to working with. So...'

Her brow furrowed as she called up her first attempt.

'Problem?' Warren asked.

'That wasn't what I'd expected to see. I've adjusted for the telescope tracking the object and the Doppler effect. It's pretty obvious that this is a satellite – but it's in a weird orbit...'

'That may be true. But I'm afraid I can't help you with that.'

'It's OK…' she replied, still totally engrossed by her work. 'Oh, shit,' she muttered under her breath, her eyes widening: 'I see what this is…'

'Siv,' Warren interrupted. 'Don't forget – this is all being recorded.'

'Yeah, alright,' she said, once more totally engrossed by her work. 'Oh, Warren…'

'Yes?'

'That's the first time you've called me by my first name.' She glanced up at him and smiled: '…and it's on the record.'

*

After about half an hour, Siv seemed satisfied with what she was getting, and she started overlaying the images.

'OK – shall we call it up?'

'Let's see what you've got,' Warren replied.

A hologram started to compose itself, hovering above the table. Siv stared at it in wonder. She found it hard to believe she'd composed this image out of the dozens of fuzzy partial views she'd had to work with. She could see now that the rugby-ball shape was indeed a reflector panel, bent in at the sides. But the harmonica bothered her. She moved her head around, looking at it from all angles.

'It's all wrong…' she muttered. 'I don't know what I've done. I'll see if…'

'No,' Warren replied. 'You haven't done anything. That's how it is.'

'Looks like someone's taken a big bite out of it.'

'A hell of a big bite. That thing's the size of a bus…'

Warren stared at it. They'd found it — this was the one. They'd caught the Enemy red-handed.

*

General Morgan sat brooding in one of the immersion seats, glowering at the image Siv had constructed. Warren had sent her home as soon as she'd saved it to the INTASSIS file. There was no point in her sticking around: she couldn't be party to this – there were probably only about a dozen people in the whole western alliance who could.

'So, if I understand you correctly,' the general began, choosing his words carefully, trying to keep a lid on his temper. 'What you're suggesting is that we allow the defence of the cities of the American Midwest to dangle precariously by this...' He jabbed his finger angrily at the hologram of the crippled satellite: '...This heap of crap?'

'No,' Warren replied, calmly. He understood Morgan's anger. The lives of millions of people were at stake. 'Not at all. The satellite arcs overlap at every point in the shield. It gives us redundancy in case one goes down. We can repurpose the undamaged platforms to take advantage of that redundancy and reform the shield. What we can't do is send up a new platform to fill the gap. If we do that the Russians will know we're on to them.'

'Anyhow, the whole question is academic,' Morgan observed. 'We don't have spare platforms, just hanging around, waiting to be deployed. If we wanted to replace BNW-55 – and for all we know, ANP-12 as well – we'd have to commission them completely from scratch. It would take months – a year, maybe.'

'So, we don't have much choice, do we? We've got one satellite down and one badly damaged. It's like a game of checkers, Leo. We can't go on indefinitely shuffling pieces forward to fill the gaps. In the end our baseline will be totally exposed. We need to know how they're doing it. And when we know that – we'll know how to stop them.'

Morgan sat forward and rested his elbows on the table: 'So, what do you propose?'

'We need to get permanent eyes on ANP-12.'

'Hah!' the general scoffed. 'And just how do you propose we do that?'

Warren looked down at his hands. What he was about to say was going to sound ridiculous – treasonable, even. He took a deep breath:

'What we're going to do, Leo,' he replied looking his old friend squarely in the eyes: '...Is kill off another one of our satellites.'

*

Siv's grandmother was stirring a large copper-bottomed stew pot, carefully bringing her *Fisksuppe* to a slow simmer, as Siv blundered into the kitchen.

'And where were you last night?' her grandmother demanded, not looking up from the stew pot. 'Come to think of it – where've you been all morning?'

'Oh, Granny,' Siv said, wrapping her arms around the old lady and staring down into the pot. 'Last night was *Nyttår* – and what I do on New Year is really none of your business, you nosy old *heks*...'

'You know it's only because I care about you.'

'It's only 'cos you want to hear all the mucky details, you mean.'

'So?' Granny shrugged, feigning innocence. 'Life gets pretty dull when you're my age.'

'OK – this is how it went,' Siv laughed, hugging her. 'You might want to sit down, though – because it gets pretty raunchy...'

*

Morgan listened impassively as Warren explained his plan:

'We take one of our surveillance satellites offline, change its orbit so that it's within, say a mile or two of ANP-12 – and all its eyes are on it, all the time.'

'But the Russkies will get its transmission, just the same as we do – it'll be an even bigger giveaway than if we sent a new platform up to fill the gap.'

'Not so, Leo. Not if the surveillance satellite only downloaded its data once in every orbit – and the signal was so narrow, so precisely targeted that it'd only be detectable from a single location...'

'Like you did with the drone...'

'Like I did with the drone,' Warren agreed.

Morgan laughed quietly to himself as he realised where Warren was going with his plan: 'Of course, you'd have to be somewhere remote to ensure you and only you – got the transmission.'

'That's right.'

'And would I be right in assuming that this location might be somewhere around the seventy-ninth parallel?'

'ANP-12's station passes over that latitude four times a day.'

Morgan sat back in his immersion chair, glowering at the wreck of ANP-12.

'You know, Warren,' he growled, 'I can't help thinking this is one Hell of an elaborate way of getting yourself back out on the glacier.'

*

'...So, this morning I wake up in a strange bed – and I'm next to the guy.'

'The one who rescued you?' Granny asked, breathlessly.

'He didn't rescue me,' Siv huffed. 'He...' Her thought trailed off as she struggled to remember exactly what he had done to save her. 'Anyway, there I was in bed, cuddling up to the guy – and do you know what happened next?'

'No – what?'

'The phone went,' she said holding up her mobile. 'Work. I got called in. That NATO tin-hat I told you about wanted me to do some stuff on an image they'd got in this morning. So, that's where I've been, Granny. Down in the depths of Jåttå – staring at screens.'

'But you're still on leave!'

Siv ladled a large lump of cod out of the pot and blew on it to cool it: 'All part of my crazy, helter-skelter life in the *Etterretnings*,' she said, stuffing the whole lump greedily into her mouth.

'But what about the guy – the good looking one?' Granny persisted.

'Who knows?' Siv shrugged, still chewing the steaming fish. 'I might see him again – I might not – depends how I feel...'

'Did you give him your number?'

'Oh, don't worry, Granny,' she said, resting her head on her grandmother's shoulder: 'He knows where to find me...'

*

Sola Air Station

Stavanger

20.00 hrs, New Year's Day

The darkness was splintered by the flashing lights of emergency vehicles. Snow was coming in thick and fast and both the station's snowploughs were working full-out to clear a pathway for the USAF Boeing C-40 that was waiting to take off, its engines screaming. All round the runway the snow was already knee deep.

'Get on — quick!' the trooper yelled as Siv swung her kitbag into the back of a waiting truck. A couple more troopers grabbed her roughly by her parka and dragged her on board. 'If you don't get off soon, you'll have to wait for the storm to pass. That might not be for days!'

Then, with a lurch that nearly shot her off the back, the truck pulled away, grinding toward the C-40, its tyres spinning, struggling to get a grip.

The snow was getting heavier, and although she knew they must be getting closer to the aircraft – the scream of its engines was almost deafening – it was invisible in the blinding white-out.

The truck paused for a second as the troopers lowered her down onto the runway, then snarled off into the swirling darkness.

'Come on Siv!' a familiar voice yelled at her. She screwed her eyes up to see where it was coming from. There was a light — a shape silhouetted against it, beckoning to her urgently. It was Warren:

'Come on – we've got to go now!'

Siv ran toward him, her boots creaking as they sank through the fresh, powdery snow. She grabbed the rails of a flimsy, fold-down stairway that raised under her as she clambered up. Warren grabbed her and dragged her in — and slammed the door shut behind her as the plane started to rumble forward.

'You couldn't have timed that better if you'd tried,' he said, tossing her kit bag onto an empty seat.

Siv looked round – apart from them the whole plane was empty – row after row of empty seats.

'You'd better get buckled in,' he said. 'This could be a bumpy take-off.'

'Where are we going?' she asked getting into the nearest seat and strapping herself in.

'Didn't they tell you on the way over?'

Siv shook her head: 'They didn't even talk to me.'

'Probably for the best,' Warren mused, throwing himself into a seat in the next bank and pulling his safety belt tight. 'By the way — sorry about the short notice!'

'Oh, don't worry,' she muttered, tightening her belt. 'I didn't have anything planned for this evening.'

The plane gathered speed, bouncing around as its wheels bucked in and out of the snowplough ruts, then lurched sharply upwards and into the sky, wrenching Siv and Warren in all directions as it struggled to reach altitude. Then, suddenly it was over. The plane levelled off. The pitch of the engines dropped – they could relax.

'I think I could do with some coffee,' Warren said, unbuckling himself and going forward, toward the crew cabin. 'Do you want some?'

'Yeah, sure,' Siv replied, getting up and following him.

Warren flicked on the crew cabin intercom: 'You guys want some coffee?' he asked.

Siv didn't hear their reply – Warren just shrugged and poured two cups. 'I don't suppose I'm very popular with them,' he muttered. 'They didn't think it was safe to take off from Sola tonight.'

'I think I agree with them,' Siv replied. 'I've never seen an aircraft take off in weather this bad.'

Warren laughed quietly: 'I've seen worse, far worse. Maybe not such a big plane. But what the Hell – we're up now. We've just got to hope it isn't any worse at Thule.'

'Thule?' Siv exclaimed. 'We're going to Greenland?'

'That's right. Then, when we get to Thule, we're going down to the port of Qaanaaq and hitching a ride on an icebreaker, that's going to take us to meet some friends who are… Well, let's just say there's an awful lot going on in the Kane Basin right now.'

'Tell me about it,' Siv replied, sipping at her coffee. 'We've been watching it round-the-clock this last week.'

Warren lowered his voice, almost to a whisper: 'We're going to use all this activity to get ourselves established back on the Humboldt…'

'At the place we saw in the sequence?'

He nodded: 'You guessed right, those were my men – it was our base that was attacked. I'd only flown out a few hours before.'

'Lucky you.'

Warren knelt down and opened up a steel cabinet.

'Are you hungry?' he asked, staring into the cabinet. 'There's not much here. MRE rations –some HOOHAH bars'

Siv knelt next to him and started stuffing her pockets with ration packs.

'What the Devil are you doing?'

'Basic survival,' she muttered, buttoning down her parka pockets after she'd stuffed them full of plastic packets. 'If you don't eat, you can't fight. Get food whenever you can. Store it whenever you can. If you can't store it, eat it – and get your body to store it.'

Warren stared at her quizzically.

'You think it's funny?' Siv demanded, indignantly. 'Do you know where our next meal's coming from, when we get off this plane? Well – do you?'

She was right. If his plan ran like clockwork there'd be no time to spare. He hadn't even thought about eating. He grabbed his own parka and started stuffing its pockets.

Siv ripped open a nutrition bar: 'So, what are we going out there for?' she asked between mouthfuls.

'To find out what happened to them – to make sure.' He stared down into his coffee. 'I don't hold out much hope. We haven't heard anything. But I owe it to them – I can't just leave them out there 'til the Spring.'

'Shitty time of year to be going out on the glacier...' Siv observed, philosophically.

'That can't be helped. And when we get out there, we're staying out there – at least 'til we find what we're looking for.'

'And what's that?'

'Ah, well, Sergeant Jagland,' Warren replied, his eyes twinkling mischievously: 'That's why I've brought you along.'

*

As the plane droned on through the night, Warren imagined the restless, storm-tossed ocean, churning beneath them. He checked his watch: they'd been in the air two hours. Pretty soon they'd be crossing the east coast of Greenland. After that it would be all ice, all the way up to Thule: endless and featureless – a landscape locked under an impenetrable, mile-deep sheet of ice.

He remembered the first time he'd ever seen it. As a boy his parents had taken him on a trip to the Pacific coast of America. Because of storms over the Midwest their plane had taken the great circle route over the polar ice cap: hour after hour of ice: white, featureless, unrelenting.

He remembered how at first he'd been excited by it. It was amazing to think that such a harsh, alien landscape existed so near to their own, cosy, comfortable world. But after three, and then four hours it had depressed and finally overwhelmed him. He'd yearned for any sign of life: an animal – even a tree, or vegetation of any kind – anything that might give him a sign that the dominion of ice was coming to an end.

That same overpowering feeling of awe had never left him – he felt it now, even though the world beneath him was cloaked in darkness. He'd spent most of his adult life up here in the Arctic and it was still alien to him – a hostile land.

But this was where the war was being fought. The silent, dirty war of death far from the prying eyes of television cameras. A war of ambush and counter-ambush; of murder on a grand scale in the fathomless depths, beneath the silent white shroud that concealed everything. An unrecorded war, without battles or monuments – or glory. A war of small, spiteful victories: of avoiding death and defeat – and holding the line.

He glanced across at Siv, curled up under her parka, fast asleep. She looked so peaceful, so innocent, just like an angel. It was hard to believe she'd spent years training to be a killer – a cold warrior. He smiled: it struck him that they were both cold warriors, but warriors of a very different breed. She was a creature of the far northern wilderness: a land of endless winter darkness and summers bereft of night. Warren had never come to love it as she so obviously did. His was a war of technology, of strategy and intellect: of second-guessing the Enemy's designs and unravelling their battle plans, anticipating their next move – and hoping against hope that he didn't get it wrong.

And in all these years he'd never got it wrong. At first it'd been a matter of sheer dumb luck. After a couple of years people ascribed it to a kind of second sight. "Trust Warren" they used to say, "He can see into the minds of the Enemy".

Nowadays his run of luck seemed so improbable that people were starting to ask questions, looking askance at him: just how did he do it? Rumours abounded that he was in league with the Enemy: that one day – when the stakes were really high – Warren would let them down.

And that would be the end.

*

Thule Air Force Base

Greenland

19.30hrs New Year's Day

The plane jumped and skittered on the frozen runway – finally slewing to an uneasy halt and burying itself in the great mounds of loose snow on the overrun pad.

The intercom crackled into life – the pilot announced the local time at Thule through gritted teeth.

Siv smiled: one of the things she loved best about the far north was the way it fucked up people's regular conventions – like time. They'd travelled four and a half hours from Stavanger, and according to the clocks they'd arrived before they set off.

She remembered a story her grandfather had once told her about the earliest NATO exercises, about how the armies of the great western powers had turned up, each one insisting that everyone work off their own time – and unwilling to surrender to anyone else's...

What a fuck-up that'd been.

Up here in the wilderness, conventional time – civilised time – didn't exist. Your time was your own, you carried it with you: the time it took to do a job, to travel a distance. Time for sleeping, time for working – time for living.

Warren heard the stairway click into place as soon as the big C-40 came to rest. He swung the locking bar up and put his shoulder against the door. It opened effortlessly – a cloud of ice splinters blasted through the gap.

'Good to have you back, Commander Warren – sir!' an American voice barked from somewhere in the darkness beyond.

'Hi, Sam!' Warren yelled into the howling wind, as he swung his kitbag down into the big master-sergeant's waiting hands. 'No let up in the storm, I see.'

'Not since Christmas, sir – hit us just after you got out!' he cried, clambering onto the plane. 'Been going strong ever since. This is the first flight we've had in – and, to be honest, we're kinda surprised to see you...'

'Needs must, Sam!' Warren replied. 'You know me – I wouldn't be doing this if I didn't have to.' He motioned toward Siv: 'This is Sergeant Jagland – the one I signalled you about.'

The master-sergeant shook her hand without taking off his gauntlet. It was so cold it stuck to her palm.

'Feels like it's pretty cold out there!' she said, throwing on her parka.

'You can say that again!' Sam barked hoarsely. 'Hit minus one hundred again yesterday!'

'But that's impossible!' Siv replied. 'That sort of temperature...'

'Fahrenheit,' Warren reminded her. 'You're at a US base, remember? Just over minus seventy centigrade...'

'Which is pretty darned cold, I can tell you,' the master-sergeant affirmed.

Siv's heart leapt as she stepped out of the plane. Sam was right, this was real cold: cold that burned the back of your throat as you breathed it – cold that made you blink all the time just to keep your eyeballs from freezing over. She swung her kitbag over her shoulder and clambered down into the swirling ice storm.

Warren stayed on the plane, directing the unloading of six small, silver crates – cautioning the servicemen to carry them with the utmost care and making sure none of them was left behind. Their contents were well-padded and the crates themselves were made from the same grade titanium the Russians used for their submarine hulls – still Warren watched them anxiously. If anything happened to any of them – if any one of them were lost or damaged, it would spell instant and irrecoverable failure for the mission.

Finally, when they were all securely stowed in the back of the waiting Air Force Humvee, Warren could relax. He climbed aboard, placing his arm protectively over the nearest crate.

Siv stared out through the windscreen at the swirling, sparkling ice that formed and reformed as the wiper blades swept back and forth, carving myopic slots that closed again almost as soon as the wiper had passed.

After three long years of waiting, she was back.

*

Siv scowled at the pile of kit laid out along a table in front of her:

'What's this?' she demanded, scornfully, picking up a jacket and examining it critically.

'Arctic survival gear,' Warren replied.

'It's blue...' she grimaced, '...and orange.'

'US Air Force issue.'

'Snow is white, ice is white – the whole fucking Arctic is white! Why make it blue and orange?'

'So you can be seen.'

Siv shook her head in disbelief: 'Why do you want to be seen?'

Warren shrugged: 'These people work on a base – they don't need to be camouflaged.'

She weighed the jacket in her hands and pulled at the seams — then raised her eyebrows slightly:

'It's well made, I'll say that for it.'

'I'm glad you approve.'

'But it's too bulky – you can't fight in it.'

'We aren't planning on fighting.'

Siv stared at him like he was a maniac: 'Nobody wants to fight, Warren. Don't get me wrong – I don't *want* to fight. But we need to be prepared for it, if we have to.'

Warren didn't have time to argue. He grabbed a pair of ice boots from his side of the table, and tossed them across to her. She caught them deftly.

'I took your sizes from your service record and sent them on,' he said, stowing his own into his kitbag.

'They're too small,' she said, striding across to a rack full of boots on the far wall and picking out another pair. 'They need to be at least two sizes too big. Your feet need to move around inside them – otherwise you risk getting frostbite, for sure.'

'It's never bothered me before.'

Siv thought a moment: 'How long do you spend outside?' she asked. 'The longest time, I mean.'

'A couple of hours, I suppose.'

'Well, there you are then,' she said, picking out a big pair of boots with jagged metal teeth sticking down from the sole and heel. 'A couple of hours is fine maybe – but any longer and you'd have lost your toes, believe me.' She dropped them heavily onto the table in front of him. 'Wear bigger boots.'

Warren stared at them. They looked enormous. Then he remembered the numbness he'd felt in his feet after every sortie – and how long it'd taken to work his toes back to life. He took the smaller pair out of his kitbag and replaced them with the ones Siv had chosen for him.

'Here – catch!' Siv cried out as she threw an old-pattern steel helmet across the room. He caught it one-handed, like a basketball:

'What do I want this for?'

'Cuts down your thermal profile better than Kevlar.'

'So?'

'Thermal imaging. Your head glows like a streetlight. The cold steel masks it. Some – not all. But enough. Better than Kevlar, anyway.'

*

Qaanaaq Seaport

Greenland

22.30hrs New Year's Day

'Fuck...' Siv muttered under her breath as she watched the caterpillar crane carrying a big, baled-up pallet of food and supplies, out along the mile-long jetty to the Danish icebreaker *HDMS Gunnar Thorson*, waiting in the bay, its engines rocking it back and forth to keep the pack ice from closing in around it.

'...You don't believe in travelling light, do you?'

'We could be out there quite a while,' Warren replied, watching anxiously as the wind swung the heavy pallet back and forth like a child's toy. 'But once it's there, it's there. If we don't use it, it'll still be good for another mission.'

Siv eyed it dubiously. There was too much stuff, she thought — way too much. How were they going to get it all up there? Warren didn't seem too bothered about it – but it sure as Hell bothered her. These damned Anglos were just like their Captain Scott – in fact they were too much like him. They placed too much faith in stuff: equipment, machines, technology – and not enough on their natural instincts. She believed in travelling light; that was the Amundsen way – the Norwegian way.

*

HDMS Gunnar Thorson

North Star Bay

Midnight, New Year's Day

Warren made a mental note of the time, as the icebreaker eased away from the jetty, its hull screeching and grinding against the pack ice:

Day 1 : 00:00 hours

He stared down, mesmerised by the great grey slabs that crowded in around the hull, grinding upwards as the ship forced its way forward, picking up speed as its momentum started to overcome the resistance of the ice that cracked and shattered, surrendering almost unwillingly – crushed beneath the weight of the ship's anvil prow.

He didn't notice Siv as she came and leant over the rail next to him.

'How long will it be 'til we get to the Humboldt?' she asked, staring out into the darkness ahead of them, as though she would make the ship to go faster by sheer will power if she could.

'It's hard to tell. In the summer I'd say a day at the most. I've never done this trip in winter. I don't think many people ever have. With luck I'd say we'll get there sometime on the third day from now.'

'With luck...' she muttered.

'Yes,' Warren conceded. 'With luck.'

*

Day 2 : 17:20 hours

The captain scowled down at the radar: 'Look at that,' he muttered, staring at the glowing green mass that filled the top of the screen. 'Just look at it! I've been sailing these waters forty years and I've never seen anything like it.'

'It's not unusual for the winter ice to come this far south is it?' Warren asked.

'Of course not!' the captain grumbled. 'But this isn't winter ice. Winter ice forms shallow and even. Oh, it can get to three and four metres thick in places – but nothing like that.' He pointed at a massive island of ice, lying straight across their path, shaking his head and staring at it.

'It's that damned earthquake. You mark my words...'

'Earthquake?'

'We had one under the Humboldt – you haven't heard, maybe? Happened on Christmas Day – a real humdinger. Broke off a lump of ice the size of Zealand – and it's heading straight for us.'

'Are we in any danger?' Warren asked, nonchalantly – not wanting to let on that he'd caused the "earthquake" in the first place.

'No real danger,' the captain replied. 'It's only advancing at maybe twenty kilometres a day. The damned thing is, how the Devil am I going to get around it?'

'Well, isn't that clear water out over there?' Warren asked, pointing to the west of the ice island.

The captain shook his head and spread his hand over the whole area: 'See all those tiny little flickers of light...?'

Warren nodded.

'...Well, they're icebergs – each one of them many, many times larger than the *Gunnar Thorson*. And there are thousands of smaller ones out there, still bigger than us, that our radar can't pick up at this range.'

'Can you get through?'

The captain shrugged: 'We might get lucky...'

'I don't deal in luck, captain,' Warren replied, turning his attention to the chart table. 'If we carry on at this course and speed, how long have we got 'til that lot starts closing in?'

'A day, no more.'

Warren didn't reply straight away. In his mind he was back in the Kjegle watching the opening sequence of Siv's first reconstruction. He drew a mental perpendicular line down from her viewpoint to sea level: ten degrees – elevation one-fifty – that gave him a surface height. He squared that with the soundings his team had taken when they'd been plotting out the disruptor pattern. Finally, he seemed to come to a decision:

'Where is it now?' he asked, staring down at the chart table. 'On here – can you show me?'

The captain pored over the map, all the time glancing back to the radar.

'Just about there,' he said, pointing to the very northernmost point of Baffin Bay.

'So it's cleared the neck of the basin at Smith Sound?'

The captain nodded.

Warren reached across and circled a patch of open sea to their west-north-west. 'Will it be ice-free out here?'

The captain stared at it: 'That's the North Water – it's normally navigable all year round. But nothing's totally clear, not this time of year – especially not this year.'

'How long will it take us to get there?'

The captain considered the question: 'About ten hours, I'm guessing.' He nodded. 'Yes, we can make that in ten hours – if the weather doesn't get any worse.'

'Alright,' Warren replied. 'I want you to take us there.'

'What?'

'Change course.' He picked up a blue chinagraph pencil and drew a cross in the middle of the area. 'Make straight for this point – understand?'

The captain scratched his head and stared at the vast expanse of open sea. 'OK,' he said, uncertainly. 'This is your mission – and it's sure as Hell easier than cruising straight into all that *Gud-forbandede is...*' He turned to the helmsman and gave him their new bearing.

While his back was turned Warren scrawled the coordinates of the cross on a scrap of paper, and stuffed it in his pocket.

*

Warren clambered right down into the bowels of the ship. Below the waterline, the screeching and grinding of the ice distorted into an unnerving, eerie banshee-screaming that echoed all around the hull, reverberating against the juddering clatter and thump of the ship's engines. Everything down here in the guts of the ship smelt of the salt-rank, brackish pools of water that had trickled down over many years, splashing and sloshing around, curdling with films of ancient oil.

Warren peered up to check he hadn't been followed. When he was sure he was alone, he took out the screwed-up scrap of paper and entered the grid reference into his mobile phone – then pressed a three-button command which encrypted the data. Reaching into his breast pocket, he drew out a set of earphones, plugged them in and pressed one of the earpieces against the thick steel plate of the hull. He watched the screen intently for a few moments. Then, seemingly satisfied, he stowed everything back into his pocket and clambered back up the corroded steel stairway.

He'd only gone up one deck when the banshee-screaming took on a different quality. He listened intently: there words in those screams. He didn't understand them – but he recognised the voice. It was coming from the other side of the hatchway right next to him.

He swung it open – and had to duck straight away, as a heavy wrench flew through the air and landed clattering on the gantry behind him.

'You horny old goat!' he heard Siv yell. 'You keep your mucky paws off me!'

Another projectile – an explosive rivet – spun across the engine room like a bullet. He didn't see where it ended up – but he heard a deep male voice bellowing as it found its mark.

This was all too much for Warren:

'What the Hell is going on here?' he yelled.

Instantly Siv's face appeared, swinging upside down – right in front of him.

'Hey – what're you doing here?' she asked, her head cocked on one side. 'You never come down here!'

Warren stared at her – she was hanging by her heels, dangling from a bulkhead: 'What's going on?' he said. 'It sounded like you were being attacked.'

'Me? Attacked?' Siv swung down, landing lightly on the grimy steel deck. 'What – by him?'

She strode across the engine room and picked up a length of thick copper pipe: 'Hoy, Bård – come out!' she hollered, banging it against a bank of steel lockers.

'Alright! Alright!' a hoarse voice grumbled from behind them. 'But don't throw anything else! I've got a lump the size of an egg on my arse...'

'Well, that'll teach you to keep your grubby hands off mine.'

An old man, not much more than five feet tall, his face mostly hidden by a straggly mane of grey hair and an unkempt bushy beard, dragged himself uncertainly from behind the lockers.

'Now you behave yourself,' Siv instructed him. 'This is the tin-hat I was telling you about – an Anglo – and a real important guy.'

'Has this ...man... been molesting you?' Warren asked – finding it hard to believe that this strange, rotund little fellow could ever pose much of a threat to a woman like Siv Jagland.

'Hah! He'd have to catch me first,' she scoffed.

'Mind, if I did catch her, I don't think I'd remember what to do with her,' Bård confessed, scratching his beard. 'She's even younger than my granddaughter.'

'Didn't stop you trying,' she taunted, poking her tongue out at her would-be assailant.

'Just stop that!' Warren ordered, irritably. 'So this is where you've been all the time.'

'Sure is,' Siv replied, grinning.

'What have you been doing down here?'

'Come on, I'll show you,' she said, grabbing his arm and leading him along a gantry, beside the clattering engines. 'Bård!' she shouted over her shoulder, 'Set up another plate!'

The old man pushed past them and waddled ahead, all the time muttering to himself and chuckling a deep, gurgling laugh.

Siv knelt down and opened up a long mahogany box. She reached in carefully and drew out a rifle.

'Do you know what this is?'

Warren shrugged: 'It looks like a hunting rifle.'

'Not just any old hunting rifle. This is a Schultz & Larsen M97 – a prince of hunting rifles. This one's got the .458 calibre barrel – it's for big game hunting.'

'So what's it doing here on an ice breaker in the Arctic?'

'Arctic patrol ships used to be issued with two of them...' Siv began.

Old Bård came waddling and wheezing back: '...In case we got iced-in and had to hunt to make our rations go further.' He shrugged. 'Of course we never got to shoot them. Global positioning meant we were never lost, so if we got stuck they could fly in supplies as soon as there was a gap in the weather. And, nowadays we're not allowed to shoot a polar bear or a walrus – not even a seal. It's more than our jobs are worth...'

'So, they've never been used,' Siv continued, drawing out the second Schultz & Larsen from the case and handing it to Warren. He stared at it appreciatively. It was a beautiful, superbly-crafted weapon – but there were a few features that didn't look right:

'I've never seen a hunting rifle with a trigger like this before,' he observed, critically. The guard was more than six inches long and instead of a conventional trigger it had been fitted with a curved steel lever that ran the length of the guard.

'It's for firing when you're wearing mittens. Of course, you can get mittens with trigger-fingers – but they're shit.'

'I get that,' Warren replied. He remembered seeing old World War Two newsreels of Soviet soldiers with similar triggers on their sub-machine guns. 'Why's the end of the barrel turned – is that to take a silencer?'

'Yeah. It looks a bit crap, I must admit, but it's all that we could think of. We've been making the silencers here in Bård's workshop. We're pretty pleased with them. Look, I'll show you.'

She reached back into the box and pulled out a short, thick cylinder, about the size of a narrow drinks can, and screwed it onto the end of the rifle.

'It makes it kind of unbalanced. But we've counterweighed it by making a larger magazine – it takes fifteen rounds, instead of the usual five. And we've bored out the stock – criminal really – so that it can take another three magazines. So you're carrying sixty rounds with you wherever you go – which can be handy if you need them.'

'And heavy if you don't,' Warren replied, disapprovingly. If their mission went to plan they wouldn't have any need for hunting rifles — no matter how well they'd been adapted for Arctic warfare.

A short clandestine mission was what he had in mind. Invisible, under the radar, the way he liked to work, the way he'd worked for years — until nine days ago. That bothered him. It bothered him very much: it was the first time one of his missions had ever been discovered, and he couldn't see how it'd happened. Why had the others been outside when they knew the satellite was overhead? It didn't make any sense — they'd been so careful… Maybe it wasn't a satellite that'd spotted them; there'd been a lot of activity round there, in spite of the storm. Maybe they'd just been unlucky. But they'd never been unlucky before…

'Hey, Warren!' Siv said, snapping her fingers in front of his face: 'Wake up!'

'Oh, sorry,' he murmured. 'Yes, it's great — really excellent.'

'Yeah, sure…' Siv shrugged — she could tell Warren was just humouring her, but she didn't care. 'Look,' she said, enthusiastically: 'Just watch this...'

She knelt down and pulled back the bolt – the first round clattered into the breech – and took aim down the gantry to where Bård had set up a steel plate, about twenty centimetres square, against a rusty old tank. Warren reckoned it was about thirty metres away – a fair distance, he thought.

With all the engine noise around them, the only way he could tell Siv had fired the first shot was from the recoil. She drew the bolt back immediately, which sent the spent shell skittering across the deck. Her face was frozen with concentration as she took aim again, and moments later a second shell sprang out, disappearing into a dark corner of the engine room.

Warren watched her shoulder kick back as she fired the third round. Then she was standing next to him once more, unclipping the magazine and drawing back the bolt to eject the last shell. The whole process hadn't taken more than twelve seconds.

'Shall we go see how I did?' she said grinning, and strode off down the gantry.

Warren followed her, and Bård waddled after them, muttering and chuckling to himself.

Siv grabbed the plate and held it up: 'Not bad eh?'

Warren looked down at it: there was a single hole, punched into the metal, exactly at the crossing point of two lines that were scratched into it.

'Not bad at all...' he glanced at the rusty old tank – it was riddled with bullet holes. 'One out of three, bang on.'

'Hah,' she scoffed, tossing the plate to the old engineer. 'Show him, Bård!'

Bård took the plate to the other side of his workshop, started up a band saw and screwed the plate into a vice. The saw screeched through the metal in seconds and Bård punched a red button to switch the machine off.

He waddled back, brandishing the two halves of the plate and handing a half to each of them. Warren examined his half: burrowed deep into the metal were the crushed remains of not one but three bullets – each one buried into the back of the other.

'Three out of three...' he muttered, admiringly. 'When I saw the other holes...' he said, gesticulating at the bullet-riddled tank.'

'You thought I'd missed?' Siv shook her head: 'That was when I was getting used to it and calibrating the sights.'

'You've used up a lot of ammunition,' Warren observed.

'We have plenty of ammunition!' Bård cried, gleefully. 'Those dimwits in Copenhagen don't let us fire the damn things – but still they send us a thousand bullets a year! Every year for the last thirty years!'

'What? You mean you've got thirty thousand rounds – for these?' Warren exclaimed, holding up his hunting rifle.

'Well, nearer to forty, actually.' Siv replied. 'They started up with a good supply. We've probably fired off fifteen hundred or so, but still...'

Warren shook his head in disbelief.

'It's .458 calibre – the same as the Winchester Magnum,' Siv continued. 'It's all good stuff...'

'No, Siv,' Warren replied, guessing what she was going to say next. 'We're not taking forty thousand rounds with us,'

'But...'

'We're not – and that's final.'

'How about ten?'

'No.'

'Two?' she pleaded, looking up at him, imploringly.

'One,' he conceded, finally.

'...Each?'

Warren glowered at her, pretending to be angry. It was obvious she'd worked hard getting these rifles ready – and dodging the clumsy advances of the amorous old engineer into the bargain.

'Alright, each,' he agreed, handing his rifle back to her. 'But you'd better get all this lot safely stowed with the other stuff – now.'

Siv looked at him, enquiringly.

'We're leaving...' He glanced at his wristwatch: '...In approximately nine hours time.'

'Have we reached the Humboldt?'

'Don't ask – just pack,' he said, then turned and went back through the hatchway.

'I'd have settled for five hundred!' she cried after him, laughing.

But Warren was already gone.

*

North Water, Baffin Bay

Day 3 : 04.50 hours

The captain stared out into the darkness. The storm of the last two weeks had passed, the winds had dropped and the stretch of open sea all around them was uncannily calm. Above them the clouds were breaking up to reveal the scintillating brilliance of the polar constellations.

'Anything on the radar?' he yelled into the wheelhouse.

'Nothing,' the first mate replied. 'No icebergs – nothing in a five kilometre radius, sir.'

The captain turned to Warren: 'We've been sat here becalmed for two hours now,' he grumbled. 'Would you mind telling me just how much longer you expect us to just sit around, kicking our heels?'

'I need you to hold your position and bearing, captain,' Warren replied. 'Only for a little while longer.'

Siv leaned over the rail and watched the cook entertaining the crew, throwing scraps of offal at a pod of orcas that'd taken an interest in the icebreaker not long after they'd stopped their engines. They bobbed up, sliding over one another, perfect black slithering over perfect white, splashing as they leapt, competing to catch the bloodied scraps, then falling back, throwing up great plumes of green phosphorescent water that drenched the laughing, jeering sailors.

The first mate came dashing out of the wheelhouse:

'Captain – sir!' he yelled. 'We've two readings on the radar!'

'How far off?'

'W-well, that's the thing,' the first mate stammered. 'They're...'

The *Gunnar Thorson* started to lurch and pitch beneath them – the sea all around suddenly started to boil and bubble – the orcas scattered and disappeared. Siv grabbed the rail – she thought for a moment she was going to be thrown off the ship into the icy waters. As she stared down into the murky sea, she thought her eyes were playing tricks on her: there were two dark shapes emerging, surging up from the depths, one on either side of them.

At first she thought they were whales – for a moment she was worried that the orcas might attack them. But whales didn't come straight up out of the water – not like this. As they rose above the waves, she realised they were submarines – really big ones. Maybe it was just that the *Gunnar Thorson* was such a tiny boat, but they looked bigger than any submarine she'd ever seen. Their conning towers loomed above them. Men in yellow waterproofs stared down at the ice-breaker through night-vision binoculars.

Warren was waving to them.

*

Siv watched in awed fascination as one of the subs moved closer to the *Gunnar Thorson*, coming right up alongside her, illuminating her with dazzlingly powerful searchlights. Then, to her amazement the whole thing seemed to open up, right along its entire length. A huge crane unfolded and swung across to the little icebreaker. It hovered above them like a predatory insect while two sailors attached Warren's pallet of supplies to a heavy steel cargo hook.

'That's the *USS Tecumseh*,' Warren said, watching as the cables on the pallet tightened and it started to rise off the deck. 'We saved her from the breakers. She used to carry ballistic missiles – but she's our logistic support now. We couldn't operate up here without her.'

'*You* saved her?' Siv replied. It was hard to believe Warren was really so important that he could stop the US Navy from breaking up one of their nuclear submarines if they wanted to.

'Well, we put in the request – begged and borrowed the necessary equipment, called in a few favours to secure the finance. But she's been so successful we've got her sister ship now...' he said with undisguised pride, pointing across at the other sub, standing a few hundred metres off from them. 'That's the *USS Madison* – her role is slightly different. You'll see how when we get to the glacier.'

The crane swung the pallet across, depositing it in the submarine's cargo bay in a single movement. Moments later it was swinging back and hanging over the *Gunnar Thorson*, expectantly.

'Now it's our turn,' Warren said.

On the deck below, the sailors had placed the six silver cases in the centre of a cargo net, together with their kitbags and the mahogany rifle case.

'Come on Siv,' Warren said, stepping onto the net next to the cases. 'We'll be over in no time.'

She stared at it suspiciously. Whilst she was perfectly at home on ice, she wasn't too keen on water in its liquid form – and she wasn't at all sure about being suspended over it like some damn-fool fish in a net.

'Isn't there some other way?'

'No,' Warren replied. 'This is the only way. If I didn't know better I'd say you were frightened...'

'Frightened – me?' she scoffed, stepping onto the thick rope netting, un-certainly. 'What's to be frightened of...?'

The sailors hauled up the heavy ends of the net and attached its steel eye-lets to the cargo hook, enclosing them in a thick rope cage. Siv felt everything around her being squeezed together as they were lifted off the deck. She could do this, she thought – it wasn't so bad at all. Moments later they were swinging, halfway between the two vessels, suspended over the waves. She felt an almost imperceptible lurch – and everything stopped.

'What's up?' Warren yelled across at the crewmen working the crane.

'Hydraulics, sir!' one of them yelled back. 'Cracked pipe – or a seal, maybe.'

'How long will it take to repair?'

'Not long sir – but we've got to find it first!'

Siv glanced up at the crane: 'You know we could just climb up this cable and along...'

'No need,' Warren replied, glancing across at the gaping cargo hold of the *USS Tecumseh*. 'We'll be safely over in a few minutes – we aren't going anywhere...'

Siv spotted something out of the corner of her eye – a dark shadow flickering through the water, darting between the two ships – making straight for them.

'*Spekkhogger!*' she yelled – pointing down at the water.

'What?' Warren replied, a half-amused smile playing on his lips. 'What's that in English?'

'Dammit – I don't know!' she cried, peering down into the murky waves. 'It's... it's – a...'

Just then an orca surged up out of the water at them, its mouth wide open, its jagged teeth bared. Siv jumped back as its jaws snapped shut – just short of the net.

'Oh,' Warren exclaimed staring at the creature, as it seemed to hang momentarily in the air, only inches below them. '...You mean a killer whale!'

'Damn right I do!'

The orca dropped backwards away from them, baring its brilliant white underbelly as it landed on its back with a mighty splash that drenched them both.

'Huh...' Siv muttered, reaching for her handgun. 'He won't do that again...'

'No!' Warren cried, putting his hand over hers. 'You can't do that.'

'Are you crazy? He'll be back! What are you – some kind of whale-hugger?'

'Don't be stupid! If you shoot him, the blood will attract the others!'

Siv didn't say anything. Warren was right – she hadn't thought about that. She stared down into the narrow channel between the two boats.

'He can only come two ways...' she said, her eyes darting up and down the channel — watching, waiting. '...Oh, shit!' she cried as the orca burst up vertically, straight out of the water. Its teeth clamped shut on the cargo net, catching in it, snagging the thick rope, twisting it – ripping it.

Above them they heard the crane creak and groan as it strained to hold the whale's colossal weight. They could feel it starting to give way – inch by inch they were dropping into the water.

The creature swung its head from side to side as it dangled from the net, snarling and blowing with each exertion. Siv backed away from it, clinging onto the far side, keeping as far from its jaws as she could.

Warren pulled out his hunting knife and launched himself at the creature.

'Cut the net!' he shouted, slashing at the mesh. 'We've got to get it off – or it'll take us down!'

Siv grabbed her own knife and scrabbled across the silver cases after him. They hacked at the rope on either side of the thrashing, snapping orca's head – its hot, rank breath was all about them, its bead-black eyes fixed on them, uncomprehendingly – bent only on capturing its prey and dragging it down into the depths.

Warren was the first to cut through the mesh – the orca's teeth clung wildly onto the last few strands – suddenly realising that it was losing its grip on its victims. Moments later Siv slashed through the other side. She dragged herself up on the netting and screamed triumphantly as she stamped hard on the killer whale's black snout with both boots.

The creature swung its head back as it fell – and caught Siv's boot between its teeth. For a long agonising moment she felt its weight dragging at her, pulling her out of the net. She wrapped her arms through the sodden rope mesh and clung on with all her might – but she couldn't hold on – it was too heavy. She was slipping. Warren leapt forward and plunged his knife deep into the orca's domed head. Instantly, its mouth opened as it let out an agonised screech and fell away, back into the black, icy depths – with Warren's knife still buried in it.

Straight away they felt themselves rising up from the water. Aboard the *Tecumseh*, crewmen laboured as fast as they could with a hand winch, winding them up and out of harm's way. Soon they were hovering over the gaping mouth of the cargo hold and being lowered into the belly of the submarine

*

USS Tecumseh

Smith Sound

Day 3 : 20.50 hours

Dan Monroe sat back in his captain's chair and tried to empty his mind of everything except the information that was coming at him from all angles: radar and sonar, echo and laser – global positioning and the fuzzy composite images coming in from the swarm of tiny guppy-drones that went ahead of the *USS Tecumseh*, picking out any obstructions that lay in wait for the submarine. He used everything, every fragment of information to build up a picture of the hazards that were ranged before him, as his craft picked its way through the archipelago of icebergs crowding in around them.

Warren watched him – he'd seen Monroe like this a few times in the years they'd worked together – and he knew better than to disrupt the captain's train of thought.

Technicians calmly called out readings from their monitors, knowing full-well the implications of every word they uttered – the awful realisation that at any time they were only a few feet away from disaster. But still they carried on, calmly calling out streams of numbers, bearings, distances: helping their captain to build up a mental picture that was going to save their lives.

'Engines reverse one quarter – five second burst. That should bring us to a standstill. You know,' he said, turning to Warren. 'the problem is that Smith Sound just isn't that deep: less than fifty fathoms in most places – and oftentimes down to as little as twenty. Some of these bigger bergs are just about bumping along the bottom…'

He turned to his navigator. 'Say, Kevin — where's the bottom round here?'

Kevin Sung stared at the three-dimensional hologram on the chart table. The light shining up on his face reminded Warren of Siv Jagland staring up at him from the black screen in the *Kjegle*.

'Thirty-five fathoms, captain,' Sung replied, without hesitation.

'Hmm... That's gonna be tight...' Monroe considered the problem. 'Well,' he said, turning back to his passenger. 'Whatever it is you're up to this time, it sure as Hell better be worth it. I've got an ice cube the size of the Pentagon sitting right in front of me, about a hundred yards ahead. If I try and go under it I'll have maybe twenty feet of clearance – that's if Kevin's bathymetry is accurate...'

'Oh, I wouldn't count on it, cap,' Sung interjected, briskly. 'These waters haven't been charted since the last century.

'And the shape of that darned thing means that if I try and go round it my only option is to surface. But if I do that, Ivan's going to know we're here.'

'But going round is the safer option – right?' Warren asked.

'If there is a safer option...' Monroe mused, half smiling to himself. '...then, yes. Going round is safer. But, like I said...'

'I don't think the Russians will try anything,' Warren replied. 'There's too much going on up there.'

Monroe looked dubious.

'Look, Dan – I know you're pretty sure you can get the *Tecumseh* under it – but are you prepared to lead the *Madison* down that way?'

Monroe took a long time to answer. The two subs were identical in every dimension. But the captain of the *USS Madison* was on his first tour of duty as commander of his own vessel. He was good – but he was green.

Monroe sighed – surfacing and going round the berg felt like a chicken option. And revealing his submarine to the Enemy went hard against the grain for a man who'd spent his whole career dealing in stealth.

'Well, gentlemen,' he said, glancing round at the crew. 'Looks like we're going up. Anyone know what the weather's like up there?'

'Cold, sir!' everyone yelled in unison: 'Damn cold!'

'It sure is… It sure is…' Monroe replied, chuckling to himself and turned to his exec. 'OK Alex, make ready to bring her up.'

As he climbed down from his chair he laid his hand heavily on Warren's shoulder: 'I sure as Hell hope you know what you're doing...'

Warren looked steadily into Monroe's eyes and smiled: 'Don't worry, Dan – people say that to me that all the time.'

*

Siv laid down her rifle — she'd cleaned it twice already — and sat down heavily on her bunk, brooding. She didn't like being in a submarine, not at all. The idea of being stuck in a metal box surrounded by all that water played on her mind.

Worse, the damned thing seemed to travel without any sense of motion – it was nothing like being rocked and tossed around in the old *Gunnar Thorson*. The only sensation of movement was the steady thrumming vibration of its engines. And, what with the cold, grey light and the air-conditioning and the cleanliness – and everyone speaking in English – it felt an awful lot like being back at Mount Jåttå.

That was what was making her feel so miserable: what was going to happen to her at the end of this mission? Would they send her back to the bowels of the mountain – discarded and forgotten? Could she really go back to that?

Warren's head appeared round the door:

'Hey, Siv!' He beamed a boyish grin: 'Come on – come up top – we're surfacing!'

*

Out on the *Tecumseh*'s conning tower in the cloudless Arctic night, Siv gazed all around in wonder at the thousands of stars blazing brilliantly in the sky and the flickering lights of the little guppy-drones twinkling in the sea beneath them. Behind, the *Madison* followed in their wake, both submarines' searchlights probing ahead as they threaded their way between the massive walls of ice rearing high above them on all sides, sheer as cliff faces, silent as sentinels.

'It's amazing...' she whispered. '...the most beautiful...'

Siv fell silent, lost for words. Nothing in English or Norwegian seemed adequate for the shimmering, deadly beauty that surrounded them.

Warren glanced at his wristwatch: 'And it's about to get even more beautiful, very soon...'

Almost on cue, the full moon appeared, glimpsed briefly between two monstrous ice mountains. A few minutes later it appeared again, higher this time – then higher as it appeared once more, finally hanging uninterrupted in the sky. Circling without setting – shining like a Chinese lantern, bathing the icescape in a delicate silver light.

'Commander Warren, sir?' A young officer, so wrapped up in a fur-lined Navy parka that only his eyes and nose could be seen, held out a radio phone. 'It's the captain, sir.'

'Hi Dan,' Warren said, taking the phone. 'How's it looking down there?'

'Pretty darned good,' Monroe replied. 'A couple more twists and turns and we're through – the Kane Basin looks almost clear.'

'Congratulations, Dan – you made it.'

'Yeah, but it's kind of out of the frying pan...'

Anything else Monroe said was drowned out as three Mikoyan *Timberwolf* fighter-bombers screamed up the channel behind them blasting their eardrums as they buzzed the submarines, one after another – each one missing the *Tecumseh*'s comms tower by a few feet – then disappearing, twisting between the silver ice cliffs.

'Christ – what're they doing here!' Siv cried, as she watched them go.

'There's not much we can do about them,' Warren replied. 'Greenland can't defend its own frontiers – and the government in Nuuk won't condone NATO operations above the 66th parallel: they don't want to antagonise the Russians. Of course we're up here – and so is Ivan. Every year it gets harder and harder to flush him out.' He shrugged and stared after the warplanes. 'Well, at least we don't have to hide anymore...'

*

USS Tecumseh

Humboldt Glacier, Greenland

Day 3 : 23.00 hours

Their searchlights played on the jagged, freshly-revealed terminus of the Humboldt Glacier. The flickering lights of hundreds of guppy-drones shuttled back and forth, probing the barrier – sending back fragments of images that the Tecumseh's computers built into a three dimensional picture of the ice wall ranged before them.

Down in the control room, Kevin Sung scoured the image, zooming it up – peering at it, scrutinising it. Finally he shook his head, disconsolately:

'It's no good,' he said, turning to Warren and Monroe. 'Everything round here is just sheer cliff face. The only decent landings are too far south – it would take you days to get to back to your base.'

'What's it like under the surface?' Monroe asked.

'Pretty much sheer, all the way down – five fathoms at its shallowest point, I'd say.'

'Well, we won't get better weather...' Warren mused.

'Are you thinking what I'm thinking?' Monroe asked.

'Very probably... Looks like we're going to have to make a whole lot of bean-counters very, very unhappy...'

*

Warren, Siv and Monroe stood in the midst of a cluster of sailors on the conning tower of the *USS Tecumseh* and watched the tracks of four torpedoes as they fanned out from the submarine and cut through the waves, then disappeared from sight, speeding straight for the ice cliffs of the Humboldt, more than five miles away. Behind them the exec counted down the time to impact.

As his countdown got to zero the whole horizon in front of them was engulfed in a single, silent sheet of flame. A few seconds later the water beneath them groaned and rumbled with the explosion. Finally, after about half a minute the air blast of the sound wave hit them.

'Well,' Warren asked, 'Shall we go see what all that wasted defence expenditure has done for us?'

Monroe nodded and turned to his exec: 'Ahead, half,' he said. 'Let's be on the lookout for new ice floes.'

The Tecumseh surged toward the glacier, cutting through the thin crust of winter ice that split and crackled as the submarine cut quickly through it.

In the clear skies above them Siv could make out about half a dozen drones, hovering overhead, silhouetted against the stars, drawn to the scene of the explosion like buzzards to carrion. But whose were they, she wondered: ours – or theirs?

*

The blast of one of the torpedoes had sculpted a whole new ice-harbour, revealing a sweeping fault that swirled up from the shore, producing a makeshift jetty and a jagged track up onto the top of the glacier.

Siv and Warren watched from the conning tower of the *Tecumseh* as the *USS Madison* disgorged dozens of heavily-armed US Marines, many of them carrying hand-held surface-to-air missiles.

'I see what you mean now…' she said as the marines deployed to take up defensive positions all around the ice harbour, disappearing into the darkness beyond the submarines' arc lights. '…The *Madison*'s your troop-carrier.'

She watched them enviously – every one of them was wearing white Arctic theatre camouflage — and glanced down at her own US Air Force blue parka, with its Day-Glo orange panels.

The young officer in the fur lined parka handed Warren the radio phone.

'Hi, Dan — how's it looking?'

'I just got a message from Colonel Law on the *Madison*,' Monroe replied. 'His marines have secured the landing area. The *Madison*'s coming back out.'

They felt a gentle surge as the *Tecumseh* moved forward to take her place.

Warren handed the phone back and turned to Siv: 'Well,' he said. 'We'd better get ready to go.'

*

Siv opened the hatchway and was confronted by a thick, blue wall of smoke. Her senses were assaulted by the reek of exhaust fumes and the deafening scream of snowmobile engines revving up, reverberating round the walls of the cargo hold.

'Shit!' she yelled as she climbed onto her own snowmobile. 'We haven't even docked yet!'

'The don't hang around,' Warren yelled back and switched on his own machine.

Ahead of them the hold doors opened, a steel gangplank lowered onto the glacier, biting into the ice, and a huge all-terrain transport rumbled out, grinding up the slope, levelling the track as it went.

'Our turn now!' Warren cried over the din: 'Let's go!' He jammed his visor down and sped out of the belly of the submarine. Siv rode in his wake, followed by a flying column of a dozen snowmobiles, their tracks snarling and skittering on steel, then biting into the ice as they sped up the ramp.

Warren stopped at the top of the slope and looked down, watching, making sure the last man made it up onto the glacier. Siv pulled up beside him and raised her visor to get a better view.

'Well – what do you think?' he yelled over the snarl of their machines.

'Think about what?' she yelled back.

'All this,' he said, waving his arm about him at all the logistics and firepower on display.

Siv smiled: 'Yeah, O.K.' she replied, her eyes sparkling with a fierce delight. 'Sometimes technology can be kind of impressive...'

*

Warren sped on, driving his column ever faster across the barren wasteland. He glanced up at the moon, shining down brilliantly on them, at the apex of its circle in the sky – it wouldn't dip below the horizon for another couple of days. But the weather reports said there was a storm coming in — it would hit them in a couple of hours, no more. The moon would be engulfed by swirling ice clouds that would blot out its light altogether. They'd be cast into total darkness for days, perhaps weeks.

Siv stared in amazement at the cracked and shattered surface of the glacier. What the Hell had happened here...? She'd never seen anything like it in her life. All these fissures – sharp-edged and newly formed – there was something unnaturally regular about them.

She spotted a raised ice-ridge just ahead, on the far side of a gaping fissure. Opening up the throttle she sped ahead of the column and gunned her snowmobile up the slope. Warren followed her.

At the top of the ridge she stopped and took out her binoculars. The moonlight was so bright she could use the optical viewer, which gave her a far sharper view. Surveying the scene from above gave her a far clearer picture: the fissures radiated up from the sea edge in waves, like ripples on a pond – except glacial ice didn't do that. Especially not on the largest glacier in the Northern Hemisphere...

'What's up?' Warren asked over the communicator, as he pulled up next to her. 'Are we being followed?'

'No... No, not at all... But look – just look at that,' she said, pointing out over the icescape. 'It's like someone's just picked up the glacier and shook it...'

'What? You broke formation – came up here – just to look at this?'

'Yeah, sure...' Siv replied, picking up on the disapproval in his voice. 'Why not? This is incredible!'

'Because we've got to get to the base and start setting up before the weather closes in, that's why.'

Siv looked up at the sky: 'How far have we got to go?'

'Five miles, maybe a bit more. Depends how many of these chasms we have to go round.'

She nodded. The weather was changing, she could feel it. Away in the east the moon illuminated great towering columns of cloud that blotted out the stars. 'You're right,' she said, simply, starting up her snowmobile. 'We need to get out of here.'

She snapped down her visor and tore off down the slope, in pursuit of the column.

*

Humboldt Glacier, Greenland
Day 4 : 00.00 hours

Warren stared at the scene of devastation that just ten days before had been his base camp. He'd seen satellite photos of it, dozens of them – pored over them for hour after hour, so that each image was ingrained in his memory – but they didn't prepare him for the reality of it.

The explosion had blown away one wing and the whole tailplane of the old bomber. What was left of the fuselage was bent and buckled like an old tin can, lying half-buried in the ice. The starboard wing was still attached: it stuck out crazily into the air, like an accusing finger – twisted by the blast so that its engines stared up at the sky, their propellers turning in the strengthening wind.

But there was no sign of the tiny fibreboard hut that'd been their home for all those weeks – every scrap of debris had been blown away, erased by the scouring storm.

The transport roared to a halt next to the bomber's fuselage and reversed back under its contorted wing. Warren pulled up next to it and scanned the horizon, flipping his night vision to high acuity, blinking at the dazzling image, straining his eyes for any sign that they were being watched from out on the glacier, but nothing registered. He looked up apprehensively at the sky – the storm was coming in. Soon they'd lose the light of the moon altogether. They'd have to work in swirling, blinding clouds of ice crystals. But at least it would hide what they were doing from the satellites — even the lowest-flying drones wouldn't be able to detect them.

Warren dismounted and struggled through the snow to the burned-out hulk of the B17. He felt his way round the battered fuselage, searching for a way in. Before the attack there'd been a few ways of getting into the plane from the underside – he was hoping they hadn't all been buried beneath the ice.

The nose was completely entombed and the ball-turret was so crushed and mangled there was no way through. But one of the bomb doors was hanging down, swinging in the strengthening wind – and as far as Warren was concerned, that was as good as a shiny front door with a holly wreath and a welcome mat.

He ducked inside and shone his flashlight around. The plane had force-landed on the glacier on its way over to Europe, a hundred years before. It had sat there undisturbed, perfectly preserved in the moisture-free Arctic air, until a botched attempt to recover her had set off a fire that'd turned the bomber into a blackened wreck – a state that'd been made far worse by the Russians' attack.

He climbed up through the bomb bay and shone his flashlight into the crew compartment. The probing beam fell on the warped and buckled skin of the fuselage, but it was practically ice free up there. The fragile, yellowed Plexiglas panels of the pilot's and navigator's canopies were still intact – even the machine gun turret was still in one piece.

He ducked back out onto the ice and beckoned to a marine wearing a gas mask carrying what looked like a flame-thrower. He nodded and trudged toward him, bowed over by the weight of two canisters on his back. Warren helped him through the bomb door, then shone his flashlight out into the darkness beyond the pool of dim light cast by his snowmobile's headlamps, straining his eyes to catch a glimpse of anyone who might be watching them...

'Do you want a hand with anything?' Siv asked over the communicator.

In his eagerness to get the base set up as quickly as possible, Warren had completely forgotten about Siv.

'Nothing we can do in there for at least an hour,' he replied.

'OK. What's he up to?'

'He's spraying the inside with a new insulator. We're trialling it.'

'Uh-huh?' Siv didn't sound impressed. 'What's so special about it?'

'Well it's completely clear – it lets light through. But it doesn't conduct heat at all.'

'What – nothing?' she scoffed.

'Not even a bit. It only needs to be a millimetre thick... But there's one small problem...'

'What's that?'

'Well, once it's set hard it's completely safe – it looks and feels like glass. But in its liquid form it's absolutely lethal. If you inhaled it or got even a drop on your skin you'd be dead in a matter of seconds.'

'And it takes an hour to set?'

'That's what the manufacturers say. We can't do anything in there 'til then.'

'Well, that's good.'

'Why?'

She tapped the display console on her snowmobile: 'I sent out an "activate" signal just now and I'm getting a distress beacon. It's very faint...' she said, pointing away to the south. '...and it's coming from over there.'

*

The driving wind threw up dense, swirling plumes of ice, that rattled against their visors, and blinded them as they rode on into the darkness. They hadn't gone more than a couple of hundred metres when their headlights fell on two figures straddling their snowmobiles, the distress beacons on their jackets flashing dimly in the darkness. As they got closer they could see they were tied both to their machines, their hands wrenched sharply behind their backs.

Their heads were uncovered, exposed to the elements.

'Fuck,' Siv cursed over her communicator: 'That's a cruel way to die...'

'It wouldn't have taken long...' Warren muttered, as he edged his machine closer. 'Their lungs would have frozen solid in minutes... Most likely their brains would've shut down before that...'

In the glare of their headlights they could see that although a few shreds of frozen flesh still clung to the corners of their jaws and cheekbones, the rest of their faces had been ripped away — ice-blasted right down to the bone by the incessant driving wind. Only the name patches on their parkas gave any indication that these inhuman ice sculptures had once been Peary and Dern.

Warren was about to dismount, when an imperious voice stopped him in his tracks...

'Don't move!' Siv barked over her communicator, practically deafening everyone around her.

Warren turned, alarmed – she was aiming her hunting rifle straight at him.

'What the..?'

'Get down – now!' she yelled, staring down her sights at him.

Warren dived off his snowmobile and launched himself sprawling onto the ice. Siv fired. He felt the bullet ripple through the air as it flew past him. The heavy .458 Magnum round thumped into Peary's frozen corpse, jerking it up – twisting it round.

She fired again.

'Siv! Warren yelled. 'What the Hell!'

He scrambled through the ice toward her.

'Stop!' he yelled. 'What are you doing?'

Siv ignored him and fired a third round. Peary's body swayed back and toppled from his snowmobile. Moments later it exploded in a blinding sheet of white fire.

'Ivan booby-traps everything,' Siv said, matter-of-factly, as she took aim at Dern and fired once more. His snowmobile went up with her first shot, throwing Dern's frozen corpse high into the air.

'But then...' she observed, carefully slotting her rifle back into its white neoprene holster: '...So do we.'

*

'I'll get the marines to bring them back in,' Warren said, gesturing toward the remains of Peary and Dern.

'OK,' Siv replied. 'But I'm still getting a beacon – and it's not coming from those two.'

'It's got to be Stewart. Let's go find him.'

Siv set off, glancing down at the direction finder on her console, listening intently to the beacon bleeping faster and faster in her earpiece — all the time peering into the darkness for booby traps and hidden fissures.

Warren followed her. Her tail light flashed brilliant crimson as she pulled up and swung her handlebars round, raking the landscape with her headlight.

'See anything?'

'Not yet. But the beacon's practically continuous – we've got to be close...'

He rode up beside her and tracked Siv's headlight beam with his own.

At the extreme end of his sweep Warren thought he saw something:

'Over there,' he said, pointing to a dimly blinking red light on top of a low *serac*, a small ice hill thrown up by the movement of the glacier.

'Do you see it?'

'I see it,' she replied. 'But it doesn't look like a body...'

'Let's get a better look.'

Warren revved up his snowmobile, giving the tracks short bursts of power as he edged forward, checking all around for anything that might be a booby trap.

Siv shrugged: 'Well, it's the right bearing,' she murmured and fell in behind him.

They dismounted and shone their flashlights at the object on the crumbling ice hillock. It wasn't a body, it was a metal chest – it had the word 'WARREN' stencilled on the side.

'It's mine,' he said.

'I'd never have guessed... So what do we do now?'

'The same as you did with Peary and Dern,' he said, drawing his rifle out from its holster.

They both took aim and fired three rounds apiece at it. Siv hit it three times out of three. Warren hit it with his final shot and knocked it off its precarious perch.

'Well,' Siv observed: 'Looks like it isn't booby trapped.'

'Maybe not,' Warren replied, standing over it. 'But there could be something inside.' He bent down and picked it up: 'We'll take it back and get it checked out.'

*

Humboldt Glacier, Greenland

Day 4 : 02.00 hours

A big, burly figure in a blue and orange Air Force parka stood silently under the bomber's wing, seemingly immune to the ice storm that swirled all around, watching Warren and Siv as they approached.

Warren waved as he recognised him: 'Hi, Sam!' he called out over his communicator. 'I didn't know you'd come along!'

'I was on the *Madison* – there were a few things I had to pick up – so I just followed on and fell in behind.'

'How's it going?'

'Pretty good. The Gomers have been real busy while you've been away.' He pointed up to the bomber's propellers: 'The wind turbines are working again – would've been better if they'd still been horizontal. But Hell, there's enough wind round here to keep 'em going...'

'What about the antenna?' Warren asked.

'All done – the whole wing's set up. Again, horizontal would've been better...'

'What about the insulator?'

'A couple of minutes yet – they're still getting readings. It doesn't set as quick as they said – not at these temperatures anyway.'

'Well, it'd better not be too long – I want you lot back on board before the storm closes in.'

'Don't worry about us,' Sam laughed. 'We ain't planning on staying round here any longer than we have to.'

Warren dismounted and unstrapped the chest from the back of his snowmobile.

'We found this out there. I want to look inside it — but I'm thinking the lid could be booby trapped.'

'So you want me to open it?'

'And blow your arms off in the process? I don't think so,' Warren replied, handing the chest to the sergeant. 'Get a couple of small charges on the spring clips. Blast the lid off.'

*

Siv and Warren watched as the master sergeant casually flicked a remote detonator. They saw a small flash in the distance, but the sound of the explosion was carried away by the strengthening storm.

The lid was flapping up and down in the wind, clanging like a tuneless bell each time it hit the chest. Warren reached out to steady it and shone his flashlight inside.

Everything was frozen together into a single, solid block. It was all just how he'd left it — except that sitting on top of it all was a card, like an oversized playing card. He brushed away the frost that welded it to the rest of the contents. It was a tarot card — a Russian tarot card. A stylised image of a sneering, raven-haired woman stared up at him contemptuously.

There was a single word beneath the image, chiseled in bold cyrillic script: *"ИМПЕРАТРИЦА"*. He sounded out the symbols: 'Im - per - at…'

'…Ritsa' Siv finished the word. "*Imperatritsa*" — The Empress.'

'You know it?'

'I've heard of it,' she replied. 'It's a calling card. An ethnic cleansing unit. They leave them tucked into the clothes of their victims.'

'Marking the bodies of the dead…' Sam muttered.

'Not just that,' Siv replied. 'They attacked one of the mining settlements north of *Sveagruva,* on Svalbard. Anyone that wouldn't leave they shot on the spot. The others they just kicked out. They wouldn't let them take their cars or trucks, they had to walk: men, women and children. It was only thirty kilometres back to *Sveagruva,* but it was February. Fifty-six set out, only two survived.

'The Northern Rangers were choppered in. They found all the bodies — each one had one of these cards, even the babes in arms. But there was no trace of the Enemy — they'd just disappeared. Of course, the Russians denied everything. As far as they were concerned nothing ever happened.'

Sam tapped Warren on the shoulder: 'I just got the "all clear" on the insulator — looks like we can get you settled into your new home.'

*

A human chain of marines passed crate after crate from the transport down to the bomb-bay, then back up to Siv and Warren, who placed them round the cabin. Siv leaned over and held out her hands as a marine passed her one of Warren's silver crates.

'Hey, Warren,' she hollered over the communicator, holding it up for him to see: 'Where do you want these?'

Warren glanced over: 'I'll take them,' he said, taking each silver crate in turn and carefully placing them on the navigator's table.

'Looks like that's it,' she said handing him the last crate.

'OK,' he replied, clambering down through the hatch and into the bomb-bay. 'We've just got one more thing to do. Come on…' He motioned for Siv to follow him out through the bomb doors.

Outside, Siv looked around. Warren was waving at her from the back doors of the transporter, beckoning her in: 'Hurry!' he cried. 'We don't have much time!'

Siv nodded and scampered across the ice to join him. As soon as she was inside, Warren slammed the big metal doors shut behind her.

Inside were two men in Arctic camouflage, one much taller than the other.

'Time to get changed,' Warren said, stripping off his Air Force parka and overtrousers. Siv watched dumbfounded as the other two men started stripping off as well. 'Well come on,' Warren said, grinning. 'You said you wanted camouflage gear.'

Siv did as she was told and exchanged clothes with the smaller man, who took her Air Force parka with the same expression of disdain that she'd had when she first set eyes on it.

'Don't worry, Zak,' Warren said, encouragingly. 'It's only 'til you get back to the *Madison*.'

The marine snorted: 'Huh. That's if I ever make it back,' he muttered. 'Wearing this piece of shit I'll be all lit up like a Christmas tree.'

'It's all part of the deception – now off you go!' Warren clapped the two marines on the back as he ushered them out of the transporter.

He glanced out of the windscreen as he scrabbled into the larger marine's gear. 'See, over there?' he said, pointing to the perimeter, where the other marines were holding up brilliant neon-pink flares. 'They're bringing Dern and Peary in. The flares will confuse the hell out of any thermal imaging – so we'll hardly register at all. Come on — back to the plane.'

They scrambled out of the transporter and darted across the last few feet of ice, clambering through the bomb door, into the sanctuary of the burned-out bomber.

Inside their new lair, they gazed through a side window at the elaborate flare-lit procession going on outside, as the marines reverentially loaded the bodies of Peary and Dern into the transporter. Siv watched in amazement: it was all too much, too overblown – too theatrical. Suddenly, everything became clear to her:

'You set this whole thing up, didn't you?' she asked, staring up at him.

'What do you mean?' Warren replied, not taking his eyes off the procession.

'You know what I mean: two submarines travelling on the surface – not one, but two – blasting their way onto the ice – then this crazy posse of marines and all the equipment. It's all a deception, isn't it?'

Warren said nothing. He just kept staring out of the window, his eyes glittering in the flickering light.

'…You made a great, big play of us coming out here in force, for everyone to see – for the Enemy to see. You *wanted* them to watch us, didn't you?'

Warren sighed as the marines finished loading the remains of his comrades into the transporter and slammed the heavy steel-plate doors shut.

'You used coming here to recover the bodies of those two guys as a front to get yourself back out on the glacier.'

'You could say that, yes,' he replied. She was right: he'd used Peary and Dern — even in death he'd used them.

'Everything...' she said, thinking it through: '...every detail – right down to those stupid Air Force parkas with their stupid orange patches. You'd thought out every bit of it... Before we'd even left Stavanger?'

He nodded: 'Way before.'

'Well, damn me,' she said, a hint of grudging admiration creeping into her voice. '...You know, you may be a *gud-fordømte* tin-hat — and an Anglo – but you're a whole lot smarter than I'd given you credit for.'

Warren glanced down at her and smiled: 'Well, Sergeant Jagland, I'd say that was quite a compliment, coming from you.'

'You're damn right it is,' she muttered, gazing out of the window – for some reason she felt suddenly embarrassed, unable to look him in the eye. 'But don't you go letting that go to your head.'

Warren didn't say anything. Instead he followed her gaze. Outside, the convoy was pulling away. Already the tail lights of the leading snowmobiles were almost out of sight. It wasn't long before the whole column was swallowed up by the swirling darkness. They were alone.

*

That night Warren laid, tightly wrapped-up in his sleeping bag staring at the thin skin of the fuselage as it warped and buckled in the storm that raged outside. He couldn't sleep: there were too many things whirling around in his head.

Murdering Dern and Peary like that was bad — but to booby-trap their bodies as well? That was new. He hadn't expected that, not at all — and he'd never even heard that the Enemy was engaged in ethnic cleansing. But Siv had. Over on the other side of the Arctic Ocean, the Norwegians were fighting a desperate, spiteful war for the possession of their northern territories, a war that made their own conflict look almost civilised.

Norway was a small, weak country — the Enemy didn't have to risk the possibility of a crippling total war; they could behave pretty much as they pleased. Murdering civilians, booby-trapping dead bodies, or even the bodies of living prisoners, was probably a commonplace over there — but it was unheard-of in this theatre.

Then there was the Tarot card. They'd found one on Dern's body. Peary's had been blown apart by the booby trap, but he guessed there would've been a card planted on him too. Someone was trying to tell him something — but what? Was it a challenge? A death threat? Who was this "Empress" — was it even a person at all?

If Siv was right, the force that'd attacked this place had come across from Svalbard. They were game-changers, they played by a different set of rules. But why had the Enemy changed tactics — why were they suddenly behaving with such confidence, such contempt?

*

Day 4 : 11.00 hours

Siv could hear the wind roaring outside, feel it buffeting the old airplane, catching at its one remaining wing and rocking it so violently that it screeched and groaned like a lost soul.

She loosened the drawstring on her sleeping bag and breathed out cautiously, watching the vapour to see what it did. If it floated in mid-air it meant things weren't too bad, if it sank it meant it was cold. She remembered one morning on exercise, when it'd been so cold the vapour had poured from her mouth and nostrils like water.

But today it was floating. She stared at it in amazement: in fact it wasn't just floating – it was actually rising. She scrabbled at the drawstring.

'Ah, you're up.' Warren said. Siv peered bleary-eyed in the direction of his voice: he was sitting over a small solid fuel stove. He glanced over his shoulder and smiled: 'I was going to wake you in a couple minutes...'

'It's warm,' she croaked, screwing the sleep out of her eyes and roughing up her hair.

He glanced at the thermometer hanging from a bulkhead: 'Four degrees – Celsius. Not bad, considering it's minus forty outside – and that's not counting the wind chill.'

'The insulator...' she replied groggily. '...It works, then.'

'Looks like it.' He nodded toward the canisters propped up at the far end of the fuselage. 'There are a few cold spots we're going to have to spray, which means one of us will have to go outside, because there's only one mask. But otherwise...' he said, handing her a mug of coffee. '...It's all looking pretty good.'

She watched in wonder as the steam rose from it. 'How long have you been up?' she muttered.

Warren glanced at his watch: 'About half an hour...' He tossed her a couple of nutrition bars: 'Breakfast's just cram and coffee – until we get ourselves sorted out, but...' he jerked his thumb over at the silver cases on the navigator's table: 'Priority number one is to get that lot working. We've got three hours 'til the satellite passes over.'

Siv stared across at them ruefully: 'So that's why you wanted me here? To do the same job I've been doing at Jåttå?'

'For that, yes,' he replied. 'But not just that. There are many, many reasons why you're the best person for this mission – maybe even the only one.'

She shot him a sidelong look, her eyes still bleary with sleep: 'Now I think you're trying to flatter me, Commander.'

Warren held up his right hand, like he was swearing an oath: 'It's the God's honest truth – believe me.'

'Believe you? Does it matter if I believe you?'

'It matters to me,' he said, drawing the conversation to a close. 'Now, get dressed.' He glanced at his wristwatch: 'We've got two hours and fifty six minutes.'

They worked together quietly, efficiently – exchanging few words as they set up the equipment. Although Siv had spent the last three years in the surveillance centre, her training in the *etterretnings* had started with field equipment that looked pretty much the same as this. It was only when she put it all together and turned it on that she realised how different it was:

'Oh, wow,' she muttered as she stared at the screen, her eyes widening as she began to appreciate what it would be capable of. She started to explore different options, different views and resolutions. Siv might have hated the daily drudge of having to work deep in the bowels of Mount Jåttå – but that didn't mean she didn't enjoy the technology she got to play with while she was down there.

'OK, I get this,' she said glancing down at Warren, who was connecting up an array of tiny packets under the aluminium navigator's table. 'So what are we looking for – or weren't you planning on telling me that?'

He looked up from his work:

'Go to "trace" in the "settings" menu,' he replied, 'and under "source" input this...'

Without hesitating or faltering, he ran off a string of thirty-six alphanumeric characters, which Siv entered unfalteringly into the source field.

'Anything else?' she asked.

'Not for now,' he replied. 'That's our start point.'

She stared at the character string. There was something familiar about it – then she realised it was one of the satellites she used to use for cross-reference. It wasn't one of the main ones. There was some reason why it didn't figure in her daily routine – but what was it? Then it dawned on her:

'We shouldn't be able to see that one,' she said. 'It's an NPGS – a North Pacific geo-stationary – what's it doing here?'

'Everyone thinks it was knocked out of action a couple of days ago – hit by a lump of space junk and sent spinning out of control. Well, that's the story we leaked to their agents – and our double agents...'

'We have "double agents"?'

'Oh yes, double and triple – we've also got freelancers working for both sides at the same time — and even a few poor souls who can't remember who they're working for anymore. The whole system works quite well, I suppose – so long as you remember where everyone is in the feeding chain.'

'So, I'm guessing this satellite isn't really spinning out of control...'

Warren shook his head: 'We took it offline and repurposed it, so now it's sitting a couple of kilometres away from ANP-12.'

'The one I did the composite of?'

'That's the one.'

'So what are we doing with it?'

'Well, now that we're out here I guess it's safe to fill you in on what we're here for. That satellite will pass over us every six hours — and when it's exactly over our location it will send a narrow signal directed at us. We don't need to do anything — it will be triggered by a command from mission control. The transmission will last exactly 30 seconds —

the rest of the time it'll look just like a dead satellite — another piece of space junk.

'And what are we going to do with one measly thirty second burst of signal?' Siv muttered unenthusiastically. 'We won't get much data from that.'

Warren smiled: she was always so sceptical about everything. Even if he told her what they'd be getting she wouldn't believe it — she'd just have to wait and see for herself…

*

Siv sat at her terminal, staring at the screen waiting for transmission: just another day at the office — except that the office was hundreds of miles from the nearest civilisation and a couple of millimetres of tin and God-knows-what from an Arctic hurricane that would kill them both in a matter of minutes if they got stuck out there.

'Ready, Siv?' Warren muttered, staring fixedly at the screen. She nodded: 'Transmission in three … two … one…'

Her eyes widened as she watched the data transfer coming in: 'Ten *Giga*bytes a second — is that right?'

'The transmission comes down an incredibly narrow channel, only a few millimetres wide. It's targeted on this little receiver,' he said, gently tapping the smallest of the silver boxes.

She watched as the data mounted up: two hundred… three hundred. It stopped abruptly at three hundred and twelve Gigabytes.

'That's it?'

'I guess so,' Warren replied, checking the download time. 'That was just over thirty seconds.'

'OK — we've got a stack of data — what do you want to do with it?'

'Well, we watch the download, see what's happening to ANP-12. Then, if we find anything, we try and work out what's causing it.'

'And if we do?'

'We transmit a single character "1" to Control, and they come and get us. That's the only transmission we make — the only one we can ever make. We keep under the radar — that's the rule, that's how we work.'

'What if we don't find anything?'

Warren shrugged: 'We keep looking.'

*

Siv started running the download:

'OK,' she said, staring at the image. 'This is sharp. I'm impressed.'

'The technology is pretty impressive,' he replied, looking over her shoulder at the screen. 'Each thirty second download gives us six hours of ultra-high definition surveillance.'

'And now we can see it properly it looks a whole lot worse than it did in the optical image.' She pointed to a jumbled mass of floating components that occupied a whole quadrant of the screen. 'Shit, just look at that — it's a mess.'

*

Siv yawned. She'd spent the last six hours watching ANP-12 in real time: just hanging there in space, with the Sun and Moon rising and falling, the stars processing majestically across the heavens and the Earth turning beneath. But, in all that time, the satellite did absolutely nothing — and absolutely nothing happened to it.

'Oh, shit,' she muttered, blinking myopically at the screen. 'It's nearly time for the next lot.'

Warren glanced at the screen chronometer: 'We've got a minute. The satellite goes into shutdown while it compiles the download. You can take a break if you want.'

'Oh, thanks, commander,' she replied, rising from her seat for the first time and stretching. 'At least when I was at Jåttå, I could go to the bar at the end of a shift.'

'Well, there's beer in the supplies if you want one.'

'What?' she cried in amazement. 'You mean you had them pack *beer*?'

Siv was stunned: this was ridiculous — it was so unlike any operation she'd ever been on before. It was inconceivable, all the energy that'd been consumed — all the effort — just to bring beer to this god-forsaken place. The thought appalled her.

'Well, we could be here quite a while, you know — I don't think we need to abstain from all creature comforts. And you do like beer, don't you?'

Siv just glowered at him.

'There's no point looking like that. I know you do. And it's here now. So…'

'Well… alright…' she conceded, grudgingly.

'Anyway, I'm afraid it'll have to wait,' he said, glancing at the screen chronometer. 'Furlough's over — the next download's about to come in.'

*

Warren was watching the download, so it was Siv's turn to do the housework. This mainly consisted of either cooking or cleaning, or clambering back along the fuselage to empty the slop bucket out of one of the waist-gunner's ports.

This time it was the slop bucket. She put her head out of the port to check the wind direction — to make sure the slop wouldn't blow back in and go all over her. Glancing down, she noticed there was a fissure in the ice below her, running right under the plane.

She shone her flashlight up and down it: it looked to be about a metre wide and about the same deep. It ran as far as her flashlight beam could reach. 'Well, girl,' she muttered to herself. 'This needs investigating.'

But, if she was going to investigate it she'd need her ice-axe — there was no telling how deep the fissure might be when she got out onto it.

She clambered back along the fuselage to the cabin. Inside, Warren was staring at the screen, his eyes flickering over the image of the satellite.

'Found anything?' she asked.

'What do you think?' he replied. He glanced sidelong at her as she picked up her ice-axe: 'What are you doing with that?' he asked.

'Some of the slop must've splashed back before it froze,' she lied. 'Just gotta chip it off.'

'Nice job,' he muttered. 'For once I think I prefer staring at the download. Have fun…'

Siv took her flashlight and ice axe and crept out through the waist-gunner's port, carefully avoiding the frozen splatters of discoloured ice, and started making her way along the fissure.

It felt good to be outside — she'd been cooped-up in that tin box for ages. Warren had forbidden any needless excursions in case they were spotted out in the open. Well, she thought, this could hardly be called "out in the open": the howling wind was blowing an almost continuous screen of ice crystals that swirled and eddied above her as she crawled.

After about two hundred metres the fissure dived under a *serac*. A mound of loose ice had built-up the along the windward side of it, filling the fissure completely. Siv shovelled at it with her heavy snow mittens, and after about five minutes of clawing and dragging, she'd cleared a tunnel through the ice and under the *serac* itself.

'Ohh, look…' she whispered, shining her flashlight around: it was made up of two arrowhead-shaped slabs of ice that'd been brought crashing into one another by the movement of the glacier, and thrust upwards, creating a sort of shallow wigwam that was wide open on the side furthest from the plane. On the opposite side, facing it, there was a triangular slot about a metre high and thirty centimetres wide at the base. She shone the flashlight through it — it illuminated the bomb doors, half-hidden now behind a mound of wind-driven ice.

Laying down she shone the flashlight beam out of the slot, to the left and right, getting an idea of the sort of traverse she'd have if she used this place as a sniper's nest. It was almost perfect: she had a full view of the whole fuselage — and if she hacked at the sides a bit, she could get a line of sight maybe a hundred metres to the left and right of it.

The shape of the hole bothered her, though. Discharging any firearm left a heat signature that would be visible to infra-red imaging. The smaller the opening, the less obvious any heat signature would be. She'd have to pack it with ice to get it right.

But not tonight. She figured she'd been out long enough. It was time to be getting back — Warren would get pretty mad if he found out she'd been disobeying orders and sneaking around outside.

*

Day 10 : 20.00 hrs

It was Siv's turn to work the download. She flicked around the screen, zooming in and out just to change the image. She didn't notice Warren tiptoe-ing up behind her, his hand closed around something — concealing it.

'Siv…'

'Uh-huh?' she replied, not taking her eyes off the screen.

'Happy birthday.'

'What?' she exclaimed, spinning round on her stool.

He was holding a nutrition bar with a burning match sticking out the top of it.

'You'd better hurry up and blow it out. I don't think I can make it last much longer.'

She blew out the match and smiled: 'You found out my birthday?'

'Not really. I was checking your service record to order ahead for your kit, and…' He shrugged: 'You see I'm blessed with a photographic memory — blessed or cursed, whichever way you look at it. Anyway, I saw it, so it just sort of …stuck.'

He reached behind him and picked up two large bottles of American beer. Knocking off their crown tops he handed one to her: 'I think we can let the file run for a while — if anything happens I'm sure we'll notice.'

Siv clinked her bottle on his and took a long swig. The beer tasted good. Her shoulders, that'd been hunched over the screen for hours, started to relax almost immediately. Suddenly she didn't feel so mad at him for bringing it.

And, after a couple more beers, she didn't feel mad at him at all.

'Warren…' she said resting her chin on her third bottle. 'I've been meaning to ask you something for ages…'

'Go ahead,' he replied, leaning back and stretching out his legs.

'Well, when we were in the *Kjegle* — and you were getting the system to authenticate you — I remember you said "Warren" twice.'

'Did I?'

'You did. I heard it.'

'Like "Warren-Warren"?'

'That's right.'

'Well, there's a pretty good reason for that…'

Siv looked at him expectantly.

'…You see that's my name.'

'No!' Siv exclaimed. 'That's crazy! But how…?'

Warren took a long swig of beer:

'Blame my Dad — it was his idea. You see, after the Soviet Union collapsed, there was a lot of collaboration between Russia and the west. My Dad's a scientist — astrophysics. Anyway, he did a lot of work with a Russian called Ivan Ivanovich Ivanov, and he signed his name I^3 — which my Dad, being a scientist, thought was pretty impressive. So, when I came along…'

'He called you Warren Warren — so that you could be W^2!'

'It's worse. I'm actually W^3. I've got a middle name…'

'No!' Siv put her hand to her mouth in amazement. 'Didn't your mum have a say in all this?'

'She's a scientist too — quantum physics. Her only objection was that W^3 didn't have any meaning in her field — otherwise, she thought it was pretty neat. They're lovely people, but…' He shrugged: '…Complete nerds.'

'So that's where you get it from!' Siv laughed. 'And is there a Mrs-Warren-Warren-Warren?'

'Ah…' he fell silent for a moment. '…There was. Not any more.'

'Divorced?'

'Dead, I'm afraid.'

'Shit. I'm sorry.'

'Don't be. It was a long time ago. She was on Lufthansa 7732.'

'The one the Russians shot down?'

'Correction: the one the Russians deny any knowledge of.'

'That was a long time ago. I was still at school, I think.'

'Well, we were pretty young.'

'I guess. Did you have any kids?'

'Come on,' he laughed. 'We were only married six months!'

'Lufthansa 7732 came down north of Svalbard, didn't it? So, is that why you're up here, fighting in the Arctic?'

'Partly. Well, totally — in the first years anyway. You see, she was everything to me…' he shrugged. '…You know what I mean…?'

'Oh…' It was Siv's turn to fall silent — she had no idea at all.

'OK, so how about you?' Warren asked. 'Is there a Herr Jagland?'

'What — my Dad, you mean?'

'Could be a husband. You're of a marriageable age, and you're not exactly hideous — except first thing in the morning.'

'Oh, thanks. I'm charmed.' She shook her head: 'No, not me. A few flings, that's about it. I tend to attract the wrong kind of guy.'

'Like those bikers?'

Siv smiled: 'Shit, that was bad, wasn't it? No, not normally that bad. …I guess I've just never…' She let the thought trail off.

'Never what?'

'Oh, nothing… Nothing at all… Anyhow,' she said, changing the subject: 'There's something else I've been meaning to ask you.'

'This is turning into a real question-and-answer session, isn't it?'

'It's my birthday — humour me.'

'OK. Fire away.'

Siv stood up and stretched, rolling her head from side to side.

'It's something I just don't get,' she said. 'And no-on seems to be able to tell me.'

'What's that?'

'Well, why are we doing this?'

'Doing what?'

'This war. No-one really knows what's going on up here. As far as most folks know everything's fine — between us and them, I mean.'

'That's how it is — and that's how it's got to stay.'

'Why?' she protested, taking another swig of her beer.

'Because if people found out there was a shooting war up here, pretty soon there'd be a shooting war all over the globe.'

'No, I mean why are we doing it?' she persisted. 'There's no more ideology to fight over. We don't hate eachother. My uncles all drive Russian cars — they're the best you can get for driving on the ice. But the firm that makes them is owned by the Germans. Our gas comes from Russia. We go on holidays there — and they come over here. So, why are we fighting eachother?'

Warren stared thoughtfully at his bottle: 'Power. …It's all about power. The power to dictate at the negotiation table, the supreme confidence that comes from knowing that, if you wanted, you can destroy your opponent utterly — and there's nothing he can do about it.'

'But that's wrong,' Siv protested. 'No-one should have that kind of power.'

'We've had it — for more than fifty years.'

'What?' Siv stared at him, genuinely astonished. 'How?'

'The shield. The thing we're trying to protect.'

'But that's only for defence.'

'Well that's just it. If we can fire a missile at the Enemy, but he can't fire back — who has the upper hand?'

'Well, OK,' she conceded. 'But we'd never actually fire first would we? And even if *they* did, we could shoot their missiles down — and we still wouldn't shoot back at them. …Would we?'

'Wouldn't we?' Warren replied doubtfully. 'We've come pretty close on quite a number of occasions.'

'But that's just sabre-rattling. Puff and bluster.'

'And who backed down — us or them?'

Siv sat down heavily. He was right: they'd backed down. Every time. Right back to the Kennedy era — before her parents were even born — the Enemy had always backed down. Always.

'So all this time… We've been dictating to them?'

'Not all the time. We've never really interfered when they've been throwing their weight around in their own back yard: Chechnya, Ukraine, Georgia, Kazakhstan — bit by bit they're clawing back the old Soviet empire. But in Europe they can't go any further — they're right up against the NATO front line states: Poland, Romania, Latvia, Lithuania, Estonia — Norway. They know they can't go any further — because they know we'll knock out their armies on the ground.

'How do they know that?'

'Because we've told them we'll do it.'

'And they believe it?'

'Wouldn't you?'

Siv pondered that for a bit. All her life she'd always thought of the West as the good guys. The idea that all these years they'd been bullying the Russians, keeping them in check with the threat of a massive nuclear strike — a threat they'd be powerless to resist or respond to… Well, it just seemed wrong.

'Isn't that what the British used to call "gunboat diplomacy"?'

'Pretty much, I suppose. But remember: that brokered the longest period of peace the world has ever known … until now.'

'But we're not at peace!' Siv protested. 'At home we're fighting an all-out war!'

'A war that nobody knows about. The average man-in-the-street, in St John's or Oslo or Trondheim hasn't the slightest idea that only five hundred miles away from his front door we're fighting to the death to preserve his right to remain totally ignorant of the sacrifice so many are making — for him.'

'But that's wrong — all wrong!'

'No it's not, of course it's not,' Warren replied. 'The world is a better place. People are free — even in the reconquered states people have more freedom than they ever had under the Soviets.'

'And that's all because of the shield?' Siv mocked.

'Yes, in a large part — and how we use it. It enables us to dictate to the Russians from a position of strength. Oh, they might bitch about it — they do it in their media all the time. A day doesn't go by in Moscow without some news story about meddling Western politicians. But, in the end, they do what they're told.'

Siv sat in silence for a while, thinking it over. She was still struggling with the idea that they might be the bad guys — and not the Russians. It was a hard thing to come to terms with. But, on the other hand, Warren was right: what would the Enemy do if they weren't always thinking about what might happen if they over-stepped the mark? What wouldn't they do?

Suddenly, she became aware that the whole inside of the plane was bathed in an eerie, pale green light.

'*Nordlys*...' she whispered excitedly.

'What?'

'Come on,' she cried, grabbing his hand and dragging him up to the gun turret at the top of the plane. 'Come on! You don't want to miss this!'

Together they squeezed into the cramped plexiglas dome. Above and all about them, ribbons of light soared — violet and green — twisting and diving, coiling and wrapping around the metal skin of the plane like endless snakes of fire.

The heavenly display grew and grew, until vast shimmering sheets of light hung right across the Arctic sky.

'Lucky we're not receiving a download now…' Warren observed.

'My God,' Siv cried, smacking him on the chest with the back of her hand: 'You damned Anglo! Have you no soul…?'

But her reproach was cut short: a great, glowing, luminous ball of light barrelled across the ice — heading straight toward them.

They felt a surge of excitement as it seemed to explode onto the turret itself — all at once it was inside the dome, swirling all around them. They laughed as they moved their hands through it. Was it just the thrill of it? It felt like the light was tickling them. Siv turned to catch a brilliant will-o-wisp, and suddenly she was in Warren's arms. They were standing face to face, holding each other tightly, surrounded by twisting tendrils of brilliant green light, that seemed to draw them ever closer together.

They were transfixed, each staring into the other's eyes. Not simply Warren and Jagland any more: they were different souls, different beings — they were creatures of fire.

Then, as swiftly as it had come, the otherworldly light that had filled the dome with scintillating brilliance was gone. The dazzling banners of flame that only moments before had stretched right across the heavens dwindled and slowly faded away.

'We can't do this…' Siv mumbled, gently pushing herself away.

Warren released his hold and let her to slip wordlessly from him. He heard her sigh, her warmth evaporating from his arms — only to be replaced by an empty chill that was only partly down to the cold.

*

Day 11 : 09.00 hrs

The download had just come in. It was sitting there in the inbox, waiting for Siv to open it. Her finger hovered over the screen. She could hardly bring herself to do it — because she knew that once she opened it, it meant she'd be committing herself to another six hours of unremitting boredom…

Suddenly she was struck by an unnerving thought — what if they'd gone too far last night? What if they'd kissed — what if they'd actually *fucked*?

What then?

Shit — what if she'd gotten pregnant? Now that would've been *really* bad. She could just imagine the look on General Morgan's face when they told him they'd had to abandon the mission because she was having a baby. Oh, that wouldn't be a pretty sight — no, not one bit…

But what if she *had* kissed him — and what if he'd kissed her back? Would that *really* have been so bad…?

She shook her head and tried to drive the thought from her mind, tapping the download folder and watching with grim resignation as the huge surveillance file slowly started to compile.

The screen flashed abruptly into life: the same old scene, the same old satellite. It looked like it was hovering somewhere over the US west coast. Wherever it was, it was daytime. Beneath it, the Pacific Ocean was a brilliant, shimmering blue — whereas up here they wouldn't even see the sun for at least another month.

She scowled at the satellite: she hated it. She knew its every facet, its every feature — every crappy square centimetre of it…

She stared at the screen and frowned, cocking her head to one side and narrowing her eyes as she scrutinised the image.

Something was wrong.

Unlike Warren, who always just sat there, with his photographic memory, staring at the download from start to finish, Siv had to find ways of fixing the image into her mind. In the end she'd broken the whole thing into quadrants and memorised the component parts of each one, then flicked back and forth comparing the same quadrant over time, going from one to another — she knew she was actually doing the same tedious job as Warren, it just didn't feel quite so boring.

But this time there was something different — something was actually different.

Something had changed.

'Get up!' she hissed, prodding Warren with the toe of her boot. He swung around in his sleeping bag.

'What's up?' he asked, blinking the sleep from his eyes.

'Look,' she said, pointing at the bottom right quadrant of the screen. 'See that cable?'

Warren nodded, but said nothing.

'The last time I looked at it, it was a "U" shape — connected at both ends.'

'OK.'

'Well, now it's a "J". It's gotten itself disconnected.'

'Or something has disconnected it,' he replied, staring hard at the screen. 'It wasn't like that when I left it. I'm sure it wasn't. Run the closing sequence of the last download.'

Siv did as she was told.

'There it is,' he murmured, staring at the screen. 'Still in place — right up to the final frame.'

'So it's happened while our satellite was downloading,' she replied.

'Or while it was compiling the download. Sometime in that ninety seconds…'

He struck his forehead with his palm.

'What's up?'

'I've been an idiot!'

She stared at him quizzically.

'We've been watching each download from end to end,' he explained. 'But we've never cross-referred the start of each download with the end of the previous one.'

'But they look just the same.'

'But we don't know that, do we?'

She couldn't argue with that: 'Well, let's have a look then,' she said, clicking on the start of the last download.

'No — I'll tell you what,' Warren replied. 'Go to the beginning of the first one. Let's have a look at that.'

The image flashed onto the screen.

'Look, tiny changes,' he muttered, flicking back and forth between the images. 'All in that bottom right quadrant.'

'Shit,' Siv cursed under her breath: 'We missed them all — every damned one. But how could we?'

'We were just looking at it the wrong way…' Warren replied, slumping back on his bunk, and staring up into space: 'Whatever's happening is happening at the same time our satellite is downloading — every time.'

'But how did they find out about us so quickly. We'd only been here a few hours…'

Warren shook his head:

'No, I don't think it's that. I think it's a coincidence.'

'Coincidence?' she replied sceptically. 'How so?'

'I don't buy the idea that they could've been on to us so quickly. The NPGS hadn't even made its first transmission, so there was nothing for them to go on. But this is the closest ANP-12's orbit ever comes to Russia, so it's reasonable to suppose that if anything's going to happen to it, it's going to happen somewhere around here.'

'OK,' Siv agreed. 'Go on…'

'Look, the two satellites are travelling at a speed relative to the surface of just over a mile a second, give or take a bit for the rotation of the Earth. So that means whatever it is that's doing this, it can only be a hundred miles away from us at most — and possibly a whole lot less.'

'But we can't see what it is because we're downloading data from our satellite at the same time.'

'That's about it,' Warren agreed.

'So, we need to get Control to delay the download, so that we can see what they're up to.'

'But we can't do that.'

'Why not?'

'Communications silence — nothing traceable — that's the first rule of these operations. If we break it, we risk exposing ourselves to the Enemy.'

*

Warren was hunched over the computer staring fixedly at the screen, his eyes flicking between images.

'What are you looking at?' Siv asked, leaning over him to get a good look.

'ANP-12's blueprints. I want to know why they're targeting that quadrant. They carved-up BNW-55 indiscriminately — this is different.'

'What's in there?' she said, pointing to the damaged area on the blueprint.

'Well that's the thing,' he replied, sitting back gloomily. 'There's nothing — well nothing of any importance.'

Siv tilted her head to one side as she stared at the screen.

'Have you got a 3-D projection?'

'Yes, it's in here…' He flicked through the folder and clicked on a file. Immediately a three-dimensional image of the platform flashed onto the screen.

Siv reached across and started to manipulate the image.

'Look…' she said, tracing a line through the platform with her finger. 'Perhaps they're trying to get at something else… ANP-12 always presents the same way to the Earth, doesn't it?'

'Pretty much. Unless we command it to change anything. But, apart from corrections, there's been no change for years.'

'So, is there anything along this line that's of any importance at all?'

Warren examined the blueprint, tracing Siv's line more precisely. He looked up: 'There,' he said pointing to a panel on the far corner of the platform. 'It's right in line.'

'What is it?'

'Behind that panel is the command control system.'

*

Day 13 : 03.00 hrs

Siv stared at the screen, miserably. They didn't need to bother making comparisons anymore. The damage was plain for any damn fool to see. They were through to the panel that housed the missile deployment backup system — already one of the retaining clips was floating around in space.

'This is stupid…' she muttered more loudly than she needed to.

Warren stirred, cocooned in his sleeping bag, but said nothing. She knew he was awake though; Warren was a restless sleeper, he was always thrashing around. If he wasn't moving that meant he was awake.

'We can't carry on like this,' she said, even louder this time. 'There's no point just sitting round watching ANP-12 gradually falling to pieces…'

Still Warren said nothing.

'…For all the good we're doing, we might as well be back in Stavanger,' she persisted. 'Look — what the Hell is up with you?' she demanded, angrily.

'I've been thinking.' Warren answered from under his sleeping bag.

'Uh-huh?' Siv replied, noncommittally. 'And?'

'Well… They carved up BNW-55 'til it was just a mass of space junk, didn't they?' he said, his voice muffled by the sleeping bag. 'But they were careful to keep the command and reporting systems active.'

'Agreed. So?'

'This time it's different. This time they're going straight for the jugular. As soon as they cut into the control system they know we'll get an alert — we'll know there's something wrong.'

'So why are they doing it this way?'

Warren unfastened his sleeping bag and rolled over to face her: 'I think… I think that they think… that once ANP-12 is out of commission, the shield is breached.'

'But we have other satellites — don't we?'

'But it'll take time to redeploy them. And in that time there'll be a thousand-mile-wide gap in our defences.'

'But you don't really think they'll attack, do you? That'd be crazy.'

'Of course it would. But what if they sent just one missile over — just to show that it could be done. No matter how bad the damage — no matter how many lives were lost — would we actually retaliate if we weren't sure about the integrity of the shield? The whole East-West balance of power would swing dramatically in their favour.'

'So we make the transmission. We've got to.'

'But if we do, they'll be on to us. Anything longer than a microsecond and they'll have our location to within five kilometres… We'll have to be ready to move out at the drop of a hat.'

'The drop of a hat?' she echoed — it was an Anglo expression she'd never heard before.

'Quickly — instantly. I'm guessing they'll probably want to know what we're up to, so they'll send another raiding party. But there's always a chance they'll just lob a missile at us and that'll be the end of it.'

Siv laughed quietly: 'At least we'll never know what hit us…'

'That's true… Look, I've been trying to work on a message that might keep us under the radar. It's not easy: we can't encrypt it — that increases its size by a factor of ten. They'd have us to within a couple of metres before we even got it off.'

'But we are going to do it — aren't we?'

'We'll have to eat and sleep in our outdoor gear and change our routines.'

'OK — and?'

'We won't need to bother going through each download. Just the beginning and end of each one. From now on one of us cooks and sleeps while the other one keeps watch.'

'That's fine — so?' she persisted.

'We'll need an escape route…'

'I've got one planned out already. And a good place to hide out if they come for us. I've been working on it while you've been asleep,' she replied, excitedly. 'So — are we going to make the transmission, or what?'

Warren looked up at her: 'I don't see that we've got much choice. Like you said, for all the good we're doing here, we might as well be back in Stavanger.'

*

They stared anxiously at the message on the screen.

'Well, there it is,' Warren said: '"delay90" — sending that out will take about 0.9 microseconds. Not much to look at: no encryption, no identification, no wrapping. It's the best I can do. We've just got to hope they understand it — and they believe it's from us — and then they act on it.'

'And if they don't?' Siv asked.

He shrugged: 'We can't risk sending another signal — not even for them to come and get us. We check the download, then we pack up and make for Thule on foot.'

'That's about three hundred kilometres — maybe four, depending on the terrain… In the dark with shitty weather…' She considered the problem: 'I guess we could do it in two weeks. Mind, it could be a whole lot longer if the weather gets worse.'

'Well, we'd better hope it doesn't. We can only carry food and fuel enough for two weeks at the most.'

He stared at the message, then glanced across at Siv. 'The next download's in an hour. Enough time for them to reconfigure the timing — but hopefully not enough for the Enemy to pinpoint our position and get a raiding party out to us.'

Siv nodded: 'Do it.'

Warren pressed "Return". The message flashed off the screen.

Siv felt a lurching feeling in her stomach: this was it — there was no going back now.

*

The next hour passed slowly. Warren took the first watch up in the gun turret, while Siv stayed below, checking and rechecking her packing. She picked up her rucksack and held it out, weighing it critically — about fifteen kilos, she reckoned. The overweight hunting rifle was maybe another five. Twenty kilos, plus short skis and poles, and the extra rounds and rations she'd stuffed into her pockets. Altogether probably just under twenty-five, well distributed. A heavy load — not too heavy. She knew she could carry a whole lot more, she'd done it before on exercise. But how quickly would she be able to move around if she did?

And this wasn't an exercise: they'd be on the move all the time — hunted, maybe. Maybe they'd have to fight their way back to Thule. She found the idea strangely appealing — exciting, even. This was the sort of action she'd signed up for when she joined the army.

Her fingers brushed against the hilt of her boot-knife, still strapped to the side of her kitbag. It was useless there, she reproached herself, unstrapping it. She unclipped it from its sheath and pulled it out, checking the short, black, triangular bade. Just ten centimetres long — too short for anything else — it was designed to kill at close quarters.

She imagined what that might feel like — taking a life, right up close.

When it came to it, would she be able to do it?

And, she reminded herself, she'd never actually fired a shot in anger. She was a good shot, she knew that. But she'd only ever practised on exercises and shooting ranges. What would she do when it came to the real thing?

Up in the gun turret, Warren peered into the darkness, looking for any light, any movement, any sign of the attack he expected to come at any moment. He cursed inwardly — he'd never done anything so ridiculous, so stupid, before. The very thought that he was risking exposing himself — exposing Siv — to the Enemy appalled him.

But there'd been no other option. He'd gone through every one again and again — even though there'd only ever been one serious choice. Whatever happened now … Well, they'd just have to deal with it.

He swung back down into the fuselage.

'How long to the download?'

'If they didn't get the message,' Siv replied, glancing across at the screen. 'It should start in five … four … three … two …'

They waited for it to start — but it didn't.

'They must be delayed,' Siv whispered, glancing up at the chronometer as it clicked away the seconds: ten, twenty, thirty… 'It's never been this late…'

'They must have got the message.'

'We'll know in just under a minute…'

They stared at the chronometer. Suddenly, Warren dragged himself away from the screen. 'Shit,' he muttered, 'if Control's got the message, that means the Enemy has too. They could be looking for us right now,' He swung himself back into the gun turret: 'Shout me if it starts to download.'

The next thirty seconds ticked by slowly. Then, precisely on cue, the download started, just the same as it had every time.

'It's coming in!' Siv yelled.

'Let me know when it's compiled — then run it straight to the last two minutes,'

'Hmm… that's weird,' Siv said as the download finished.

'What's that?'

'It took a second longer than usual.'

'That's the Doppler effect. The satellite's moving away from us — the signal's stretched.'

'Oh, right…' she muttered. '… smartass.'

'I heard that!'

'Yeah — I meant you to.'

It took another couple of minutes for the download to compile. Then, when it was ready, Siv opened it, went to the end and manually scrolled back two minutes.

'OK,' she cried, 'We're ready to roll!'

Warren swung himself down and together they watched the last two minutes of the download.

There was nothing there — nothing changed, nothing at all.

'Well I don't know what I expected,' Warren said finally. 'But I did expect to see something.'

'Let's try slowing it down…'

They tried it at half speed, then 0.1, still no change.

'I'm going to give it a go at 0.01,' she said. 'After that the resolution starts to break up.'

'That'll take two hours to do two minutes.'

'So? It's not like we've got anything better to do.'

'We might not have two hours…'

'OK!' she chided him, pointing up to the turret. 'You get back on watch — I'll tell you if I find anything.'

Warren had just clambered back into the machine-gunner's seat when Siv called him straight back down.

'Look,' she said, pointing to the centre of the screen. 'See that flash?'

Warren watched. A tiny red light flashed, just to the right of the plate that covered the main weapons control panel. A few moments later it flashed again.

'There isn't normally a light there…' he said under his breath.

'We've never seen it before,' Siv agreed, glancing down at her toolbar. 'Six second intervals at 0.01 — so it's pulsing at just under a twentieth of a second — too short to be seen at faster speeds…' She tapped a scroll bar on the screen. '…Let's try going across the ranges…' She scrolled into the highest frequencies, up above the UV range, then back through visible light and down into the bottom end of infra red.

'Ooh…' she breathed, pointing at the bottom of the screen. 'Just look at that.'

It was impossible to miss. Right above Siv's finger, Warren could see an almost impossibly fine line of light, flickering up from the Earth.

'What is it?' Warren whispered.

'I don't know. It's at the very bottom of IR, almost into microwave. You could cook with it…'

She rolled the sequence back, and drew down two rulers. 'Right, you little sucker, let's see how big you are…'

She was totally engrossed in her work, her eyes wide as saucers, tapping her teeth with her thumbnail: 'OK. The first time it touches the satellite it's lighting a patch two micrometres by 0.3 millimetres… Over a period of ten seconds that grows to 0.7, then 2.2 — but it stays at the same width — two micros …'

'It's cutting like a blade,' Warren observed.

'Yeah, but there's not much energy in it. It's incredibly fine.' She zoomed tight into the patch of light. 'But look — you can see, how it's scratched the surface already.'

'Yes, and tomorrow that scratch will be a score — then in a few days' time it'll be a hole.'

'Oh, my God,' Siv muttered. 'They're going straight for it.'

'What do you mean?'

'Well I thought they were cutting through the screws to release the cover plate, but they've stopped doing that…'

Warren stared at the screen, suddenly alarmed: 'You're right — they're cutting straight into it.'

'How long 'til they get through?'

Warren called up the blueprint: 'Well, it's not exactly armour plate. Aluminium. Three millimetres thick. How deep's the cut?'

Siv shook her head as she called up the image again: 'Hard to tell — there's no cast shadow. Could be anything between 0.1 and 0.3 millimetres.'

'Can we find out where it's coming from?'

Siv frowned and shook her head: 'Not from this, not on its own. We'll need a second download.'

Warren considered the problem. They were in exactly the same position as the Enemy: they needed a second download to get a fix on the source of the cutting light — in just the same way as the Enemy needed them to send a second message, to get a fix on their location.

'Alright… we wait. We fix its location, transmit it back to control, and get them to bomb the Hell out of it — then we high-tail it out of here as fast as we can. Let's get our packs, our rifles, everything up by the waist-gunner's port — we may have to make a quick exit…'

*

Day 13 : 14.50 hrs

A thunderstorm was brewing out to the west. Siv watched it from the pilot's seat, staring out through the yellowed Plexiglas canopy. Every few moments a flash lit the far horizon, briefly illuminating the desolate, featureless landscape of the glacier.

She put on her helmet and blinked her way through the visor options 'til she reached the chronometer. It was a lazy, stupid way to check the time, but it was a whole lot quicker than stripping off her gauntlets and mittens, then scrabbling up the sleeves of her various garments to get to her wristwatch.

If they delayed the next download by 90 seconds, it'd be due in five minutes. It was time to go to work. She flipped up her visor and clambered stiffly out of her seat, tapping Warren's boot as she passed the turret:

'You still awake up there?'

'Sure am. Looks like there's an electric storm coming.'

'Yeah, I saw it,' she replied, checking everything was ready to receive the signal.

'Handy for keeping a look out. Lights everything up like daylight.'

'I guess so. Download's in five minutes — you coming down?'

'I'll stay up here. Let me know when it's ready.'

Siv poured herself a coffee and passed one up to Warren. Sometimes this job was a whole lot like being back at Jåttå — little routines, little rituals.

'Normal download time's passed,' she said, settling in front of her screen.

It started precisely ninety seconds later. Siv watched the chronometer as it started coming in: ten seconds, fifteen… she wanted to see if it would run to 31 seconds again, and prove Warren's smartass theory was right.

It stopped. At eighteen seconds — it stopped dead.

'Warren!' she yelled. 'We've lost the signal!'

'What?'

'We lost it.'

Warren swung down from the turret.

'Shit — that's bad!'

'How bad?'

'Very bad…'

He stared at the screen, searching for some clue to the malfunction. 'They could've knocked out the NPGS,' he muttered. 'Or they could be jamming the signal…'

Suddenly the whole plane was bathed in brilliant, flashing blue-white light. The thin skin of the fuselage screamed and warped — buckling like it was being crushed by a great weight.

'… Or they could be coming down the signal to get to us!' he yelled, ejecting the memory from the computer and initiating a "total erase" sequence. 'It's time to go!'

Siv stared up through the gun turret — lightning was crackling all around them. Her ears were assaulted by a deafening, screaming snarl and the boom of a distorted baritone voice haranguing them unintelligibly. Powerful searchlights probed up and down the whole length of the bomber.

'Let's go!' Warren yelled, shouldering the bulkhead door open and scrambling up the fuselage.

But Siv didn't follow him. Instead, she clambered down into the bomb bay, scrabbled the gas mask over her face and opened the valves on the insulation canisters. Then she darted back up and kicked the bulkhead door closed behind her as she scampered along the fuselage.

'Where the hell were you?' Warren demanded over the deafening cacophony.

'Just a little surprise for our visitors,' she grinned. Then, reaching up and grabbing Warren's shoulder, she pulled him down and kissed him full on the mouth.

'What was that for…?'

Siv shrugged her pack onto her shoulders and smiled up at him: 'We could be dead in a couple of minutes — I wanted to know what it felt like!'

She took her rifle out of its holster and checked all around, waiting for the probing searchlight beams to pass — and swung herself out of the plane.

Warren was about to follow when her head popped back up: 'Oh, yeah,' she said, glancing down. 'Keep to the left — I don't think the last slop bucket's fully frozen yet.'

Siv dropped from the gun port and scuttled along the fissure. Warren checked the track of the searchlights then jumped out after her, just as the air was rent by the clatter of machine guns and the rattle of bullets zipping and pinging round the belly of the old B17.

*

'This way!' Siv hissed, as Warren scrambled into the ice cave. 'Switch off your visor — it leaves a trace!'

Warren turned in the direction of her voice.

'Come slowly,' she whispered. 'Don't breathe heavily.'

He crawled up beside her. She was lying back from the pillbox slot she'd made in the ice, peering down her rifle sight at the wreck of the B17 as the Russians peppered it with machine gun fire. The Enemy craft — whatever it was — was coming down, throwing up a cloud of ice crystals as it landed on the far side of the old bomber. All they could see of it were the fingering beams of its searchlights as they turned the Arctic night into day.

Moments later they saw the forms of men running, lurching and struggling through the snow — all the time firing their machine guns into the wreck.

'I don't think they're too bothered about taking us prisoner…' Warren whispered.

'Don't talk…' Siv hissed, still peering down her rifle sight. 'Put ice in your mouth. Breathe over it. Breathe slow.'

Siv watched them as one by one they crawled in through the bomb bay doors.

'How long does that insulator stuff take to kill a man?'

'The manufacturers said a couple of minutes — but I don't know how they could tell…'

'We'll soon find out,' she said, glancing across at him and smiling wickedly as the last man scrambled through the snow and up into the plane.

'Don't say anything,' Warren whispered. 'I'm putting my communicator on. See if I can…'

'Wha…' Siv exclaimed, alarmed — Warren placed his gauntlet up to her lips for silence, and listened. Seconds later he made a "thumbs-up" — followed by a "thumbs-down", drawing his gauntlet across his throat, then switching off his communicator.

'One of them got the word "gas" out before everything went quiet. Let's see what they do next.'

The second wave came more cautiously — and they were wearing black, special forces-issue PPM-100 "pig-face" gas masks. Warren put his hand up for silence, then turned his communicator back on.

The second wave was in the plane now. He listened to them muttering and cursing as they checked the bodies of their comrades for signs of life:

… Anatoly dead … Evgeny … Gregor …All dead…

He heard them clambering up into the fuselage, all the time reporting their every move to their control:

… No, no sign of them … Can you see this? … Yes, bring it in …

He switched off his communicator. 'Won't be long now…'

There was a brilliant white flash in the fuselage. Moments later the whole plane was engulfed in a raging red fireball.

'What the fuck was that?' Siv muttered under her breath.

'Looks like the insulator is flammable too…' Warren observed. 'I'll have to mention that to the manufacturers…'

'But what happened there?'

'The anti-tamper device on the tracking equipment went off.'

'You mean it was booby-trapped?'

'Well… Yes — of course,' Warren replied. 'We couldn't let it fall into the hands of the Enemy…'

'You could have told me!'

'You saw me laying the charges!'

'Dammit — I thought they were signal boosters!'

'Shh…' Warren pointed out of the pillbox slot. The Enemy craft was taking off, throwing up great plumes of ice and soaring clouds of vapour that concealed it completely. Moments later sparkling lights flashed through the ice-clouds and the landscape all around them was spattered by a deadly hail.

Bullets thudded into the walls of their cave, bringing down huge lumps of ice and ripping apart the whole front of their lair. They scrambled back further into the cave and huddled behind an ice boulder to get out of sight.

'How the fuck did they spot us?' Siv cursed as the cloud-swathed monster lurched away to the east.

Warren shook his head: 'They didn't see us. They were using gatlings — carpeting the whole area with indiscriminate fire. Just spite, that's all — blind rage.'

They watched anxiously, waiting to see if it would come back for a second pass.

'Well,' Warren said, getting up and brushing shards of shattered ice off his parka. 'They know now that we weren't in there…'

'How?'

'We laid some pretty lethal booby traps — we'd look pretty stupid if we'd waited round in the plane to watch them go off, wouldn't we?'

'Pretty stupid?' Siv chuckled: 'We'd be pretty dead, that's for sure. But why did they just leave like that?'

'I'm guessing they ran out of bodies…'

'…Or too many bodies.'

'Whatever,' Warren replied, slinging his rifle over his shoulder. 'They'll be back soon — and we don't have any more surprises up our sleeves. It's time to get out of here.'

Siv nodded in agreement and clambered out of the ice-cave. For a moment she just stood staring at the blazing wreck of the Flying Fortress, feeling the fierce heat on her face.

Then she shrugged dismissively and turned her back on the scene of devastation, putting it out of her mind — almost as though it was nothing. She knelt down and clipped on her short skis. Then, without a backward glance, she pushed down hard on her poles and set off into the night.

*

Day 13 : 20.00 hrs

'Shit!' Siv yelled over her communicator. 'I've got my visor on full — and I can't see a fucking thing!'

Suddenly, a storm blast swept her off her feet and sent her, rolling and slithering across the ice like a rag doll.

'Warren!'

'I've got you!' he said grabbing her shoulder.

'This is madness!' she yelled as he dragged her to her feet. 'It's building into a *Piteraq* — an attack storm!'

'We've got to get under cover!' Warren yelled back as the wind buffeted them, driving them stumbling across the ice. 'It's going to kill us!'

They clung together to keep themselves upright, to fight the wind.

A great black void loomed up on her screen, straight ahead.

'What's that?' Siv yelled.

'What's what?'

'It's a ravine!' she cried as the storm blasted them over the edge.

They fell, clinging together, sliding, clutching despairingly at the walls of the ravine, until they landed in a bank of crackling snow.

'Well… at least we're out of the storm,' Siv observed, drily.

'Are you OK?' Warren, asked, spluttering and momentarily blinded — he'd landed face-down in the snowdrift.

'Think so,' she replied, lying on her back, sprawled out, hardly daring to move. She blinked to her right to turn on her helmet light and examined their surroundings. 'The ravine's narrow. A couple of metres, not much more. Looks like we're on a snow bridge — and it's a long way down from here. The snow's attached to an overhang in the ice wall,' she said, pointing, stabbing her gauntlet to her left, cautiously. 'It's only about a metre away. If we can get to that…'

They both shifted uneasily on their precarious snow perch. With a sickening lurch, they felt it start to give way beneath them.

'It won't take both of us moving at the same time,' Warren said. 'You're lighter than me, you've got a better chance of making it.'

'Afraid not, commander.'

'Why not?'

'Well, first, you're nearer, so you've got a better chance than I have. And second — you've got the memory chip. So that makes you more important than me, doesn't it?'

It made Warren sick to admit it, but she was right. Their lives didn't matter — the only thing that mattered was getting the chip back.

Siv reached over her shoulder and detached her ice-axe from her rucksack, twisting the leash around her wrist as she gripped it tightly and braced herself for the fall she knew could only be moments away.

'OK, Warren,' she muttered, her heart beating fast. 'I'm ready — off you go.'

He inched toward the overhang, ready to throw his axe into the hard ice as soon as the snow gave way. Every time he moved he heard the slithering and patter of snow falling as their support started to disintegrate beneath them. He was almost there. He edged the leash along his wrist as far as he dared, to extend his reach, then swung his axe hard into the solid ice.

It bit — and held fast.

But the motion was too much for the precarious snow bridge. It crumbled and fell away.

'Siv!' Warren cried despairingly, staring down into the void. But there was no sign of her — she'd gone. He struggled round, still half-dangling from the overhang. But he couldn't see her.

Warren spun himself around, still dangling from his ice axe: 'Where are you?'

'Hmm…This isn't going to be easy…' she muttered thoughtfully.

He clambered up onto the overhang and peered down. She was about three metres below on the far side of the ravine, hanging one-handed from her axe — suspended against a sheer wall of ice.

'…No way up — no hand holds, no foot holds. …Tricky.'

They both fell silent as each one considered the problem. The only sound was the wind roaring above them.

'Any ideas?' Siv said, finally.

'Yes,' Warren replied. 'Keep very still…'

Moments later Siv felt a shattering thump against the side of her leg — and she was spattered with ice.

'What the Hell was that?'

'Foot-hold,' Warren replied. 'I made you one — it's just above your right ankle.'

'OK — how did you do that?' she demanded, wedging the toe of her boot into the hole. With all the extra weight she was carrying, it felt good to take the strain off her arm.

'I shot it. Thought it was best to use the silencer…'

'You did what!?'

'You heard.

'But you're a lousy shot!'

'Didn't hit you, did I?'

She had to give him that one. He hadn't shot her — not yet.

'So,' he continued. 'Where do you want the next one?'

'What! You're going to shoot at me again…?'

'That's right. And again. All the way up.'

'And you want me to tell you where …to shoot at me?'

'Yep.'

Siv weighed up her options. Asking to get shot at by someone who couldn't shoot straight was a pretty poor prospect — but, as the alternative was plummeting to certain death…'

'OK,' she said, breathing in deeply and bracing herself. 'Above my right shoulder and slightly out to the right.'

'Not to the left?'

'That would be the middle of my head.'

'Only joking. Here goes…'

Siv looked away, waiting for the impact and the sickening burst of pain that would surely accompany it — but, instead her helmet was showered with ice as the bullet hit its mark. She turned to inspect his handiwork — it was almost exactly where she'd have put it herself. She slid her hand into it and straightened up.

'Two out of two,' she said, glancing over her shoulder at him. 'Lucky for you.'

'On the contrary, you're the lucky one. Where next?'

'Left of my knee,' she said, swinging over to the right.

And so they went on, Warren shooting and Siv edging her way up the ice face. Finally she reached the safety of a narrow shelf that'd formed the other side of the snow bridge.

She scrambled up and they sat facing eachother across the narrow ravine.

'Well,' Warren said cheerfully, his legs dangling over the edge. 'This is nice.'

'Nice?' Siv echoed. Sometimes his humour eluded her. 'How is this nice?'

'Let's see… We haven't been killed by the Enemy, or by the attack-storm — and we haven't plummeted to our deaths … down there.'

He leaned forward and peered down into the chasm. His light didn't reach more than twenty metres or so — but there was no sign of the bottom. Nothing but huge white snowflakes drifting down and disappearing into the inky, blue-black darkness below.

'Not yet,' Siv corrected him. 'So what do we do now?'

He looked around.

'There's an ice cave behind me,' he said, stripping off his pack. 'Goes back quite a way. We can wait out the storm there.'

'OK, that sounds cozy — but first I need to get over there with you.'

*

'This isn't going to work,' Siv muttered as they edged their way along either side of the ravine.

'The gap's getting narrower,' Warren replied. 'We could almost reach across now.'

'Yeah, but I'm running out of ledge. In fact,' she said, staring off to her side. 'I've pretty well run out now.'

'Ah.'

'Yeah. "Ah".'

Warren shone his helmet lamp across Siv's side of the ravine: 'It looks sheer, all the way up.'

'And down,' she replied, shining her light into the gloom below.

'Do you think you could jump it?'

'I could jump the gap,' she said, considering the problem. 'I might get my axe in, I might not — but there's nothing else to hold onto. If you tried to catch me I could pull you down… Not good.'

'OK. I've got an idea.'

'Is it as good as the last one?'

'No. But it's all I can think of right now. Throw me your pack.'

'You want to leave me to die over here?'

'Don't be stupid. I want to get all your stuff on this side before we start.'

'OK…' she said, stripping off her gear and tossing each item across the divide to him. 'You want all of it?'

'Not all. I don't want you to freeze to death,' Warren replied, catching her rifle and propping it against the ice wall. 'Now comes the tricky bit.'

He knelt down and started hacking into the ice ledge with his axe.

'That should do it,' he muttered, then opened his parka and pulled out a small titanium case.

'See this?' he said, placing it in a crack in the ice. 'The memory chip's in here. If we both make it through this, that's fine. If we both fall, too bad. If one of us falls and the other doesn't…'

'The survivor takes the chip. I get it — but what the Hell are you up to?'

'Well,' he said, swinging his axe into the ice and lowering himself over the edge — and wedging his fist into the hole he'd cut into the ice. 'I'm turning myself into a human scramble net. Jump across and grab me, then use me to climb up.'

'You're crazy.'

'Not really,' he said, moving his shoulders from side to side. 'I'm feeling pretty secure. Go ahead. Just let me know when…'

'OK — here I come!' she yelled and launched herself across the void.

Suddenly he was showered with ice — he felt her weight slam into his back and her arm locked round his throat.

'Shit!' she yelled. 'It worked!'

He felt her scramble up his back. A heavy, spiked ice boot pushed hard on his shoulder — and then she was leaning over the edge, looking down at him, smiling. Warren scowled back:

'I was rather hoping you'd give me a countdown.'

'I figured I'd do it straight away — I didn't want to think too much about it,' she said, grabbing the scruff of his collar. 'Would you like me to help you up — or are you planning on staying down there?'

*

'OK,' Siv said as they hauled the last of their kit into the ice cave. 'We're going to be here a while, so we might as well make the most of it. The rucksack frames pull out to make a temporary bed…'

She slipped the sack off its frame and snapped out the telescopic tubes.

Warren looked it up and down: 'Doesn't look much like a bed to me.'

'Sleeping on a rucksack frame isn't much fun,' she agreed. 'There's no slats, no mattress, no creature comforts, in fact they're downright uncomfortable. But it keeps you off the ice, and that's all that matters — because keeping off the ice is the difference between living and dying.'

Siv got the chemical stove going while Warren stretched a flysheet across the mouth of the cave. When he'd finished he came and sat down to warm his hands over the stove.

'It doesn't give off much heat, does it?'

'It's not supposed to,' Siv replied, dropping crushed-up ice into the top pot and clamping down the lid. 'It's heat efficient — the energy goes into the cooking, not out into the air.'

'And what're we having?' he asked.

She pulled off her balaclava and ruffled up her hair. 'To be honest, I didn't look at the pouch when I slotted it in, but I'm pretty sure it'll be high-fat stew.'

'Mmm... my favourite.'

Siv looked up from the stove:

'So, "mister strategy" — what's the plan?'

Warren took out his knife and stared drawing on the floor of the cave with the point:

'Well, if I was the Enemy, I'd expect us to strike out west to the glacier's edge, the way we came, to meet up with a submarine. That's just what we'd have done if we'd had chance to send a rescue signal.'

'But we didn't.'

'No,' he said, drawing a heavy line in the ice: 'We've come south. Not far — only a few miles. And now we've disappeared altogether. So, when the storm passes, we carry on south — as fast as we can for as long as we can.'

'Our own guys will be looking for us too — won't they?'

'Maybe. They'll have seen the attack, just like you did back at Jåttå. But only the Enemy knows we got away.'

'So?'

'So, in the meantime, we eat, we sleep, we keep warm, we wait for the storm to pass. Then, when it does, we go south and we keep going south.' He looked up and smiled: 'We try not to get caught and we try not to get killed.'

'And that's it?'

'That's it.'

That night they slept with their frames pushed together, each cocooned in their own sleeping bag. Enveloped in an insulation bag, they huddled together to share whatever warmth they could with eachother.

'Siv…' Warren murmured.

'Uh-huh?'

'You kissed me today.'

'Yep. I sure did.'

'It was nice — I liked it.'

'Yeah, me too,' she replied. 'Now go to sleep.'

*

Day 15 : 11.00 hrs

The storm had blown over. They emerged from their lair into a moonlit world, brilliant beneath the dazzling northern stars — so bright that they could see without the help of lights or image-enhancing visors. Siv looked around at the landscape and smiled.

'We could ski good a long way today,' she said, waving her ski pole across the flat ice and snow stretching out as far as the eye could see: 'Fifty — maybe even a hundred kilometres if the weather holds and the ice is kind. It's a good thing that those crazy cracks all run from north to south. If they'd cut across us it'd take us weeks to get off the glacier — we'd probably starve before that.'

'Lucky for us,' Warren agreed. He still hadn't told her he'd created them in the first place.

'Are you ready?'

He nodded and gripped his ski poles.

'OK,' Siv cried, pushing away: 'Let's go!'

*

Warren was starting to slow down. The ever-present cold that crept in like icy fingers through the slightest gaps in his clothes, was taking its toll on his body: every move he made felt stiff and laboured as the fluid in his joints began to thicken; each breath seemed to crumple his lungs.

Siv was somewhere up ahead, but he couldn't see her. He could feel his mind starting to wander. He needed to keep alert, to concentrate. He glanced down at his GPS:

'Hey!' he cried over his short-range communicator: 'We've gone nearly eighty kilometres!'

'Yeah,' Siv replied, breathing heavily. 'Well, we have been going ten hours — and we've only stopped twice. Another hour and we'll be off the glacier!'

'We'll make camp as soon as we get to the broken country,' he croaked. 'It'll be good to stop.'

'Yeah, but not 'til then. If we stop out here we start to freeze. Stop too long and you won't start.'

'Bloody slave driver…' he muttered.

'Hey — I heard that!'

'You were supposed to!' Warren laughed — it sounded more like a cackle — and pushed harder on his poles to try and catch up.

'Not far now!' Siv called back as she surged forward along a sheet of compacted snow. She glanced over her shoulder at him: 'Hey, come on slowcoach!' she yelled. 'You can't…'

Siv stopped in mid-sentence and turned sharply, bringing her skis crunching to a halt. Staring out into the distance behind Warren, she pointed back the way they'd come.

'What the fuck …?' she muttered.

Warren turned and followed the line of her hand. Far off to the north, something was flying low and fast — it was coming straight for them.

'What is it?' Siv said under her breath.

'I don't know, but I don't want to be out in the open when it gets here.'

They scrambled down into a crack in the glacier, dragging snow and ice over themselves.

'Well, it's not a drone, that's for sure,' Warren replied, watching as it approached. 'You can't remote pilot a drone that close to the ground…'

'Do you think it's seen us?' Siv whispered as the thing approached.

'I don't know,' Warren replied, staring at it intently. 'It looks like it's following our tracks.'

It was nearly on them — hovering like a giant blowfly with a bloated, elongated tail. They were suddenly aware of a strange noise, unlike anything they'd heard before — a sort of humming, crackling noise. Siv pressed herself closer to the ice, hardly daring to breathe, as the thing flew straight over them and carried on toward the broken country beyond the glacier. She stared at it in amazement as it went — it was a man.

'B-but, how…?' she stammered.

'Shh,' Warren hissed urgently. 'He's coming back.'

Siv drew her hunting rifle out of its holster and laid it flat beside her: 'Shall I bring him down?' she asked.

'Only if we need to. Let's see what he does first.'

They watched as he flew around them in a wide circle, peering left and right as he swooped down like a bird of prey. Now he was closer they could see that what they'd taken for a bloated abdomen was actually some kind of insulating cocoon. Then, as he soared up into the sky, they could see he had a long, white, delta-shaped wing on his back, perfectly camouflaged for the arctic landscape — it emitted a cold blue light.

He swooped again and flew so close that they they could see the instruments flickering on the inside of his visor. Surely he must have seen them, Siv thought. But if he did, he didn't show any sign of it.

Suddenly, about fifty metres away, he swung around and stopped; hovering — his anonymous, visored face staring straight at them — more like an insect than a human being.

A red light flashed in the corner of their visors. A targeting system had locked on to them.

Siv raised her rifle and took aim — she wasn't going to wait for him to shoot first.

But, as suddenly as he'd stopped, he appeared to nod and shrug — as if he was acknowledging something. Then, turning in mid-air, he swept off back north and away from them.

When they were finally sure he'd gone they crawled out from their hiding place, knocking the snow and ice off themselves.

'What the hell was that?' Siv exclaimed, still staring after it, as though she thought it might come back at any moment.

'It's a jetwing — they were popular for a while around the turn of the century. The US Army trialled them and rejected them. Too slow — and sitting ducks for heat-seeking missiles.'

'I never felt any heat when it flew over.'

'Me neither. And that's the interesting thing. The blue light — and that crackling sound — must be some kind of cold propulsion system.'

'Could be…' Siv replied, still staring into the distance. 'But why didn't he fire at us? He was locked on. He had us. So, why…?'

'Well, isn't it obvious?' Warren said, glancing across at her: 'Now they know where we are, they've decided they want to take us alive.'

*

Day 17 : 02.00 hrs

'I wish we were back on the glacier…' Siv muttered as she dragged herself up the rock face.

'Me too,' Warren agreed as he reached down and hauled her up.

They leant against the rock wall and looked back across the terrain they'd covered — a broad band of jagged, blasted hills and lifeless lakes of trapped, immovable ice, many times more ancient than human civilisation.

'Christ,' he said, breathing heavily. 'I've flown over this place countless times. Takes about five minutes.'

Siv checked her GPS: 'Two days — we've done less than twenty kilometres.' She did a quick mental calculation: effort and energy — and time. Climbing consumed more energy; they needed more food to keep going. When they got off the glacier they still had they still had food and fuel for ten more days. Two days into the broken country and they were down to six — less if they carried on like this.

'Come on,' Warren said, squaring his rucksack on his shoulders, and picking his way up the craggy hill face. 'Like you say: "if we stop we freeze".'

He peered up ahead as they rounded the shoulder of the hill.

'Ah…' he muttered, staring up at a steep ridge that lay right across their path.

'Another climb?' Siv said, coming up behind him.

'Yep — and look,' he said, pointing straight ahead with his pole at a field of loose rock. 'That's scree. We go into that, we'll go straight down — which means we'll have to keep on going up.'

'I like going up,' she said, tapping him on the shoulder as she passed him. 'At least you can see where you're going.'

*

'Nearly there,' Siv muttered, barely able to get the words out — her lungs hurt so bad.

They dragged themselves to the top of the ridge — and gazed down into a long, broad, ice-filled valley that spread out before them.

'Ah, just look at that,' Siv said, barely able to suppress a smile. 'It just goes on and on.'

'I'll bet it goes all the way to the sea,' Warren said, admiringly. 'You've done it, Siv. You've got us through.'

She flipped her visor to binocular and surveyed the scene below. The ice sheet was practically flat, running as far as she could see. In her mind's eye she tried to imagine what lay beyond: a cascade of slowly moving ice, grinding down the valley in its relentless procession to the coast — they'd found a glacier.

'We'll need to keep over to the western edge,' she said, planning their route in her mind. 'That'll give us a better chance of finding cover…'

Just then they heard a low thrumming noise behind them. They turned just in time to see a drone cresting the ridge — no more than twenty metres above them. It bore the familiar grey splinter-pattern camouflage and the white star and bar of the USAF, boldly emblazoned on its side.

They waved at it frantically, jumping up and down and shouting joyously, even though they knew the drone had no sound detectors. It described a lazy circle over the valley below, then came back, straight for them, tipping its wings to the left and right as it crested the ridge.

'It's seen us!' Siv yelled, still waving. 'It's seen us!'

'Well, I'll be damned!' Warren exclaimed, leaning on his poles and watching the drone as it disappeared over the horizon. 'They were looking for us after all. Well, I guess we'd better get down off this ridge and find a good landing place for our rescuers.'

'My God, Warren,' Siv said, smiling broadly, with tears standing in her eyes. 'You can't imagine just how good that sounds.'

*

Siv counted each step as she strode along the glacier: 'sixty-seven, sixty-eight, sixty-nine… *Faen*!' she muttered, skipping across a long, shallow crack in the ice — small enough to jump over with ease, but large enough to wreck any plane that tried to land there.

'We need to find a better surface,' Warren said, waving his pole across the glacier. 'Get closer to the centre. It looks better over there.'

'But we'll be a long way from any cover…' Siv replied, dubiously.

Suddenly, she dropped flat onto the ice, and dragged Warren down with her.

'What's up?'

'Look…' she hissed, pointing toward the edge of the glacier. '…Over there.'

Warren stared in amazement. Less than half a mile away, a mother polar bear and her two pink-white cubs were slowly making their way up their side of the valley, coming straight for them.

'The wind's blowing our scent away from them,' Warren whispered. 'We can carry on when they've passed.'

'It's not that,' Siv said, peering all around, anxiously. 'They shouldn't be out here. It's too early. They should still be hibernating. Oh, you might see an adult coming out if they're hungry. But those cubs are too young — way too young. Something's happened — something's disturbed them…'

Warren tapped on his short-range communicator and drew his hand across his throat: '…They know we're here,' he said, pulling down his ice-mask. 'They're waiting for us.'

'How?' she replied, shaking her head uncomprehendingly.

'Satellite, I guess — they must have been tracking us.'

'But their satellites are hopeless, Warren — you know how crappy they are. We'd barely register — a faint heat smudge, that's all we'd look like to them — nothing, nothing at all.'

'Yes, but we've had clear skies since the storm. And they had our exact location pinpointed by our flying friend. All they had to do was look for two heat signatures moving close together — then keep tracking them.'

Siv stared down to the southern end of the glacier: only a few minutes before it'd seemed they couldn't get there quickly enough. Now it was the last place she wanted to be.

Warren racked his brains for a way out of this, a way to shake off the surveillance… Then it came to him: the mental timetable he'd lived his life by, for all those long months he'd spent up here, suddenly clicked back into place.

'… Hmm…' he muttered thoughtfully to himself: 'It's 0415.'

'So?' Siv replied, irritably. 'So what?'

'How close do you think we can get to them?' he asked, pointing to the polar bears.

'What the Hell are you talking about?' she asked, dumbfounded. 'Get near a mother *isbjørn* — *with cubs*? You're a fucking crazy man.'

'How close?' he persisted. 'A hundred metres — less?'

'Well, I guess — if we keep downwind…' Siv shrugged, still confused.

'We need to disappear for just over an hour. Lose ourselves under the ice. Then, with a bit of luck the satellite will pick up the bears' heat signatures and start tracking them.'

'Why?'

'Because their surveillance gap starts in an hour's time. They'll be blind for two hours and we can make ourselves scarce.'

*

The wind was strengthening from the east. They clambered up onto a craggy outcrop and watched, mesmerised, as the mother and her cubs passed right beneath them. They could see the wind ruffling her fur, and how she always kept herself between her cubs and the piercing icy blasts.

Suddenly, she stopped and held her head up to sniff the air.

She turned — and for a moment she seemed to be staring straight at them.

They stared back, not daring to move. She'd seen them, Warren was certain of it — but what should they do? Then, for no sensible reason that he could think of, he nodded to her as if to say "it's okay".

Almost at once the mother bear grunted to her cubs and nudged them on their way.

They stared after them as they shambled off into the night.

'I've never seen that before…' Siv whispered.

'Me neither — it just seemed right at the time,' Warren muttered under his breath. 'Well, now we dig in and wait.'

*

'Can you hear that?' Siv said.

Warren scrawled back his balaclava. After a few moments he heard a high-pitched buzzing snarl.

'Snowmobiles?'

Siv nodded: 'Two of them, I think.'

Just then they crested the ridge, their engines screaming and racing as their riders struggled to negotiate the cracked and rutted terrain.

Siv and Warren watched them down their rifle sights as they approached.

'Do you think they know we're here?' she whispered.

'They wouldn't come on so openly if they did. They were waiting for us to come to them. And now they think we've gone back up the glacier. They're following the polar bears.'

'There'll be more where they came from.'

He nodded in agreement, then fell silent. Siv recognised the silence — Warren was thinking.

The Enemy was nearly upon them.

'How long do you think it'll be before they realise their mistake?' he asked finally.

'Depends…' Siv replied. 'The *isbjørn* will hide with her cubs as soon as she hears the snowmobiles. But if they see her first and realise their mistake…'

'That's what I was thinking. I reckon we should count on them seeing her first — then turning round and coming straight back.'

'So, I'd say about half an hour. Not much more.'

'That's not enough time,' he said, shaking his head. Not enough. We don't want an enemy in front of us *and* behind…'

They were almost level with them now. Siv could see their eyes in the reflected light of their visors.

'Do you want me to kill them?'

'No. That will bring the rest of them straight here…' He screwed his eyes up and stared blinking into the wind, not daring to use the image intensifier on his visor. 'How far away could you get a reliable hit on their fuel tanks?' he asked.

'Won't that blow them up?'

'Only in the movies,' Warren laughed quietly. '…But you'll have to use your silencer.'

Siv weighed up the shot in a few seconds: the snowmobiles were bucking around a bit, but they were making plenty of noise — they wouldn't hear the impact. The silencer would reduce the accuracy, but she didn't have to rely on a single shot — just so long as the Enemy didn't realise they were being shot at.

She recognised the make of snowmobile they were riding — a *Russkaya Mekhanika*. Her uncle had one just the same — and she knew exactly where its tank was. She reckoned she'd have a sixty centimetre target circle, maybe a bit less. Under normal conditions, with a static target, she could probably have hit it from half a kilometre away.

'Moving target, with the silencer: a hundred and fifty — two hundred metres at most. I'll have to cover the muzzle or they could see the flash in their wing mirrors. Yeah, call it one-fifty.'

'Go on then,' Warren said, as the snowmobiles snarled past — so close they could feel the spray from their tracks.

'You mean it?' Siv replied, her heart pounding with excitement.

'They're all yours.'

'What if I miss? What if…?'

But Warren cut her off: 'If they find out we're here — then we'll fight it out. Do it.'

Siv nodded and focussed on her task. There was an obvious place, just before a steep rise, where they would have to slow down then rev up their engines to get over it without flipping over. She drew a bead on it. Then, with the back of her pole, she bored a channel in the snow along the line, widening it at the far end to give herself a small traverse. Screwing on her silencer, she ran the rifle halfway along the channel, set her telescopic sight for 150 metres and drew the bolt back to bring the first round clattering into the chamber.

Then she waited.

The first rider rode his machine right into Siv's cross-hairs. Warren heard a hissing thump and Siv snapped back the bolt to send the first spent shell spinning into the snow. He heard a second thump — and Siv muttering to herself:

'*Faen*,' she cursed as she pulled back the bolt a third time and took aim.

The second snowmobile was about to mount the bank as Siv's shoulder jerked back. She lay there, motionless, staring down her rifle sight at the Russians as they disappeared into the darkness.

'You got them?' Warren asked.

Siv looked over her shoulder and grinned: 'For a second I thought I'd shot one of them in the ass. But, he didn't jump up so I guess I must've missed him.' She laughed quietly: 'But I got both tanks — well, let's say I holed them right where the bottom of their tanks are. So, as long as they aren't armour-plated — which they aren't — then yeah, I got them good.'

*

Day 17 : 05.20 hrs

Siv scampered across to where she'd holed the snowmobiles and knelt down, sniffing the ice. As she struggled back to her feet she waved to Warren and stuck up both her thumbs — two petrol tracks.

'You didn't have to do that,' Warren reproached her as she trudged back to him. 'I would have believed you…'

'I wanted to make sure I'd got both of them,' she replied, grinning like a mischievous child. 'Two can ride on one snowmobile faster than we can walk. And we'll have to walk now — we can't use the skis, not 'til we're sure we've lost them.'

She pointed up to the right, to a long, jagged, winding fault in the rock about twenty metres above them. 'We'll go that way. It'll give us some cover,' she said, simply. Then, without another word, she shouldered her rifle in its white neoprene holster and started off, clambering up the rocks. Warren watched her go. She really was amazing, he thought — it was almost as though she was enjoying this whole thing.

She stopped, and turned around. 'Well? Are you gonna hang around here 'til they come back?' she demanded impatiently, her hands on her hips.

Warren didn't protest: he squared his backpack on his shoulders and scrambled up the rocks after her.

*

They flipped their visors to binocular view and peered down from their eyrie, high up on an escarpment in the black rocks that topped the barren hillside. Beneath them, they could see about twenty figures, all white-camouflaged: some lurking in the cracks and fissures in the ice, others were gathered together in small knots, staring up the glacier, waiting — waiting for them.

'Quite a welcoming committee,' Warren said, turning off his visor.

'Yeah, that's one welcome I can do without,' Siv said, edging her way back down the rock. 'Come on — we need to get as much distance between us and them as we can.'

Warren was about to follow when he saw one of them gesticulating, frantically. He turned on his communicator, but all he could hear was static and wordless chirping — they were too far away to hear what they were saying. After a few minutes the men saluted, then ran to their snowmobiles and set off up the glacier.

He watched as one of them strode to what looked like a short, stubby totem pole. Warren realised it was a jet wing, standing upright. He flipped his visor back to binocular and watched intently as the Russian turned and struggled awkwardly into the insulating cocoon, and pulled down a console with two hand-held controls. The jetwing lifted off and hovered momentarily over the ice before its engine glowed brilliant blue and it tore off after the others, quickly overtaking them.

He crawled back down the escarpment to where Siv was waiting.

'Well?' she asked, as Warren dropped back down onto the ice. 'What's happening?'

'Looks like mother bear heard them before they saw her,' he said. 'They're all high-tailing it back up the glacier.'

'It was a good trick, Warren,' Siv admitted. 'I thought you were crazy…'

'I know you did,' he laughed: 'To be honest, so did I. But, you're right, we need to get as far away from here as we can. I want to get back down onto the glacier so that we can use our skis, but we're too close to their camp — I don't want to risk being seen if any of them come back.'

Siv nodded in agreement and eyed the hillside, critically: 'Not straight down — not yet. …O.K. — looks like there's a good track that way,' she said, making chopping motions toward the rocks with her gauntleted hand. 'If I'm right it'll lead us back to the glacier gradually. Maybe a few kilometres that way — but it looks like good terrain. We wouldn't be much faster going straight down then using the skis — and we won't be leaving any tracks.'

*

Siv stopped and scanned hillside.

'What's up?' Warren asked.

'This path's coming down more quickly than I expected. Look…' she said, pointing ahead 'You can see a fold in the fault line. It's going to bring us back down on the glacier about two or three kilometres behind the Enemy camp.'

She peered up the hillside, switching her visor to binocular view: 'Looks like there's another path, maybe a hundred metres up there. But there's no telling what we'll find when we get up there.'

'The wind's getting up,' Warren replied. 'If it turns into a storm I'd rather be holed-up in a nice, warm crack in the glacier than stuck up here on the hillside, scratching around for shelter.'

'OK,' Siv agreed. 'We go down…'

Warren grabbed her shoulder and pulled her down behind a boulder.

'Look out…' he said, pointing back up the glacier.

Siv saw a blue flicker out of the corner of her eye. It was the jet wing, flying low, skirting the rocky margins of the glacier, looking for them.

'Shit,' she muttered.

Warren watched as it passed close — dangerously close — maybe only ten or twenty metres below them: 'Another quarter of an hour…' he muttered under his breath, '…and it would've caught us out in the open.'

He flipped on his communicator. He spoke pretty good Russian, but already the signal was starting to break up. He caught the words "no sign" and "go back" — but then the Russian was completely drowned out by another much louder signal:

'Myers to base … quadrant sixteen … I think there's something down there … I'm not sure what it is …Going down for a closer look…'

They heard the drone of a light aircraft. Moments later they saw a USAF C41-A dropping down from the southern skies. Unarmed — and with its searchlights blazing, it made an easy target.

The jetwing hovered menacingly in the sky. They watched impotently as the hapless spotter plane came straight for it. Warren switched on his communicator: 'Myers!' he yelled. 'It's a trap! Abort your approach — do you hear me? Abort!'

The jetwing faltered, its pilot peering left and right for any sign of his quarry — and for a moment it looked like Myers would get away. But instead of pulling out of his deadly flightpath, he carried on, all the time signalling to his control: *'Myers, sir! Quadrant sixteen — it's Warren — I heard him, sir ... He's alive...!'*

A pencil-thin vapour trail shot from the jetwing. The tiny missile glinted briefly in the moonlight, before it slammed into the defenceless plane, turning it instantly into a blazing ball of orange fire.

'Shoot the jetwing!' Warren yelled to Siv, forgetting his communicator was still on. 'Bring it down!'

But the Russian must have overheard Warren's order. The jetwing twisted in the air and sped off into the distance before Siv could even take aim.

'I'm sorry!' Warren said, staring at the smouldering wreckage as it floated, spiralling onto the glacier. 'I've put us in danger. I shouldn't have done that.'

'You did the right thing, trying to save him,' Siv reassured him. 'And he didn't die for nothing. He got his signal off — they know we're here now. They'll be here soon — and they'll sort that bastard out, for sure.'

'You're right,' Warren replied, mastering his rage. 'We'll get him later — but we can't stick around here. They know our communicator range — they know where we are. We've got to get as far away as we can.'

'Then we go down onto the glacier,' Siv said. 'The wind's getting stronger. It'll cover our tracks in minutes.'

*

The weather closed in. The brilliant moon and stars, that had illuminated their path these last few days, disappeared behind mountainous, lowering clouds. They skied on desperately, through the worsening weather, the storm-winds battering against their backs, driving them on into the formless void — with only the ghostly shadows on their image intensifiers to warn them of what dangers lay ahead.

Warren glanced at his GPS — they'd only done twenty kilometres. Only twenty — in six hours.

'Siv…' he croaked.

'Huh?' she replied, her voice thickened with tiredness.

'Time to stop.'

'Yeah.'

They stumbled to a hollow in the ice, barely big enough to crawl into. Siv scrambled in first. As he watched her go, it seemed to Warren's fatigue-addled mind that she was crawling into a grave.

Her voice came over the communicator: 'It's good … opens out. Come on — this'll do.'

He crawled in after her, following Siv's torchlight. Shining his own light all around he was surprised to find himself in a small ice cavern, about the size of an igloo.

'It is good…' he muttered.

Siv didn't reply, she was dragging out her sleeping bag and snapping her backpack frame into shape. Warren did likewise, then stripped off his white outer kit and kicked off his boots. They were too tired to even think about making a meal. Within minutes they were both inside the insulation bag, curled-up together like two wild creatures, fast asleep.

*

They were woken by a slow grinding rumble that flipped them off their frames and sent them sprawling across the cavern floor. Siv sat up, suddenly alert.

'Glacier's on the move,' she said, shining her torchlight back the way they'd crawled in. 'Thought so,' she muttered, ruefully: 'damn thing's closed up on us.' Then, without another word she rolled over and snuggled back down into her sleeping bag.

Warren stared at her, surprised by her reaction: 'Well,' he asked. 'Shouldn't we dig our way out?'

'No point,' she replied, from inside her bag. 'Might as well get some sleep. 'Won't be any different when we wake up — might even be better.

But we won't be so tired. Anyway, it'll be better if we fug the air up a bit.'

'Oh, why?'

'That way we'll know where the fresh air's coming in. Get some sleep, Warren.'

*

Day 18 : 17.30 hrs

Siv woke and sniffed the air — and smiled.

'It's fresh,' she said, scrambling out of the insulation bag. 'So, let's see where it's coming from.'

After a few minutes exploration she found a new hole in the ice that led back up to the surface, not as wide as the one they'd come in by — but it would do.

'Come on then,' she said. 'Let's get digging. As my old grandpa used to say, if you get stuck in a glacier there's only two ways out: either you dig — or you wait for the glacier to spit you out the other end.'

'Oh?' Warren asked, looking up from the burner where he was heating their morning meal. 'And how long does that take?'

'Between fifty and a thousand years — depends on the glacier.'

'Well, if you put it like that,' he said getting up. 'We'd better make a start.'

They hacked and clawed their way out of their ice-hole like two creatures emerging from hibernation. In the sky above them the moon shone fitfully between broken clouds: the weather had cleared. Siv passed the backpacks and all their gear up to Warren and crawled out after him. As he helped her up, she handed him a small foil packet.

'Nutrition bar,' she said, stripping the foil off her own bar and gnawing into it, ravenously. 'It'll replace the energy we used up digging our way out. Go on — eat it while it's still soft.'

'But how did you keep it warm?' Warren asked.

'How do you think?' she replied, chewing through a mouth full of carbohydrate-enriched nutrients, proteins, saturated fats and vitamins.

Warren placed his hand on her arm: 'Don't move,' he said, pointing up to the sky.

Siv looked up and saw the flickering blue light of a jetwing flying high above them, moving south. She instinctively went for her rifle — but Warren shook his head.

'There's no point,' he said. 'He's way too far away, you wouldn't get him. Besides, I don't think he's seen us…'

'He might have.'

'Maybe,' Warren conceded. 'But if you shot at him the muzzle-flash would give away our position for sure.'

Siv nodded, conceding his point. 'Dammit — I thought we'd got away in the storm,' she said, ruefully.

'We've been under the ice for nearly twelve hours. Who knows when the storm cleared? He's looking for us — but they obviously think we're much further south.'

'So what do we do now?' Siv asked.

'We carry on. But they could be close on our heels…'

'Yeah,' she replied, watching the jetwing as it disappeared into the distance. 'If they aren't ahead of us already.'

*

Day 21: 2300hrs

Siv crunched her skis to a halt as the glacier dropped away into an icefall, and waited for Warren to catch up with her. She watched him lurching forward uncertainly, making heavy work of every movement, he really was hopeless on skis — it was a miracle he'd made it this far.

'My GPS says eighty kilometres to Thule — that's only fifty miles!' Warren said, laughing, and breathing heavily as he caught up with her. 'That's a day, maybe two…'

Standing side-by-side they looked around, taking stock of their surroundings. The glacier had joined other glaciers, flowing down from the broken country, spreading out into a great field of ice that stretched as far as the eye could see, gently sloping down toward the coast.

'… Maybe less,' Siv replied. 'But I think we may have a bit of a problem…' She pointed her ski pole out to the east. A solid wall of cloud was rolling toward them.

'Oh, yes,' Warren replied, sombrely. 'I see what you mean…'

'It's moving fast,' Siv said. 'I reckon it'll hit us in less than an hour.'

Warren watched it approaching. She was right, it was moving fast. But there was one cloud that seemed to be moving faster than the rest. As he watched, it seemed to detach itself from the storm front, racing ahead, its base skirting across the ice.

'Do you see that?' he said, fascinated: 'What do you make of it?'

'I see it,' Siv replied, switching her visor to binocular view. 'And it's not a cloud. There are flashing lights in it — and it's making straight for us.'

They didn't need to say anything — they both realised what it must be. Siv pushed hard on her poles, sending herself skittering down the icefall. Warren pushed off and went hurtling after her.

Down at the base of the slope Siv could see the ice was fractured into hundreds of jagged *seracs* as it tumbled down the icefall. They could get lost in there — if they could only get there before…

Suddenly, she felt something thump against her helmet, throwing her head forward. She glanced to either side — as much as she dared. There were other skiers: three or four, more maybe — she couldn't tell how many. They were coming across their line, trying to cut them off — and they were firing at them.

'Stick with me!' she yelled over her communicator. 'Keep close!' She crouched down into a racing position and kept pumping her ski-poles. Hitting the broken ice at this speed could kill them — but it was their only chance.

Glancing across she could see the other skiers had a better line down the icefall. They were going to get there first. It wasn't going to work — they weren't going to make it.

She was dimly aware of the clatter and flash of machine guns, but they were firing wildly as they skied — all their shots went wide of her.

The Russians were ahead of them now, stopping behind a rounded ice hummock— getting ready to take aim.

Siv saw that one of them had got his machine-gun sling caught in his ski pole.

He was straight ahead of her — she went straight for him.

Launching herself off the hummock, she glanced both skis off his head. She felt the slightest of movements as his neck gave way under the force. She lifted her knees and carried on, hitting the snow hard and bowling head-over-heels — finally coming to rest by a small serac. Bullets zinged past her as she kicked off her skis and scrambled for cover.

Warren followed her, making straight for the gap she'd made in their firing-line.

Siv pulled out her rifle and started giving covering fire. She hit one of them, watched him slump onto the ice. The others kept their heads down.

She watched in amazement as Warren hurtled down the ice: he was going to make it. It was incredible — suddenly he could ski, really ski. He leapt into the sky, just like she did — but he landed perfectly on both skis. He was coming straight for her! He was going to do it…

Suddenly he lurched forward, releasing his poles and falling, sprawling, spiralling across the ice toward her, finally coming to rest a few metres away.

The Russians were shooting at them from cover now, peppering everything with gunfire — sending showers of ice spattering over her.

'Get over here!' she yelled at Warren. But there was no reply. Three times she tried to crawl across to him — and three times she was driven back by a spattering hail of machine-gun fire.

Suddenly they were engulfed by a cloud of swirling ice and snow. A screaming noise deafened her — all around the air crackled with electricity.

Siv took her chance — she scrambled out from her hiding-place and grabbed Warren, rolling him over on his back. Her mind raced, urgently: *She couldn't see any blood! Where was the blood? Where was it?*

'Warren!' she yelled, smacking him across his mask and pounding on his chest. 'Get up! For God's sake — get up!'

But he didn't respond.

Warren was dead.

She could hear voices, yelling to eachother, getting closer. There wasn't much time — she knew what she had to do. Ripping open his parka she scrabbled around his tunic looking for the memory chip. Tears streamed from her eyes, freezing into tiny pearls of ice as they fell onto her visor.

Her fingers touched on the tiny titanium case where Warren stored the memory chip. She grabbed it. As she stuffed it into her pocket, she felt Warren's warmth rising from his body, dissipating — as though his soul was leaving him.

The Enemy was getting perilously close, but she couldn't bear to leave Warren open to the cold like this. They were almost upon her now: if it weren't for the swirling clouds of ice crystals all around they would have seen her long ago.

She wasted valuable seconds closing-up his parka, then scrambled back to the cover of the serac, just as half a dozen figures descended on Warren's body. Siv couldn't hear what they were saying, so she risked turning on her communicator — but her Russian was too bad and they were talking too fast.

The ice crystals were settling now and the Russians were in plain view — she could have taken them all out before they had time to return fire.

But that would've given away her position. And, now that Warren was dead, the only thing that mattered was getting the memory chip back to the base at Thule.

The men standing over Warren's lifeless form fell silent as their commander approached. One of them knelt down and held something against Warren's neck.

'It's him!' he reported, enthusiastically.

'Very good,' the commander replied. 'Get him aboard.'

'But what about the other?' one of the men asked.

'Who cares? If we have Warren, we have everything.'

They roughly hauled the body up and carried it away. Laughing and joking, they threw it across the back of one of their snowmobiles, strapping it down like a reindeer carcass.

Then Siv heard a word she did understand. It took her breath away.

One of them said "*narkotik*" — narcotic.

Warren wasn't dead. He was drugged.

*

Warren was still alive — that changed everything.

The Russians were out of sight, but she could still hear them over her short-range communicator — they couldn't be far away. Siv took out the titanium box and stuffed it down a small crack in the ice, then ripped the locator beacon out of her jacket and pushed it in with it. Then she set off in pursuit.

It didn't take her long to catch up with them. They were up ahead, picking their way across the rugged ice, riding two to a snowmobile carrying

Warren and the bodies of their fallen comrades slumped across the backs of their machines.

She was close enough to kill them all. In her mind's eye she imagined them all lying, bleeding into the snow, while she tore off with Warren on one of their snowmobiles, flying back to Thule and safety. She was about to take aim when the Russians were joined by a larger contingent of maybe a dozen more men — too many — where the hell had they come from?

Then she saw it, behind them, nestled in a depression in the glacier: massive — but perfectly camouflaged — the Enemy mother-ship. At first she'd just taken it for a *serac*, thrown up by the glacier's relentless progress to the sea. But now she was close-up to it, she could see it was a sleek, shallow disk— like a cross between a stealth bomber and a flying saucer.

She couldn't help but admire it, it was a perfect counter-surveillance design: no radar profile; cold propulsion; flawless camouflage — and it threw up its own ice screen as it went, which made it almost invisible to the naked eye, even in good weather. But, cloaked by the Arctic storms, it was almost completely undetectable. She realised just how lucky she'd been to spot it on the satellite surveillance — but that was only because there'd been heat sources moving all around it, which had given its position away.

They were unstrapping Warren from the back of the snowmobile and dragging his inert body aboard. Siv edged closer to the mother-ship as the Russians got ready to take off, yelling at one another as they bucked their snowmobiles up a ramp and into the craft's cavernous cargo hold.

As the hold doors started to shut, she darted out from cover and sprinted, stumbling, across the ice, making straight for the undercarriage. The air all around started to crackle — ice crystals sparked electric blue. The long steel compression legs of its landing gear flexed as the mother ship started to lift off. Siv launched herself at the nearest one, and clung on tight.

With a droning, juddering motion it started to retract, drawing her up into the undercarriage bay. She felt a pressure on her thigh, moving down her leg — it was closing on her. Then, with a metallic clank, the landing gear snapped into place — trapping Siv's ankle.

The undercarriage doors started to close — if she didn't move quickly they would decapitate her. She squirmed herself up tight against the compression leg and, ignoring the screaming pain in her ankle, contorted her body so that she could force herself up into the shallow space around the undercarriage.

The doors slid together, brushing along her cheekbone as they closed.

*

Day 22 : 0300hrs

The confined space of the undercarriage bay was dark and claustrophobic. Siv hated being in confined spaces — really hated it. To stop herself from panicking she tried to think rationally, to focus on her situation.

One: she couldn't move much more than a couple of centimetres in any direction and she was starting to cramp up — that was bad.

Two: she could breathe — that was good. As they'd started to take off, she'd suddenly realised that if this thing got anywhere near the altitude of even a commercial airliner, she'd die in the thin air. So, breathing was a good — very good.

Three: her ankle hurt like Hell — bad. But she kept flexing it and it didn't feel like it was broken — good.

Four: she was cold, but not frozen. It'd taken her a while to realise why this was: the undercarriage bay was lined with small heaters that kept the temperature just above zero, so the landing gear wouldn't freeze up. Definitely good.

So, good wins 3 - 2. That was OK, she could live with that.

She blinked on her chronometer: the screen flickered into life. They'd been in the air for just over two hours and they'd travelled about five hundred kilometres, due north.

Then it went blank.

That startled her. She could feel the panic rising up again.

'Come on, Siv,' she muttered through gritted teeth. 'Think — you need to think... What does that tell you?'

In her mind's eye she tried to visualise the map of Greenland. They were going back over the Humboldt Glacier right back the way they'd come, and further north. Five hundred kilometres — they'd be skirting the north west coast now. She tried to imagine what they were flying over: jagged black hills and fjords running down to the winter ice-sheet that covered the Kennedy Channel. She racked her brains to think where they could be going. Russia? Not very likely: they were doing less than three hundred kilometres an hour — at that speed it'd take them days to get across the Arctic.

The dull hum that had been reverberating all around her, subtly dropped a semitone, then another. Suddenly the bay doors started to open, sliding along Siv's cheek and blasting a flurry of ice crystals into her face. Outside, the dark of the night seemed bright compared to the cramped, lightless space she'd been confined in.

Then, without any warning, the undercarriage dropped.

It all happened so quickly. As it swung down Siv tried to cling onto it — but her arms and legs were so cramped they wouldn't obey her command.

'Oh, shit…' she muttered.

The landing gear snapped into place — Siv was catapulted off.

'Ohshitohshit!'

For a brief, sickening moment she was hanging by her trapped foot, dangling upside-down, the wind blasting her face. Everything down below was just a grey blur. She summoned her strength and tried to swing herself up to catch hold of one of the compression legs — but the motion dislodged her foot.

'Ohshitohshitohshit!'

She was falling: twisting in mid-air, spiralling, head-over-heels.

Silence — nothing but the rushing wind.

Then everything went black.

*

Day 22 : 1900hrs

Cold — that was the only thing Warren was aware of. Cold — real cold, right through to the bone: tomb-cold, ash-cold. Inescapable. So cold he couldn't remember ever being warm…

There was a noise, reverberating at the back of his mind. A mournful moaning, rising and falling — like the groaning of lost souls.

Now there was something else, another feeling.

Hands. Gripping him — shaking him. Slapping his face again and again. The taste of blood in his mouth…

'Wake up, Commander Warren!' A harsh staccato voice — a woman's voice. Not Siv.

Not Siv…

A sudden jolt of panic brought him round: where the Hell was Siv? What had happened to her?

A hand on his face, gripping his cheek — hard. Nails digging into his skin. Eyes staring deep into his eyes, probing, examining him like a specimen: purple irises, dark, heavy make-up — not Siv.

Strong perfume — sultry, overpowering — definitely not Siv.

'Who are you,' he mumbled, shocked by the heaviness of his voice.

'Don't you know me?' The eyes creased at the sides. Smiling — only the eyes didn't smile. 'I'm disappointed, Commander Warren. I thought you of all people would have heard of me by now…' Nails running down his face — the smell of blood.

'Sorry…' he muttered, shaking his head.

'Oh, now I really am disappointed. Especially after I left you that nice calling card…'

'The Empress…' The words slipped from Warren's lips automatically, without thought, without intention. He wondered if he'd been given a truth serum.

'Clever you,' she replied, mockingly. 'But *you* don't need a calling card — do you, Commander Warren? Everyone knows you: "Warren the wizard" — "Warren the thinker" — "the man of a thousand strategies"… You've been a thorn in our side for many years…'

A mirthless laugh, like ice crystals falling on steel.

'… And now I've caught you.'

*

Siv flipped her visor to night vision — it flashed on briefly, then went out. She blinked at the screen, trying to call up the options menu — still nothing. As she moved her arm down to grab her flashlight she heard a familiar creaking, pattering sound that told her she was was buried in a snowdrift.

'Thank you God...' she muttered to herself. When she thought of all the things she could have landed on — hard stuff like rock and ice — she knew she was incredibly lucky to be alive. She wriggled around to check if anywhere hurt — which brought a cascade of fresh powdery snow down on her. No pain. Even her ankle had stopped throbbing: but that could be down to the cold.

She wondered how long she'd been down here, and reached down to get to her wristwatch — the movement brought down another pattering deluge. Better to get back up on solid ground first.

She'd been getting herself out of snowdrifts ever since she was a little girl. She knew that if she tried to stand upright she'd sink — and keep on sinking 'til she got to the bottom. The trick was to lie flat and disperse her weight, then do a sort of swimming crawl through the compressed snow, moving gradually upwards, and trying to keep a pocket of air in front of her face.

But to do that, she had to get free of her damned helmet or she'd suffocate. As she scrabbled it off her hand fell on something unfamiliar. She shone her flashlight onto her helmet — there was the crumpled remains of what looked like a small calibre hollow-point bullet embedded into its power pack.

'Well, Siv,' she said to herself, twisting it out and staring at it: 'Now you know why your visor isn't working...'

She shone her flashlight around, looking for any faults in the snow that would make crawling easier — there was a good way, almost straight ahead. Shining the beam straight up through the hole she'd made in the snow, she figured she was only about two or three metres down. For some reason that didn't seem right to her: as far as she could remember, she'd fallen from a long way up. She should've been buried a whole lot deeper. But what the Hell, she thought as she started to crawl her way out — maybe she'd just got lucky.

After a couple of minutes of crawling, she began to realise things weren't going exactly as she'd expected. Instead of moving steadily upwards she felt pretty sure she was actually going more or less in the opposite direction. The snow was slipping away from underneath her — faster than she could crawl.

Up ahead a whole mass of it slid away, leaving her face exposed to the night sky. All her questions and doubts were answered in a single, gut-wrenching moment: the snowdrift she thought she'd fallen into wasn't a snowdrift at all. It was a snow sheet — a snow sheet that was halfway up a mountainside.

Everything started to drop away beneath her — and Siv went with it. Above she heard a rumble and realised with alarm that she'd triggered an avalanche. She was falling — great lumps of snow and ice, some the size of houses, were crashing and tumbling all around her.

She curled herself up as tightly as she could, made herself into a human ball — an automatic reaction, something she'd been told when she was a kid. Ice boulders buffeted her, sent her spinning. There was nothing she could do, just go with it and hope that when she got to the bottom — if she was still alive when she got there — she wasn't buried under a mountain of snow and ice.

*

The woman gripped Warren's skull in both hands, peering at it, surveying it with hypnotic fascination.

'So much knowledge in this little place,' she muttered, running her fingers through his hair, twisting his head around, searching, probing. 'So many secrets — so *many* secrets — but how do I get them out? How?'

He felt a fingernail cutting into his scalp, describing a line across his cranium.

'A little incision here, perhaps?' she mused. '…a drill there?'

As she wrestled his head around it dimly registered in Warren's mind that she was only wearing a blouse, and it was unbuttoned to the breastbone. Why wasn't she freezing when he was so cold? How could that be?

As he slowly became more aware of himself, he realised he was naked. He tried to move — but he couldn't. He was manacled and shackled to an ice-cold steel chair. He wrenched his body against it — but it didn't budge. He knew there was only one explanation for that: it had to be bolted to the floor. And there was only one reason he could think of for bolting a steel chair to the floor — so it wouldn't fall over while the subject was being beaten.

*

Siv felt something pulling at her wrist, tugging it, shaking it violently from side to side. There was a snarling, growling noise — it rose and fell in time with each tug. She lifted her other arm and the snarling stopped. Forcing her body up through the mound of snow on top of her, she rolled over to get a good look at her assailant.

Lying back on its haunches, ready to spring, staring fixedly at her with its coal-black eyes, its head cocked slightly to one side was a *fjellrev* — an Arctic fox, so brilliantly white it glowed in the moonlight.

'Ah, did you think I was dead, little feller?' she asked as she got up and batted the snow off her. The motion startled the fox and it jumped back — but it stayed there, staring at her, his big bushy tail moving lazily from side to side, as though he was thinking he might still have a chance of turning Siv into prey.

'You must've thought all your Christmases had come at once, didn't you? Finding a big lump of carcass just lying there in the snow like that.'

But there fox didn't make a sound. He just lay there, staring at her.

Siv stared right back — and it suddenly struck her that there was something very odd about him…

'My, my mister fox — you're a fat little fucker, aren't you…?'

In the depths of a hard winter like this, *fjellrev* were more likely to die of starvation — but, if anything, this little creature was looking positively overfed.

'… I bet I can guess where you've been scavenging for scraps…'

*

Warren was thinking more clearly now. He quickly took stock of where he was: a small grey-walled room. If he could stretch out his arms he'd be able to touch all four walls from where he was sitting. Above him, the room was lit by a single ceiling panel. Below was a metal floor, it felt cold under his feet.

The woman was circling round him, brushing her hip against his shoulder each time she passed. He took stock of her too: white blouse, Russian Navy dress uniform. Rank insignia: Captain-Lieutenant. Her shoulder patch said she was in the elite 61st Kirkenes Naval Infantry Brigade — but he knew that wasn't right. Back at Control they had files on every serving member of that unit — Warren knew the faces of every single one of them. And he would definitely have remembered this woman if he'd come across her picture — definitely.

She looked a little older than Siv — but not much. Similar height, but a completely different build: Siv was tough and lean. This woman was slim, but… Well, she was a very different creature. Hair short and spiky, like Siv's, but dyed jet black with purple and blue highlights — retro-punk — it was a popular look all round the world this year.

Looking at her, she reminded him of a pampered Persian cat. He couldn't imagine she'd even get through basic military training, let alone the tough, gruelling ordeal Russian marines had to undergo to earn the coveted black beret of the Kirkenes.

So, who was she? What was she?

'You know,' she mused, idly to herself, perching her bottom on his shoulder: 'You really are a big catch for a little country girl like me. Oh, yes you are.' She sighed: 'But I'm afraid it doesn't look like I'll be able to keep you. As soon as the weather clears I have orders to send you back to my superiors for more detailed interrogation.'

'Sorry to hear that…' Warren replied. He started to laugh, but he was brought up short by a stabbing pain in his back that took his breath away.

'Oh, yes. I was just about to mention that,' she said, running her fingernail down his spine: 'You have a hypodermic bullet lodged between your shoulder blade and your ribs.' She pressed her finger hard on the entry wound, forcing his shoulder blade down. Warren felt metal grating on bone — the pain was so bad he almost passed out.

'Oh, dear,' she cooed, sympathetically. 'I imagine that must be quite agonising.'

'Quite…' Warren replied, through gritted teeth.

'Ah, but lucky for you, I trained as a field nurse.'

'Lucky me.'

'Indeed. So, before I send you back to the motherland, I'm going to cut that naughty little *pulya* out of your body.'

'You don't have to bother…'

'Oh, it will be no bother, Commander Warren — in fact it will be my pleasure.'

*

This was getting her nowhere, Siv thought as she and the fox competed with one another in a staring contest. She needed to get him moving — to go foraging for food — but he wouldn't budge. And she didn't want to scare him off.

She needed a plan.

Of course, Warren would have figured out what to do ages ago, she thought. But she wasn't Warren — that was painfully obvious.

She pulled out a nutrition bar and stripped back the wrapper — she figured she might as well keep her energy levels up while she was waiting. Immediately, the fox jumped up and started circling around, eagerly.

'Oh, so that's what they've been feeding you, is it?' Siv taunted him, holding the bar over him, just out of reach. 'Well, you can't have this one,' she said, firmly — and stuffed it back in her tunic.

The fox glowered at her, as though Siv had cheated him of his rightful reward.

'Go, on!' she said, waving him away. 'Go find some dinner!'

It gave her one last long, hard stare, then trotted past her and off into the darkness.

Siv followed him.

*

Day 22 : 2300hrs

Warren heard a door open and close behind him. Something clattered as it was set down — a tray with metal objects on it? He listened intently as the woman whispered an order to a man: she didn't want to be disturbed, she wanted to be left alone with the prisoner for one hour and no longer. The man just grunted in reply.

The door closed.

Standing behind him, the tone of her voice became very businesslike: 'Of course, one of the benefits of the Arctic environment is that there is very little chance of contracting an infection in a gunshot wound. I suppose we could let it go gangrenous, but that would be sheer laziness…' Her voice brightened: 'But, anyway, as my old babushka used to say: "better safe than sorry".'

He heard a hiss — at once it felt like his shoulder was on fire.

'Acid?' he muttered through gritted teeth.

'That — and iodine, plus some other ingredients. Capsicin …and a bit of petrol, I think. We keep it to treat our prisoners' wounds.' She paused, thoughtfully: 'Not that we take many prisoners…'

'I bet you don't…'

It was a perfect opportunity. More than anything he wanted to know about Siv — where she was, if she was still alive. But he couldn't appear too eager. If he did, they'd know that she was important to him.

'Speaking of prisoners…' he said, as nonchalantly as he could manage: 'What happened to my minder?'

'Your what?' she replied, distractedly. He could hear her moving metal items around.

'My minder, my bodyguard…'

'Oh, him. He's just down the corridor. I have to say, he's being very helpful. *Very* helpful indeed.'

They didn't have her. Siv had got away.

She leaned forward, her face next to his: 'Now,' she said gently. 'I'm sure you don't really expect me to give you any anaesthetic for this. Obviously, I'm going to make sure it's very, very painful.'

'I rather thought you might…'

'But, because you've been such a nice man, I'm going to give you something just to chill you slightly.'

He felt a jab in his arm, just below his bicep. Moments later a familiar sensation washed over him — like he was hovering inside his own body. The walls of the tiny room seemed to be closing in — but the inside of his head felt vast, like the interior of a cathedral.

'SP-117?' he murmured. 'You know that won't work, we're trained to control it…'

'Ah, but this is SP-117*S*,' she corrected him. 'The twentieth incarnation of our old and trusted friend. Oh, it's the usual mix of scopolamine hydrobromide, plus a little sodium pentathol, a twist of sodium amytal and a soupçon of sodium thiopental — but over the years we've added a few more exotic ingredients. To that we add intense pain — which, as you know, you are about to experience — and then finally, one very special ingredient.'

'I can't wait.' Warren replied, struggling to master himself — not to succumb to the drug. SP-117 worked as an anti-inhibitor, releasing all self-control and making the subject susceptible to suggestion — and all-too-eager to please their inquisitor. He had to fight it — and to do that he had to focus on something important. He tried to cling on to the thought of Siv. He didn't know how long he'd been knocked out for, but he reckoned by now she had to be getting close to the military base at Thule. She was alive — and she was free. And that was all that mattered now. Siv was safe.

*

Day 23 : 0000hrs

Siv was alive — and she was close to a military base — but it wasn't Thule.

She'd followed the little *fjellrev* as it went in search of an easy meal — and now she was lying hidden, watching as it scampered across the snow toward a shanty of low-lying camouflaged cabins, clustered around a small, squat turret. Behind it, the VTOL had lowered itself flat onto the ice, its splinter-pattern camouflage breaking up its outline so that it would be all but invisible from above.

The terrain all around her was flat, as far as the eye could see — all the way back to the mountains behind her. She was right out on the winter ice: three metres beneath her, maybe four at the most, the dark waters of the Arctic Ocean surged south on the strong Nares Strait current — which made Siv's stomach churn just thinking about it.

Ahead of her the ice field was strewn with the remains of half a dozen polar bears and what looked like a couple of seals — all at various states of wind-erosion, with snow banked up against their sides. At first they'd puzzled her — but when she checked out the base more carefully she realised what had happened: the perimeter was ringed with proximity-triggered machine guns. They'd been lured to this place, probably by the smell of food — and then mown down in a hail of automatic gunfire. From the appearance of the corpses it looked like some of them had taken a while to die. So, how the Hell was she going to get through?

*

The woman's face was next to his once more, he could feel her breath on his cheek.

'We're going to have to work together now,' she whispered. 'I've got to widen the wound so that I can insert the probe to locate the bullet, and then the forceps to pull it out. I'm about to make the first incision, Warren. It will hurt you, but you must stay very still… Very, very still.' She placed her hand on his shoulder. 'Do you understand, Warren? You'll have to trust me. You do trust me — don't you?'

He wanted to shout out, to tell her exactly what he thought of her — but he couldn't. He felt his head nodding slowly, obediently. He was losing control — he could feel his will to resist ebbing away — but how could that be?

'That's good,' she whispered, kissing the nape of his neck. 'Now, as I cut into your flesh, I want you to think about all the men and boys you murdered in that submarine, their grotesque and needless deaths… Friends and fathers, brothers and sons — crushed like insects. Their deaths on your conscience…'

The pain screamed into his shoulder as the scalpel sliced through his skin and down, deeper — until it scraped along the bone of his shoulder blade. He struggled to master himself, not to cry out. He clamped his teeth together so tight he thought they'd break.

'Very good…' she murmured. 'This second cut is for all my men you murdered in your booby traps. Twelve good men. Friends and fathers, brothers and sons. …Their deaths on your conscience…'

She cut slowly, pushing the scalpel into the wound, then drawing outwards, so that it dragged at his flesh before it cut. Warren nearly blacked out with the pain.

Now her face hovered before his, staring into his eyes — her beauty exaggerated by the effects of the drug.

'Oh, my dearest dear…' she whispered as she held his face gently in her hands. '… You're being so brave…' Then she kissed him on the mouth, her lips full and soft, her tongue probing. He wanted to bite it, to give back some of the pain. But he couldn't. He felt his own tongue responding to hers, eagerly forcing it into her mouth.

And then she was gone. Her voice behind him once more.

'And this cut is for me. You ordered your man to shoot me down as I hovered, helpless in the sky. You wanted me dead…'

'No…!' Warren cried out as the scalpel went in. But he wasn't crying out with pain. He wanted to protest his innocence — he could never have wanted her dead. Not her — not her. The image of her hovering in the sky above him burned into his drug-addled brain — she was an angel.

An angel.

His will to resist was slipping, receding into the far distance — inconsequential. Siv was gone. All that mattered to him was this woman who consumed his mind completely, giving pain and pleasure in equal measure — she was everything to him.

'Now I insert the probe…'

He felt it digging, tugging, grating on the bone of his shoulder blade. Sweat dripped from his every pore — even though he was freezing. Waves of nausea swept over him.

'…And now the bullet forceps…'

More tugging — more pain. Warren was falling into unconsciousness…

A clatter of metal on metal.

'There,' she muttered. 'Now, before I stitch you back up, I'm just going to pour a little of our home-made antiseptic into the wound…'

Warren lost all control of himself as the capsicin coursed through his veins, wreaking havoc with his nervous system. His body convulsed violently, involuntarily.

Time melted into nothingness. All sense of pain, all sensation, drifted away. There was something he knew he needed to cling onto, something vitally important — but he couldn't remember what it was.

Then she was in front of him again. Hitching up her skirt, sitting astride him, kissing him long and deep and hard. He was powerless to resist — he didn't want to resist. All he wanted was her. He felt the blood surge as she reached down and stroked him. He felt himself harden under her hand.

She smiled as she guided him inside her.

'Oh, Commander Warren,' she cooed as she arched her back and pushed down on him, forcing him deep inside her. 'How can you possibly expect to control your tongue — when you are so perfectly in my power…?'

*

Day 23 : 0020hrs

Siv watched in amazement as the little fox trotted blithely across the killing ground and disappeared behind one of the huts. How the Hell had he done that?

She figured there had to be a blind spot in the perimeter. Either one of the proximity sensors wasn't working or there was a gap in the traverses of the machine guns. Whatever it was, it'd let her little companion through. But would the gap be big enough for her?

There was only one way to find out. She checked her boot knife — the only weapon she had left after the avalanche — making sure it was securely strapped in place. Then, with her heart pounding uncontrollably, she got up and followed the tiny, pointed *fjellrev* tracks in the snow.

'This is so stupid…' she muttered as she passed the frozen carcass of a giant polar bear. It looked like it was just sleeping, that at any moment it would spring back to life and grab her in its huge paws. Up close though, she could see that some small creature — perhaps the little fox itself — had gnawed its face away, right down to the bone.

'It's alright…' she whispered to herself as she reached halfway mark. 'You're nearly there…'

She stopped dead in her tracks — one of the machine guns stirred into life and slowly turned in her direction. She stared helplessly as it stopped. Its mechanism clicked and whirred, trying to move further round, to get Siv in its sights — but it couldn't.

Maybe it was at the end of its traverse, she thought, her mind racing frantically. She tried to persuade herself that was it — maybe ice had gotten into its mechanism. That was it — that had to be it.

But whatever it was, the gun couldn't get her in its sights. And, after a couple of seconds, it stopped trying and fell dormant once more.

*

Day 23 : 0100hrs

The woman was gone and Warren was alone.

How long had he been left there? An hour? A day? No time at all?

He remembered the woman — the pain and the pleasure she'd inflicted on him he remembered with every fibre of his body. It was the only clear memory he possessed. But what he'd said, what he'd told her — what information she'd managed to extract from him — he had no idea. His mind was in shattered fragments, like a broken mirror. All his senses, everything around him — cold, light …pain — it all seemed to merge together in an incomprehensible swirling mass of confusion.

The door behind him clanged open — the sound of it reverberated round inside his skull. He was dimly aware of being released from the torture chair. The staccato clatter of shackles and manacles assaulted his ears. His skin shrieked with agony as his captors roughly manhandled his limbs back into his clothes. The words "heightened sensitivity" drifted into his consciousness — but he had no idea what they meant…

Now he was being hauled up — his legs buckled under his own weight. He felt himself being dragged like a sack, his feet slithering on the steel floor.

Another door slammed open, booming against a metal wall — his brain collapsed into shining sparks. He was propelled into the darkness, falling to the floor like a heap of rags. Then another mind-shattering clang — and the darkness became total.

His head still reeled — nothing made sense. He felt himself sliding back into the warm reassuring oblivion of unconsciousness. He tried to fight it, but he couldn't remember how. He felt insubstantial — like he didn't exist at all.

The only thing he was aware of was pain.

Pain — he knew what that was — that was real: the one fixed point in his universe. He clung onto it, struggled to focus on it.

Gradually, the single fact of being in pain separated into two distinct areas of pain. He remembered their names: "face" and "shoulder". He used them to re-acquaint himself with the rest of his body. He shifted his shoulder, and his arm twitched back into life — he felt slight movements in his fingertips. They were close to the pain in his face. He touched it: it flinched away from his touch, and he became aware of another sensation — a sweet-salt taste. His mouth was full of thick, congealed blood.

And all the time there was the continuous haunting, groaning noise that seemed to come from all around him. He focused on that. After a while he realised there was another sound in amongst it. He tried to remember what it was...

Then it came to him: it was the sound of sobbing. Somewhere in the darkness, very close to him, someone was crying: wretched, forlorn — hopeless.

'Who's that?' Warren croaked, his voice dry and parched.

The sobbing stopped. The silence deepened.

'Skipper?' the voice whispered, nervously. 'Is that you?'

*

Siv scrambled the last few metres past the perimeter defences. Ahead were half a dozen weatherboard huts, shrouded in camouflage netting, clustered close up to the squat tower. She skirted around under the netting, searching for anything that might be a door — but she drew a complete blank. They were all interconnected — but there didn't seem to be any way to get in.

She thought about trying to hack her way in. That wouldn't be easy, though — she figured the walls would have maybe a metre of insulation. And it wouldn't be quiet. She imagined the welcoming party that would be waiting for her as she finally broke through the inner skin — no, that was a bad idea.

But she'd have to think of something fast. The wind was getting up and she was starting to freeze. If she didn't find a way in soon she'd be joining the silent menagerie of corpses that littered the ice field.

She heard a frantic whining and yelping and ran stumbling and lurching through the snow to see what it was. The little *fjellrev* was scrabbling frantically against one of the huts. After a few moments a concealed hatchway opened at the bottom of the wall and a small cascade of steaming scraps issued out — which the fox immediately started to devour before they froze.

It was so intent on its meal it barely noticed Siv as she nudged it to one side and knelt down to investigate the hatchway. She pulled at it — it opened easily, but it was heavy, weighted down to stay shut when it was buffeted by the Arctic winds.

Lifting it and peering up inside, she could see it was at the bottom of a metal garbage chute — big enough for her to climb up, but only just. She stripped off her pack and parka and dragged them into the chute behind her.

Up above there was another hatch door. A thin chink of warm amber light showed round its edges. She pushed at it gently, but it didn't budge: like its counterpart below, it was weighted to resist the storm winds. She climbed up on top of her pack and wedged her boots against the sides of the chute — then pushed hard up through her shoulders. The hatch lifted slightly. A blast of warm musty air rushed over her face. She peered around — she was in some kind of drying room: parkas and overtrousers were slung over racks, boots balanced precariously on pipes.

Siv listened intently. There were muffled voices coming from a doorway off to her right, but they didn't seem to be getting any nearer. She wedged the hatchway open with her boot knife, hoisted her kit through the gap, then swung herself up after it. For a second she sat perched on the top of the garbage chute, her legs dangling, then lowered herself down gently, so that her heavy ice boots only made the slightest sound as they touched the floorboards.

*

A faltering hand brushed against Warren's shoulder.

'Stewart?' he muttered as the pieces of his mind began to fall back into place

'Afraid so, sir.'

'I thought you were dead.'

'Wish I was,' Stewart replied, sniffing back his tears. 'I wish they'd just kill me and be done with it.'

'What do you mean?'

Stewart laughed, a hollow, desolate laugh: 'I don't know why they didn't just leave me there with Dern and Peary. I should've died with them. Not carried on …like this.'

'Look, I'm sorry…' Warren was struggling to remain conscious — maybe it was him, but Stewart didn't seem to be making any sense. 'I'm not really with it, I'm afraid,' he muttered, his voice slurring. 'They've filled me up with drugs, and…'

He felt Stewart grabbing at his tunic, pulling him closer.

'No, I'm the one who should be sorry,' he said, placing his hands on either side of Warren's face. 'They've been interrogating you — did they torture you? What happened?'

'No, no.' Warren replied, shaking his head, trying to make sense of what had happened to him. 'Well, yes, I guess you could call it…' He paused in mid-thought. 'I don't know. …There was a woman. … She was…'

'That would be Yekaterina,' Stewart said, excitedly. 'You've met her?'

Warren could still smell her strong, heady perfume on his body, feel the scratches from her fingernails on his flesh, the searing pain in his shoulder. 'Yekaterina — that's her name?'

'Yes, yes…' Warren could feel Stewart nodding his head. 'She's beautiful, isn't she?' he enthused. But, before Warren could reply, the young man started sobbing convulsively again.

'Come on Stewart,' Warren said, trying to sound comforting — though, in truth, as he was still trying to pull together the unravelled threads of his memory, he was beginning to find Stewart's histrionics irritating. 'What's wrong? What can be so bad?'

'It's her,' Stewart replied, between sobs. 'Her face — it's the last thing I ever saw.'

'I don't get it.'

'Don't you? Don't you understand? I'm blind, sir.'

'We're both blind, Stewart. It's pitch black in here…'

'No, sir.' he replied, his voice faltering on the edge of tears. 'They blinded me — *she* blinded me.'

In his confused state this last piece of information seemed more bewildering than anything else.

'But why?' he asked — it was all he could think of to say.

'She said it was an experiment,' Stewart said, bitterly. 'She works with lasers — you know that, don't you?'

Warren's mind might have been a mess, but he knew he shouldn't answer that. What if they took Stewart away and tortured him? 'No, I didn't,' he replied bluntly. 'What… What does she do?'

'Nano technology — small things, deadly things. She said she needed to calibrate a nano-laser. She used the lens of my own eye to focus its beam onto my retina. The first time she did it, she only burned a small patch away. I could still see out of the sides of my eyes — but nothing in the centre, nothing at all. The next time she increased the intensity, burned all the way down the optical nerve. From that moment on, my world has been total darkness.'

*

Siv stripped off her ice-boots and overtrousers, then bundled all her kit together and stashed it in the darkest corner of the drying cabin. But, as she stood up straight, her head started to swim — huge black spots appeared, dancing before her eyes.

It took her a few moments to remember from her training what was happening to her: oxygen levels at the poles are no different to other parts of the world — but the intense cold meant that her lungs had had to work much harder just to breathe in and out. She'd been living outside in the cold of the Arctic winter for the last ten days. Here in the warmth of the cabin it was much easier to breathe — and now she was overdosing on oxygen.

'Whoa, Siv,' she murmured as she propped herself up against the wall. 'Take it steady, girl.' She sat down heavily on a bench and started to breathe more slowly, taking shallow sips of air. Gradually everything began to settle down.

She took out a nutrition bar and gnawed on it, all the time looking around the drying cabin: there were boots and parkas, skis and snowshoes, probably enough equipment for about twenty men. She stared warily at the doorway — that was where the sound of voices was coming from. If anyone came through there now, while she was like this — that would be it, all over. She was too weak to fight.

After a few minutes the spots started to clear and she could breathe normally again. Siv got up and crept stealthily toward the open doorway in her stockinged-feet, clutching her black-bladed boot knife. She could still hear the sound of voices, but they seemed to be a long way away.

Looking round the doorway, she could see two more wooden doors, both open, immediately to her left. Straight ahead, down a short corridor was a closed metal door — that had to lead to the tower. The sound of mens' voices was coming from the other side of it.

She edged her way to the first doorway and peered inside. It was dark and cold in there, and there was no sign of life. She crept inside, all the time keeping her knife at the ready. In the dim light all that she could see was a single massive object — all pipes and boxes and tubes — that occupied practically the whole cabin, looming right up into the roof.

As her eyes became accustomed to the gloom, the massive object assumed a familiar shape. She'd only ever seen them in satellite images — never up close like this. But it was unmistakable: a Redut 7 surface-to-air missile array, the Russian Navy's latest — and most powerful — anti-missile defence system. The NATO files on this were still pretty sketchy, but if what they said about it was true, it could engage up to fifty targets simultaneously — with complete accuracy.

She peered into the next cabin, all the time straining her ears for any sound of someone coming. She didn't have to wait for her eyes to adjust to the darkness this time. Another Redut array lurked, massive and threatening. Siv was amazed: it was ridiculous, incredible — this place was better protected from air attack than most Russian cities.

*

Day 23 : 0200hrs

'Thanks for coming to get me, skipper,' Stewart muttered.

'Don't mention it.'

Warren could feel his mind coming back together. Everything was fitting back into place: he was starting to think clearly again.

'…I mean,' Stewart continued. 'I know you got caught. But there are bound to be others coming to rescue us, aren't there?'

Warren shook his head in the darkness: 'I wouldn't count on that,' he replied. 'No-one knows we're here. And, to be honest, I don't have the slightest idea where "here" is.'

'I don't think we're that far from the base,' Stewart said. 'When they took me, we weren't in the air very long. Less than half an hour, I'd say.'

'You were conscious?'

'Oh, yes. Yekaterina made me watch as they tied Peary and Dern to their snowmobiles. She ripped off their headgear and exposed them to the full force of the ice storm. It didn't take long for them to fall into unconsciousness. She kissed each one of them on the cheek before they died.'

'She likes kissing her victims, it seems,' Warren observed.

'She does that, sir.'

Warren tried to visualise the Enemy VTOL as it had approached them across the ice field. How fast had it been travelling? Not fast, he thought. Much slower than a conventional jet. It wouldn't have got far in half an hour.

So, the Enemy was maybe about a hundred miles from their base, perhaps even less. And what was it Siv had said, back at the *Kjegle*? She'd tracked it for between a hundred and a hundred and fifty kilometres, then she'd lost it. But she hadn't lost it. It hadn't flown on — she'd tracked it right here, right to its lair. So, its precise location was already on the database back at the JWC in Stavanger. All he had to do was get that information to his control and get them to blast it this place to oblivion — but how was he going to do it?

*

The sound of mens' voices got louder. Siv darted under the Redut's missile cradle, just as she heard the clang of the metal door being swung open. No second clang — the door was still open. She watched as three pairs of feet sauntered past her hiding place, then slowly clambered up into the Redut's control module. After a few seconds she heard the thrum of small electric motors as they fired up the weapons system. Siv realised at once what they were up to: it was a routine warm-up — this was the sort of thing she'd spent the last three years in the surveillance centre looking out for.

NATO forces in the Arctic had practised exactly the same routine: a missile system couldn't be allowed to freeze up — but if it was kept warm it was an obvious target. The solution was to regularly fire up elements at the core of the system and run them until the heat had permeated almost to the outer surfaces, then switch off. The whole thing would warm up to about a couple of degrees above freezing. She guessed that was probably why they'd left the metal door open, to allow a tiny amount of warm air to circulate and break up the heat profile of the missile platform.

Siv bobbed her head out from under the missile cradle and checked to see if the coast was clear — then scrambled out. At the doorway she looked around and listened: another team was warming up the other Redut. The coast was clear — she made a bolt down the corridor and through the metal door.

Siv stopped dead in amazement.

'What the fuck...?' she cursed under her breath. On the other side of the door it was nothing like what she'd expected. She wasn't exactly sure what she'd expected, but it was nothing like this. A steel gantry led to a spiral stairway that looked like it went up to the top of the tower — but the same stairway also went down, down as far as she could see.

What kind of place was this?

*

'How long has it been?' Stewart asked. 'Since the attack, I mean.'

Warren thought for a moment: 'About a month.'

'A month? God, you really loose track of time in here…'

'I suppose you do.'

'So, have you been looking for me all this time?'

'Not to start with. Remember, I was ordered to Stavanger. Then there was a big storm. Everything was grounded for more than a week.'

'And after that? What did you do then?'

That was another thing Warren didn't want to talk about to Stewart. It was all for his safety — the less he knew, the less they could beat out of him. He got up and started pacing the cell, with his hands held out in front of him.

'What the Devil are you doing?' Stewart asked.

'Getting an idea of the dimensions of this place,' Warren replied. 'One, two, three … Four paces wide, by…' He backed himself against the door and started to pace toward the far wall: 'One, two, three, four … Ow! What the Hell was that?' he felt a sharp pain on his knee.

'Steel toilet, built into the wall. If you want a drink, you've got to catch the flush in your hands.'

'What about washing?'

'The same.'

'Anything else in here?'

'Nothing. You, me — and one steel toilet.'

Warren was thinking clearly now: he needed to find a way of getting out of this place. There had to something he could work with, something he could use.

'What about food?' he asked. 'When do they come to feed us?'

'They lift a flap at the bottom of the door. No-one ever comes in here.'

Warren peered around the cell. Everything was pitch black, there wasn't even the slightest chink of light coming from around the door, it was completely sealed. But the air was clean. He reckoned he'd been in this place for about an hour — and God only knew how long Stewart had been imprisoned in here. The air ought to be thick and fetid, especially if the door was sealed — but it wasn't. He remembered what Siv had said when they were trapped under the ice: he needed to find out where the clean air was coming from.

Reaching up as high as he could, Warren stretched out his fingers to try and touch the ceiling — he couldn't feel anything.

'Stewart,' he said. 'Can you come here and kneel down on all fours?'

'I beg your pardon, sir?'

'I want to climb up and find the ceiling. There has to be an air duct up there. I'm betting it'll be right here, in the middle of the cell.'

Stewart shuffled across and Warren climbed up on his back. He reached the ceiling easily — it could only have been a few inches away when he'd reached up before. There was a square slatted panel, about two feet wide, right in the middle of the ceiling. He ran his fingertips around it: it was held in place by eight screws. He forced his thumbnail into the slot of one of them and tried to twist it out. He cursed under his breath as his thumbnail split: the screw wouldn't budge.

*

Day 23 : 0400hrs

'Shit…' she muttered under her breath as she came to the end of a long corridor and realised where she was, 'I'm on a fucking submarine.'

But where was the crew? Apart from the men working on the missile systems, she hadn't seen a single soul. The only sounds she could hear were the humming of generators reverberating up and down the corridors and the moaning and shrieking of the ice as it ground against the hull — it was like being on a ghost ship.

She made her way back the way she'd come. The corridor seemed to run the length of the boat. Siv crept stealthily through hatchway after hatchway, listening for any sound, opening each door, getting to know the layout of the submarine, looking for Warren, looking for weapons and food — and places to hide.

About half-way down she opened a door and stepped into a cavernous bay. It looked like a small helicopter landing pad. Above her were sliding doors, with massive pressure locks, like in the cargo bay of the *Tecumseh*. On the deck beneath her feet were numbers and arrows, cyrillic symbols and lights that looked like landing directions — but the whole place was far too small for even the tiniest of helicopters.

Siv looked around for any clue to its real purpose. Over on the far side of the bay, lurking in the gloom, she saw six jetwings, lined up together, each one linked to a thick, umbilical cable. They stood with their domed helmets nodding forward, their thick, bulky cocoons unfastened down the middle — looking like giant impaled bugs.

She checked inside one of the cocoons: there were two hand controls — one looked like a joystick, she figured the other had to be a thrust control — it all seemed pretty straightforward. At the end of the thrust control there was a large red button with the word "активировать" on it. Siv sounded out the letters: 'A-K-T-I-V-I-R-O-V-A-T…' She didn't need to be an expert at Russian to work that one out. It had to be the start button. There was a flip-top on the joystick and another button underneath it — it looked like some kind of weapons control.

She imagined escaping with Warren in their jetwing fliers, soaring into the skies, leaving the Enemy far behind — but to do that they'd have to get out of the landing bay. Siv searched all around for any way of getting the massive sliding doors to open — without any success. So much for that good idea, she thought miserably.

She made her way back along the corridor to the place where she'd boarded the sub. Up ahead she could hear voices now, laughing and joking, the clatter of cutlery on metal plates. Warm wafts of highly-spiced cooking assaulted her nostrils. That was why she hadn't encountered anybody: they were all in the galley. She must have arrived just as the Russians were having dinner.

She turned round a corner — there were three sailors straight ahead of her, not more than ten metres away. They were having a heated discussion about something. If they looked up, if they looked in her direction at all, they'd see her for sure. She ducked into an open hatchway and closed the door behind her. It was dark, she couldn't see a thing. She pressed her ear against the door — she could still hear them arguing. They were getting closer.

Then they passed, the sound of their voices getting quieter — until she couldn't hear them at all.

'That was a bad mistake…' she reproached herself. 'Too confident — careless — stupid.'

*

Warren sat with his back against the cold steel wall, brooding in the darkness. There had to be a way out of this. If their captors didn't open the door, not even to feed them — then they'd have to get out through the ventilator.

'What do they feed you on?' he asked.

'Eh?' Stewart replied, sleepily. 'Sorry, I was just taking a little nap. … Um, *kasha* mostly, with vegetables and some meat. Actually, it's pretty good — but it does go straight through me…'

Stewart's lack of interest in getting out of here irritated Warren. It seemed like he'd just accepted his fate. Alright, so he was blind — but in this darkness they were both blind. Once they were out of this cell, Warren would get him to safety — surely he didn't think he'd leave him behind?

'Do you eat it with your hands?'

'Uh, no. A spoon.'

'Plastic spoon?'

'No. Metal I think — at least I think it's metal.'

'Do you have one now?'

'No, they normally give me about half an hour, then they come and bang on the door and I send the bowl back, with the spoon.'

Warren relaxed. He'd soon have his screwdriver — he'd soon be out of this place.

But what if they were being watched — where were the cameras? He checked all around the cell, but he couldn't see any. There was no light at all in the cell so they'd have to be using image intensifiers. Warren peered into the darkness for any sign of a minuscule light source — even an infra red source would be visible in this complete darkness — but if there was, he couldn't see any sign of it.

He went to the door, feeling all around it. There was a blank metal plate where the handle would have been. The locking mechanism was probably behind it. There were no screws, but maybe he could break it off. To do that he'd need something hard and heavy. He went back to the toilet and started yanking it up and down.

'What the Devil are you doing?' Stewart asked.

'I want to see if I can wrench it off the wall.'

'What! If you do that they'll hear you.'

'Maybe — but if they think I'm wrecking the place, they'll want to find out what I'm up to — and to do that they'll have to open the door.'

*

Day 23 : 2000hrs

Siv stopped dead in her tracks — there were voices up ahead. She looked around: no doors — nowhere to hide. She turned and ran, swinging through hatchways — and barrelled straight into a ladder, sending it skittering across the deck. Siv turned as she ran on: a pair of legs were dangling from an inspection hatch in the ceiling, she could hear muffled cursing from the void above.

She tried the handle of a storage locker. It opened and she dived in. A few seconds later she heard a lot of laughter and more cursing. She held her breath. Shadows loomed over the vents in the locker door, blocking out the light as they passed. Then they were gone.

Siv slumped down on the floor — a cascade of mops and brooms fell all around her. This was getting too risky. She had to find Warren soon before her luck ran out. But she'd searched practically the whole submarine and there was no sign of him — where the Hell was he?

Doubts started to creep into her mind: what if he was still on the VTOL? Or, worse, what if they'd taken him someplace else — and he wasn't here at all? She had to think — think like Warren. There had to be a way of finding him. There had to be…

Her thoughts were interrupted by a metallic clatter and the sound of someone whistling. She peered out of the vent: a young sailor was coming down the corridor, carrying a dinner tray with a small bottle of white wine and a neatly rolled white linen napkin next to a plate covered with a highly-polished silver dome — the whole thing was set off with a small glass vase containing a delicate posy of flowers. It seemed incongruous to her that anyone should be served so lavishly on a warship.

But that was it, she thought: food. They'd have to feed Warren sometime — she didn't suppose he'd be eating in the galley with the crew. There were cabins on the decks above the galley, but she'd already searched up there. So, if they were going to take any food to Warren, the only way they could come was right past her in this storage locker. If she followed the trays of food from the galley — one of them would lead to where they were holding him. All she had to do was stay put here and wait —

and hope that nobody wanted to get any cleaning materials while she was here…

*

Warren was waiting, waiting for the same thing as Siv — waiting for feeding time, when his captors would bring him the one thing he needed to get out.

He tried to visualise the sequence of events when they pushed the food through the flap at the bottom of the door:

There would be some light, maybe only for a few seconds, no more — he'd have to be poised, ready to use that time to get a good look at the cover on the ventilation duct.

He'd only have the spoon for half an hour — he tried to imagine what could go wrong: the metal might be too thick, he might have to make adjustments to it — how would he do that? Could he get all eight screws off in the time? Maybe not, but he could slacken off each screw and get them off by hand later if he ran out of time.

But, right now, all he could do was wait.

*

Day 23 : 2127hrs

Siv was munching on a nutrition bar when the whistling sailor came back along the corridor. She checked out his tray as he passed: two aluminium bowls full of some disgusting-looking glop and two spoons — now that looked more like the sort of crap they'd feed to prisoners.

Two bowls, two spoons — it looked like Warren had company.

She waited 'til the whistling sailor was a decent way ahead, then stuffed her half-eaten bar into her pocket and slipped out of her hiding place. She watched as he tripped nimbly down a spiral staircase. Siv waited at the top, peering down through the gaps in the stairway, watching as he went all the way down, right to the very bottom.

He jumped off the last stair. Siv heard the bowls and spoons clattering on the tray. She looked to see which way he'd gone — but she couldn't see him. She scrambled down the stairs — but when she got to the bottom there was no sign of him.

'Dammit!' she cursed under her breath: 'Where the fuck is he?'

She heard two voices, laughing and talking loudly together and set off cautiously toward the sound. Peering round a corner she watched as the whistling sailor handed his tray to a man in a black uniform, who spat into both of the aluminium bowls, then shoved the tray unceremoniously through a flap at the base of the door beside him.

After exchanging a couple more words, the sailor set off back along the corridor — back towards her. She bolted under the stairwell and made for a steel door marked: "не входить". She dragged it open, and held it together, peering out of the gap — watching as the sailor skipped lightly up the stairway, three steps at a time, still whistling to himself.

*

Warren was dazzled by the sudden influx of light as the hatch flipped open. He got a momentary glimpse of the ventilation grille. It was just as he'd visualised it. Then everything went dark again as the flap was closed and locked from the outside.

He grabbed a spoon and tapped it on the tray. It was metal, but it felt light: could be aluminium. He ran his finger along the edge: thick, but possibly not too thick. Anyway, he'd soon know.

'Quick,' he hissed. 'Get over here.'

'Are you sure about this?' Stewart whined as he shuffled to the centre of the cell. 'They're not going to be too happy if…'

'We're not here to make them happy — we're here to get out.'

Stewart groaned as Warren climbed up on his back: 'I don't think I can hold you for long…'

'Just stay there.' Warren reached up and pushed the edge of the spoon into one of the screws. It fitted. He turned it carefully and after some initial resistance, he could feel the screw coming out. He moved on to the next, and the next, slackening each screw so that he could remove it completely later.

'Sir…' Steward whispered, pitifully. ' I don't think I can hold you…'

'What? Stay where you are — only a few seconds longer.'

'I can't…'

*

Siv froze. There was a voice just above her. A woman's voice: strident, imperious — issuing short, clipped orders. She risked shifting around to get a look at where it was coming from. Up above her, much further away than she'd first thought, there was a dark-haired woman in a shimmering white lab coat that seemed to fluoresce in the violet light that bathed everything around her.

The light illuminated a single, gold cylinder. It was three, maybe four metres wide, down here at its base, tapering as it went up through the submarine — it looked like it went all the way up to the conning tower. All around it were gantries and steel stairways. About half way up men were ranged around a bank of computer consoles. The woman was standing over them, pointing to their screens, making comments, giving instructions. The men simply nodded obediently and continued with their work.

There hadn't been anything like this on the American submarine, Siv thought as she eased her way back out of the door and closed it quietly behind her. This had to be it. This was what they were looking for.

*

Warren felt Stewart start to wobble, then he collapsed altogether, sending them both sprawling on the floor.

'For Christ's sake!'

'I'm sorry, sir,' Stewart moaned. 'I'm just not as strong as I was…'

'Alright,' Warren replied, struggling to hold back his simmering wrath. 'We'll do it the other way. Come on, I'll hold you up.'

Without another word he picked up Stewart like he was a child and lofted him up on his shoulders.

'Here,' he said, passing him the spoon. 'Use this.'

'But how?' Stewart replied, feebly. 'I'm blind.'

'Don't be stupid — we're both blind. Use your fingers, feel your way around.'

Warren seethed with frustration as he heard Stewart dithering and scratching around — how could he make such a hash of something so easy?

Just then he heard a metallic clatter on the floor below.

'I'm sorry, sir,' Stewart whimpered. 'I'm afraid I've dropped it.'

Warren cursed, and was about to reach down to pick it up — when a muffled "boom" shuddered the door. Stewart panicked and toppled from Warren's shoulders, bringing Warren crashing down with him.

*

Siv stole back to the corridor. The guard was sitting on a chair, leaning back against the door where he'd shoved the tray only a few minutes before. His outstretched legs were propped-up on the opposite wall of the corridor, his arms folded across his chest. It looked like he was asleep.

He had a pistol hanging from his belt, butt-forward and strapped-down. Siv smiled: obviously he wasn't expecting any trouble.

OK, so he looked like he was asleep — but Siv wasn't taking any chances: she wanted him facing away from her. Rummaging in her pocket, she pulled out her half-eaten nutrition bar and weighed it in her hand. She could almost hear her Granny admonishing her for wasting food, but it was the only thing she had to throw.

She tossed it backhand in a shallow arc down the corridor. It was a lousy throw: she watched, dismayed as the loose wrapper span round like a rotor blade, just missing the guard's nose as it skittered down the corridor beyond him.

He woke at once and turned to see what the noise was. Siv sprinted up behind him, silent in her stockinged-feet:

'Don't turn around,' she kept repeating in her head: 'Don't turn around — don't…'

As she closed on him her thought changed:

'Can I do this? Can I kill him? Can I…?

Then she was on him — and her training took over:

Left hand — wrap around the top of the head, pull back — hard.

Right hand — plunge knife into spinal cord between the occiput and the C1 vertebra — hard.

Leave the knife in. The subject is alive — but immobilised.

As the Russian slumped back into Siv's arms his china blue eyes stared up at her, uncomprehendingly. His lips moved — but no sound issued from them — his lungs had ceased to obey his command.

She let him fall heavily against the door he'd been guarding, then stripped him of his pistol. She stared at it momentarily — an old Grach special forces pistol, not standard navy issue. But there was no time to wonder about that now, she thought. She checked the clip and felt around his belt for any ammunition. He didn't have anything else on him, but at least the clip was full. Better than nothing, she thought and stuffed it into her hip pocket

She unlocked the door and swung it open. Her jaw dropped, her eyes opened wide with amazement at the scene that confronted her: two men lying, sprawled out on the floor, one on top of the other — and both of them covering their faces, shielding the light from their eyes.

'Shit,' she said, smirking: 'If I'm interrupting something — I can always come back later…'

'Siv?' Warren exclaimed, angrily. 'What the Hell are you doing here? I thought you'd got away safe!'

'Yeah, well,' she shrugged. 'I figured I'd tag along and see how you were doing.' She chuckled: 'Who's your boyfriend?' she asked, as she dragged the paralysed Russian into the cell.

'This is Lieutenant Stewart.'

'The one we couldn't find?'

'That's him. He's coming with us.'

'No, no! You can't do that!' Stewart protested. 'I'll only slow you down.'

'He's blind,' Warren explained.

'Oh, OK…' This was bad, Siv thought. She figured their chances of getting out of this place were pretty slim already — but dragging some blind guy along with them? They'd just dropped from slim to zero.

Warren glanced down at the Russian: 'Is he dead?'

'Not yet,' Siv replied, drawing her knife out of his neck and wiping off the blood on the Russian's tunic. 'He'll black out pretty soon. He can't breathe. He's dying and there's nothing he can do about it — but he can't feel a thing.'

'Quite humane, really,' Warren observed.

'If you call killing another human being "humane".' Stewart muttered.

'Yeah, well,' Siv replied, helping Stewart to his feet. 'I guess I could've gone up to him and asked him nicely to let you guys out — but he had a gun and I didn't, so…'

'Did you get his gun?' Stewart asked, excitedly.

Siv stared at him: 'Do you think I'm stupid…?'

'Never mind that,' Warren interrupted. 'What have you found out about this place?'

'We're on a submarine, part submerged under the sea ice, pretty much due north of the Humboldt — in the Kennedy Channel, maybe,' Siv replied. 'We're at the bottom level, directly below their jetwing bay. I figured that would be our best way out, but…'

'See?' Stewart whined, miserably. 'I told you I'd be holding you back…'

'They've got some weird-looking device,' Siv continued, ignoring him. 'It runs the whole way from here, right up to the top of the conning tower. I don't know what it is — it could be the laser — but, whatever it is, it looks pretty important. The whole place is ringed by proximity-activated machine guns and protected by a Redut missile system. I've seen two arrays, both housed in cabins outside the sub…'

'Two?' Warren echoed.

'At least. I've seen two — but there could be more.'

'So it's pretty much impregnable to attack from the air…'

She nodded: 'It'd be a miracle if anything got through.'

'Well, it looks like we'll have to destroy it ourselves, then,' Warren concluded.

Siv jerked her thumb over her shoulder: 'It's just down there.'

'OK, let's have a look at it.'

They bundled Stewart out of the cell. As she closed the door, Siv glanced back at the inert form of the Russian, lying on the floor. She hoped he'd already blacked-out from lack of oxygen — she hated to think of him suffering for too long.

*

They dragged the heavy steel hatchway slightly ajar and peered through the gap at the golden cylinder. They could hear people moving around on the gantry above them.

'I could try and shoot a few holes in it,' Siv whispered.

Warren shook his head: 'Looks like it's made of titanium, coated in titanium nitride. You might not even dent it.' He thought for a moment: 'What about repurposing one of the Redut arrays and aiming it back at the sub?'

Siv nodded: 'Yeah, that would work.' She glanced at her wristwatch: 'They should've finished their routine warm-up by now.'

'Can you get us up there?'

'No problem,' Siv grinned, strapping her knife back onto her boot and pulling out the pistol. This suited her fine: destroy the submarine and its laser weapon, then get into cold-weather gear and get the Hell out of here, back out onto the ice. Nice simple plan. It sure was good having Warren back.

'No time to waste,' Warren said. 'Siv, you lead. I'll take Stewart. Let's go.'

Siv led the others back to the spiral staircase climbing it stealthily, her pistol held out before her, safety off, ready to shoot anyone who got in their way. Warren followed close behind, leading Stewart, who shuffled behind them, stumbling up each step.

*

'OK,' Siv said as she helped Warren haul Stewart up the last stairs. 'This is the level we need to be at — but we're a long way down the back of the sub — right down by the reactor. It's quiet here. We've got to go that way…' she said, pointing up the corridor, through the hatchways. '…But that's where the crew are.'

'The laser's behind there,' she whispered as they passed two doors marked "не входить, then pointed her pistol further along the corridor, off to her right: 'That's where we need to be…'

She heard the sound of voices up ahead, boots clattering on steel gantries. Siv froze as half a dozen sailors issued from the galley, laughing and joking. They spotted them immediately — stopping dead in their tracks, staring at them. One of the sailors ran off — the others started edging toward them. Siv backed away, and motioned for Warren and Stewart to do the same.

A sailor in a black crew-neck sweater came forward with a pistol. He raised it and took aim. Siv did the same. For a long, silent moment they faced eachother — like duellists.

She felt a shove from behind as Stewart blundered into her.

'Get down!' she hissed, pushing him back behind her.

The Russian took advantage of her distraction and fired. The bullet zinged past her shoulder. She fired back — a half-aimed shot. The Russian jerked backwards and dropped his gun. Another sailor made a lunge to grab it. Siv shot again and he slumped to the ground. The others backed off.

'Go back!' she yelled over her shoulder. 'We can't get to the Redut now!'

They grabbed Stewart and roughly dragged his squirming body back the way they'd come.

A door opened right next to them — a sailor with a pistol stood framed in the doorway. Siv fired — a reaction shot. He fell backwards. Behind him was the woman in the white lab coat — staring at her, ashen-faced and defenceless.

Suddenly, the air was rent by automatic fire. Siv felt the bullets' heat as they zinged past her face, ricocheting all around, throwing up blinding sparks as they thumped into the steel door, clattering on the metal walls beyond.

Siv turned and fired off three rounds in quick succession — the automatic fire fell silent. But when she turned back the woman was gone.

'This way!' Warren yelled, falling back to the jetwing bay. Siv ran after him, firing behind her. Together they span the hatch-wheel and dragged the door open. Bullets spattered and clanged against it as they dived through the hatch and into the jetwing bay, shoving Stewart ahead of them.

The Russians were close — too close. Siv fired blindly at them, then hauled the door shut and span the wheel to seal it.

'Find something to lock it!' she yelled to Warren, throwing her body against it, holding the wheel tight shut.

Warren looked round frantically — and snatched up a long, heavy torque-wrench, lying on top of a toolbox.

'I can't hold it!' Siv cried, straining at the wheel. 'Here,' she said, tossing her pistol to Stewart. 'You take this.'

Stewart caught the gun and stared at it, wide-eyed — then pointed it Siv:

'Let go of the door!' he cried, his hands trembling.

'Stewart? Warren said, staring at the pistol. 'What the Hell are you doing?'

'W-what does it look like?' he cried, pushing it into Siv's face. 'Just get away from the door!

Warren didn't move. 'You mean you're a double agent?'

'Sure he is,' Siv replied. 'He's no more blind than you or me.'

'Eh?' Stewart whined, his confidence faltering. 'How did you know?'

'You don't shield your eyes from the light if you're blind. It's a test, Stewart. The gun's empty — check the magazine.'

Stewart twisted the Grach in his hand and stared in horror at the empty hollow where the magazine should have been.

Warren sprang forward and brought the wrench down hard on the traitor's wrist. The bone snapped — and the Grach fired into Stewart's thigh. He screamed in agony as it fell from his grasp.

Warren grabbed the gun and tossed the wrench to Siv, who wedged it into the wheel. Just in time. It flexed and rattled angrily as the Enemy tried to turn it from the other side — but it didn't move.

'Shit…' Siv muttered. 'I forgot the round in the chamber…'

'I thought you might have,' Warren replied. 'I saw you unclip the magazine — I guessed you were up to something.'

'And you let me carry on!'

'I figured you knew what you were doing…'

'I could've been killed…!'

'Look, will you please stop bickering,' Stewart muttered through gritted teeth. 'It doesn't make any difference — you'll both be dead in a few minutes, anyway.'

Warren ignored him and gazed round the bay. 'Is there another way out?'

'There's the roof,' Siv replied, gesturing up to the massive steel panels above them. 'But we can't get out that way. I couldn't find a control…'

Warren turned his attention back to Stewart, still squirming on the deck, his lifeless hand hanging from his forearm.

'I must say, I take my hat off to you,' Warren said, watching the traitor writhe in agony. 'You sailed through every single security check — you were the perfect candidate for the mission. But as soon as we got out there things started to go wrong, didn't they? …You were out on the glacier with Tanner when he died… You lost the signal from the drone — and it must've been you who kept Peary and Dern out on the ice while the Russian satellites were overhead.'

Stewart struggled to his knees, cradling his shattered arm: 'I can't take credit for Tanner,' he muttered through gritted teeth. 'He was a lousy rider — drove his snowmobile straight down a crevasse…'

He looked up, smiling, his eyes glittering with malice: '…But, as for the rest — guilty as charged. The signal wasn't lost, I just pulled out a cable from the back of the monitor. And once you were gone, all I had to do was shift the chronometer back while they were asleep. I couldn't do it while you were around, you'd have noticed.'

He shrugged — and winced with pain: 'Peary and Dern were … careless, easy targets. I was telling the truth when I said I watched them die — but I was the one who exposed their heads to the cold.'

'Why?' Warren demanded.

'To please her — why else?'

'*Drittsek*,' Siv muttered, raising her fist to strike him down — but Warren held her back:

'Not yet. You can have him in a minute.'

'Norwegian?' Stewart said, leering at her. 'Oh, the crew are just going to love you. They all like a bit of corn-dolly…'

Warren brought his fist down sharp on Stewart's nose. The traitor squealed as it snapped, exploding blood over his face.

Ignoring Stewart's plaintive cries he knelt down and grabbed him by the throat: 'So that's why there were no cameras in the cell — why they put me in with you — why you were always asking questions…'

'A lot of good that did me, didn't it?' Stewart croaked, wiping the blood from his face with the sleeve of his good arm. 'Stuck in a stinking little box all that time, pretending to be blind — what a load of bollocks that was. I didn't find out a sodding thing — well, not 'til she turned up, anyway.'

'What do you mean…?' Siv demanded, suddenly alarmed.

They were interrupted by a mechanical grating on the other side of the hatch door. Stewart glanced across at it:

'Ah, they're jacking it off its hinges. It won't be long now.' He turned his attention back to Siv: 'We needed to know if you'd found out what we were up to. And now we do — thanks to you…'

'Now *you* know,' Warren corrected him. 'We kill you — they're none the wiser…'

'But you won't do that, will you, Warren? Kill an unarmed man? That's not very sporting, is it?'

'No, but I would.' Siv replied, grabbing his damaged arm and twisting it. Stewart screamed in agony.

Warren checked the door — the hinges were coming apart. He gazed around the bay: 'We need to get in the jetwing suits.'

'But we can't get out,' Siv protested.

'Maybe — but they're armed with rockets — we'll kill a lot more of them with those than we can with one knife and a pistol.'

Siv nodded: 'What about him?'

'Tie him up.'

Siv looked confused: 'Why don't we just kill him?'

'Not yet — but don't worry, we'll kill him if we have to.'

'OK, Commander,' she said, saluting — then grabbed Stewart's hanging arm and wrenched him to his feet.

Warren watched as she dragged him over to the other side of the landing-bay and wrapped a length of flex round his neck, then hoisted him up so that he had to stand on tiptoe to stop himself from choking. She really did have a vicious sense of humour, he thought. It was one of the many things he loved about her…

He stopped himself in mid-thought. It was the first time he'd actually admitted to himself that he loved her…

'Help me into this thing,' he yelled as he uncoupled a jetwing from its power cable. Siv nodded and scampered back to him.

As she helped him clamber into the cocoon, Warren turned and took her face gently in one hand — then kissed her, full and hard on the mouth.

'Wow!' she exclaimed, when he released her. 'What was that for?'

'Well,' Warren smiled, 'Looks like we're about to get killed again. I wanted to see if I liked it as much as I did the first time.'

'And?'

'What do you think?' he said — and drew up the fastener on the cocoon.

'Well, come on Warren,' he muttered to himself. 'Enough of romance — let's get this show on the road.'

He pressed "активировать". At once the visor display lit up. On the right of the display was a launch sequence menu — one of the options was "open doors".

'Siv!' he cried, then realised she couldn't hear him. He unfastened the suit. 'Siv!' he yelled. 'There's a control! We can get out!'

'Well, what are we waiting for?' she cried, and scrambled into the next jetwing. Warren heard his communicator crackle into life. 'Come on,' she said. 'Open the damn things and let's get out of here!'

Warren blinked at the "open doors" option. At once the great steel panels started to draw back. There were stars in the sky above them.

'Come on, *somlebøtte*,' Siv yelled, launching herself into the air. 'Let's go!'

At the same moment Warren saw a flash — a single tracer bullet fired from the conning tower above them. The shot was aimed to meet Siv as she flew through the bay doors. Their paths seemed to converge in slow motion…

Suddenly, Siv jerked back violently — her suit was still joined to its power cable. Her jetwing faltered and fell spiralling down until she landed, sprawling on the flight deck.

'Ow, shit!' she muttered. 'That was stupid…'

'Didn't you see that?'

'See what?'

'There's a sniper on the conning tower. Nearly got you. If it hadn't pulled you back you'd be dead.'

'No shit.'

'Oh, yes — shit.'

'Fuck…' she muttered. 'So, how the Hell are we going to get out of here…?'

*

'You can't do this!' Stewart screamed as they bundled him into a jetwing, his hands bound behind him — and dragged it into the centre of the launchpad.

'Don't worry,' Siv said, merrily rapping on his visor. 'I'll be right behind you!'

'You'd better be,' Warren said, clambering back into his cocoon, facing Stewart. 'You've got to be out before he reloads.'

Siv wiggled into her jetwing and pressed "активировать". 'I'm ready!' she cried, as it sprang into life.

Warren reached across and activated Stewart's machine. 'We'll be going up together. Only you'll be between me and the shooter.'

'Don't do this!' Stewart whimpered. 'Please don't!'.

Warren noticed his visor was beginning to mist up. He smiled at him: 'Don't worry, Stewart. You never know, he could miss. And I'll have to let you go once we're out — at least you'll have a better chance than Peary and Dern…' He grabbed hold of both thrust controls. 'Ready, Siv?'

'Ready!'

'OK. On three … One … Two … Three!'

Warren and Stewart soared out of the landing bay, followed moments later by Siv.

'No, no!' Stewart protested. 'Please…'

The sniper made a perfect head shot. Warren watched in horrified fascination as the inside of Stewart's visor was instantly coated red. Moments later it shattered, revealing the remnants of the traitor's face spattered around the inside of the helmet.

He released his grip on Stewart's machine and it careered out of control. He didn't look to see what happened to it.

'Go South!' Warren cried, fastening his cocoon.

'Wait!' Siv yelled back. 'Just a minute…'

Warren threw his jetwing into a clumsy turn, just in time to see her firing a tiny rocket at the conning tower. It exploded in an all-consuming ball of orange flame.

'Wow!' she exclaimed. 'I want one of these!'

'For Christ's sake!' Warren barked. 'We need to get away — not stick around taking pot-shots…'

'I'm doing a bit of damage!' she yelled as another rocket slammed into the conning tower. 'I want to put it out of action for a while.'

Warren was taken aback: she was right, of course she was. He'd been so intent on getting away he'd forgotten about the attack capability of these things. He circled round and joined her, firing two rockets in quick succession into the sub's conning tower.

But, as the smoke and flames cleared, they could see that, apart from a few bent and twisted antennae, their attack hadn't caused any damage at all.

'We're not doing any good here,' he said, as he turned his jetwing round and set off back southwards.

'Yep,' she agreed falling in behind him. 'Time to go home,'

*

Warren picked up a feint, crackling message on his communicator.

'Are you getting that?' he asked.

Siv didn't reply. Just the same crackling, only quieter this time. Warren brought himself upright and swivelled in mid-air. He scoured the skies and the ice below — she was nowhere to be seen. With his heart pounding he set off back the way he'd come.

'Siv!' he yelled over his communicator. Another indistinct response, louder now. He thought he could pick out some syllables. 'Siv!' he yelled again.

'…Warren…?'

'Yes!' he replied, relief washing over him. 'Where are you?'

'Lost sight…' he heard over the crackling: 'Can't make it … … … damn pile of crap…'

He spotted her on the radar — dead ahead. A couple of seconds later he got a visual. She was still flying, but so slowly it was a miracle she was still airborne.

'What's up?' he asked as he circled around her.

'Don't know. Got the throttle full open, but it keeps getting slower and slower.'

'Look — grab the end of the cocoon. I'll see if I can tow you.'

'I don't think that's going to work, Warren.'

'Why not?'

' 'Cos I've got three traces on my radar. They're coming out of the north and they're coming fast — and I mean real fast. You've got to get out of here.'

'I can't leave you. It's only two against three. We can make a stand…'

'Don't be stupid. They know what they're doing — and I'm a dead duck. Look, if you don't get back Control will never know what's happening. Go! For God's sake go!'

Warren soared up into the sky above her, then hovered, waiting. He had a visual on their pursuers. They were slowing down. About a mile away they stopped: hovering, like vultures. Waiting.

He realised what they were waiting for: Siv's jetwing was losing altitude as it lost power. She was only about a hundred feet above the ice. Soon she'd run out of power altogether. She was stranded, helpless.

She came over the communicator: 'If you're not going to go,' she said, resolutely. 'Then you'd better cover me.'

Warren watched in horror as Siv's jetwing turned and crept toward the waiting enemy. She fired off a rocket. It fell short and petered out, falling harmlessly, skittering onto the ice.

He checked his own manifest: he had three rockets left.

'I'm sorry, Siv. I can't just leave you here,' he said, pushing his thruster forward and swooping down on the enemy.

'No!' She yelled, nearly deafening him. 'Don't be an idiot!'

Warren made straight for the middle jetwing. The targeting system on his visor flashed yellow as it locked on and he fired off all three of his rockets together, then banked steeply and swerved away.

The enemy scattered — but one rocket pierced the cocoon of the middle flier.

For a long moment nothing happened.

Then the darkness of the night was banished by a dazzling light — Warren was swept up into the heavens like a dragonfly sucked into a tornado.

Day 24 : 0200hrs

Warning signals flashed all round his visor. His horizon appeared and disappeared, spinning, flipping, rolling in every direction — but he didn't know which way was up. His altimeter told him he was falling — but which way was down?

A blast on the engine — it was all he could think of. It might stop him from spinning — but if he got it wrong it would send him careering back to earth in an unstoppable dive. He checked his altimeter: fifteen hundred metres, fourteen, thirteen — it was now or never.

The horizon came back into view — he pushed the thruster, his eyes fixed on the altimeter. The jetwing surged forward, spinning and bucking, buffeted by the air resistance. He was still losing height — but it was slowing. The horizon appeared, right at the top of his visor. He pulled his joystick back to correct his angle, and one by one the warning signals went out.

He checked his instruments: he was flying straight and level, 200 metres above sea level, heading south-east. Something nagged at the back of his mind — there was wrong with that. But what was it? Suddenly it came to him: if he was flying at two hundred metres, south east of where they'd been, he should be crashing into a mountainside any time now.

He blinked on his night vision: there was nothing ahead of him — nothing at all. Flipping to map view didn't make any difference; nothing registered. He pulled the view out, then out again. Finally, a feature came into view, a very familiar feature: the seaward edge of the Humboldt Glacier — and he was making straight for it.

The blast had dragged him in, then spat him out — nearly two hundred miles away.

But where was Siv? Had she survived the blast? She'd been further away than him. But he'd been hurled up into the sky — that was probably what saved him. She might not've been so lucky…

An alert flashed on the side of his visor. He brought the radar up: two contacts, approaching fast out of the north. Range: thirty miles — and making straight for him. He checked his weapons control: it was showing a single machine gun — but it was flashing red, out of action.

He couldn't stand and fight, so he wrenched the jetwing round due south, and pushed the thrust control to full power — he had to make a run for it.

The jetwing surged on into the darkness. Warren kept flipping his view between the radar behind him and night vision ahead. If he could get to the jagged peaks and crags of the broken country, south of the glacier he might be able to lose them. But every time he flipped back to the radar, his pursuers were gaining on him — they were flying at more than twice his speed. How could that be? Was his jetwing grinding to a halt, just like Siv's? At this rate his pursuers would overtake him while he was still over the open ice.

Indicators around his visor screen gradually changed from green to amber, amber to red. Maybe if he could get this damned thing to blow up he could take his pursuers down with him. They were coming up fast now. In a couple of minutes they'd be onto him.

His communicator boomed into life:

'Unidentified aircraft, this is RCAF zero-one-niner. You were detected making an unauthorised entry into Canadian airspace at 23:55 hours. We have clearance to pursue into Greenland airspace and intercept. Identify yourself — or we will shoot you down.'

Warren was just about to reply when two Typhoons, emblazoned with the maple-leaf roundels of the Royal Canadian Air Force, roared past him. He was almost laughing with relief as he responded to their challenge:

'RCAF zero-one-niner, this is Warren. Request escort to USAF Thule. Please relay confirmation to General Leonidas S Morgan, NATO Joint Warfare Centre, Stavanger.'

'Roger that, Commander Warren. Good to have you back, sir. You've had the whole of NORAD out looking for you.'

*

Thule Air Force Base

Greenland

Day 24 : 0305hrs

Warren hovered over the runway. He could see the lights of fire tenders and safety vehicles flashing directly beneath him. He pulled back on his thruster — he immediately felt himself lurching toward the ground, dropping like a stone.

'Whoa…' His eyes widened as the runway soared up to meet him. 'Too fast, way too fast.' He realised with horror that he didn't have the slightest idea how to land this thing. Worse: he'd never even seen one landing, so he couldn't even guess how it was done.

He pushed the thruster forward and his descent slowed — then pulled back again and it dropped.

'Alright, Warren,' he muttered to himself. 'You can do this…'

He rocked the thruster back and forth little by little. Gradually he brought it closer and closer to the ground. He was only a few inches above the surface — he pulled full back on the thruster. His whole body sagged with relief and exhaustion as it came to rest on the runway.

Suddenly he was surrounded by people in full CBRN suits, swarming everywhere, waving Geiger-counters all over him. He couldn't see their faces, but from their movements, they didn't look very happy.

One of them stuck a sucker cap onto his visor:

'Commander Warren — can you hear me?'

'Loud and clear. What's up?'

'This whole thing's pretty heavily irradiated. But we're going to risk getting you out.'

'Oh, thanks.'

'Can you see that operative over there?' he said, pointing off to the right, to a person waving at him. 'When we open this up I want you to go over to her, as fast as you can. She'll check you out. Got that?'

Warren nodded: 'She'd better be quick. I'll freeze to death in seconds out there.'

The voice didn't reply. Moments later Warren felt a blast of icy air as they opened up the cocoon. He scrambled out and ran barefoot across the ice. The woman waved her Geiger-counter over him:

'You're all clear, commander,' she said and pointed toward a waiting truck. Warren sprinted to it — he'd already lost all feeling in his feet. A big figure in a white Marine parka reached down from the tailgate and dragged him in.

As the truck pulled away, he threw a thick survival bag over Warren and thrust an insulated mug of hot coffee into his hands.

'Christ, Warren,' he said, 'You look shit.'

Warren glanced up over his mug. It was Leo.

'I've just sent a message to you — in Stavanger.'

'Don't worry. It'll get to me. Did you find out what it is?'

Warren nodded. His head was swimming — he felt as though he might black out any minute: 'Nano laser — high-intensity,' he muttered, forcing himself to focus. 'Pinpoint accuracy. Little cuts every day — adds up to total dismemberment over weeks and months.'

'Do you know where it's coming from?'

'Submarine — about a hundred miles north of the Humboldt. Siv found its location on that first day at Stavanger — we just didn't know what we were looking for.'

'Where is she?' Leo asked with genuine concern in his voice.

Warren shook his head: 'I don't know,' he said, his voice hollow, staring into his coffee. 'We were both caught up in the blast…'

'We saw that. Reports estimate it at four kilotons — about the same as a theatre weapon. What was it?'

Warren nodded back at the jetwing: 'One of those things going up.'

Leo cursed under his breath as he stared back at it. 'We'd better tell those guys to go easy on it, then.'

'Might be a good idea,' Warren replied, laughing, dog tired. '…I was blown up into the air — the next thing I knew, I was careering back to earth about two hundred miles away. I still don't know why I'm not dead. Siv was further away, but lower down, near the ground. I don't know what happened to her, Leo…' he shook his head, sadly: 'I just don't know.'

Morgan put his big, heavy arm over Warren's shoulder. 'You look dead beat, son,' he said, gently. 'You get a couple of hours shut-eye. We'll ramp things up after that.'

Warren shook his head: 'No …no time for that. They're going straight for the control system. They must be nearly through to it by now. We've got to stop them, Leo — we've got to do it now.'

*

They were alone in the briefing room, their faces illuminated by the eerie light of a display console.

'We're reforming the shield,' Leo said, pointing to a 3D graphic floating in front of them: glowing points with reference numbers hovered next to them, circling around a virtual globe like an impossibly intricate astrolabe. 'We started just after they hit you. …But it hasn't been as easy as we thought.'

'Why not? You've had ten days to do it.'

Leo sighed: 'It turns out the shield isn't quite as … comprehensive … as we thought it was.'

'That doesn't sound good.'

'It isn't. The recession back in 2008 knocked the stuffing out of defence spending. We had serious commitments on the ground — so, something had to give.'

'The shield…'

'That's it. Or, to be more precise, the maintenance programme. For about ten years no work was done. And by the time it was picked up again about fifteen percent of the platforms were… Well, to put it politely, they were no longer operational.'

'So, the politicians have done more damage than the Enemy ever could.'

'That's about it. We're redeploying the whole shield. But if ANP-12 goes offline, the only way we can protect the US Midwest is to leave Northern Europe exposed — and the Enemy will see us doing it. They might even be expecting it — it's possible they already know which platforms are no longer operational. After all, the only satellites they've attacked so far have been live ones.'

'What about the surveillance satellite?' Warren asked. 'Can't we use it to block the laser?'

'They took it out the same time as they attacked you. We can see it, it's operational — but it's not responding to any command signals.'

'So, we've got to destroy the laser itself…'

Leo nodded: 'That's about it,' he said passing his hand through the image. Instantly it was replaced by a ground plan of the Russian base.

'This was constructed from satellite images using the co-ordinates from Sergeant Jagland's analysis…' he said, pointing to the different features: '…the submarine, a cluster of what look like small buildings. We're assuming this large disc is the VTOL.' He glanced at his wristwatch: 'We're going to hit it with a missile strike in twelve minutes. Knock it out completely, just like we do every time they try and get a foothold on our side of the Arctic…'

'It won't work,' Warren replied, staring at the image: 'Siv said they've got two Redut arrays, and maybe more. A missile attack will be useless — and it'll scare them off. They'd be able to slip away — and start up again somewhere else.'

'Damn,' Leo muttered: 'Well, what about our subs? A couple of torpedoes should finish it off.'

Warren shook his head: 'Underwater, the sea ice is sculpted by the currents into all sorts of weird shapes. Radar and SONAR will be useless — they'd be lost among thousands of underwater features — and we won't be able to get close enough for a visual.' He fell silent, considering the problem: 'We can't hit them from the air and we can't attack them from under the ice — but we've got to finish them now, while we know where they are…'

'So, what do you suggest?' Leo asked.

'Where are the *Tecumseh* and the *Madison*?'

'They're still up in the Kane Basin, about a hundred miles south.'

'That's good,' Warren said, thinking through a plan as he spoke. 'We dispatch them tonight. They break through the sea ice as close as they can get, and we make a ground assault.'

'What would they be up against?'

'Siv said it's ringed by proximity-activated machine guns. We know they've got some special forces on board, but we've already taken out about a dozen of them. I don't know how many they have left, but they must be a weakened force. The naval personnel may fight out on the ice, they may not — we'll have to assume they will. But if they try to submerge and get away — that's when they'll be visible to our subs. We'll be waiting for them.'

'Their SONAR will spot the *Tecumseh* and the *Madison* as they approach.'

'They'll see us before we can see them, that's for sure…' Warren stared at the image on the table: 'But they've been there a month at least. That's a long time to have ice building up all around it. I doubt if they could even fire a torpedo — and if they did, the chances are it'd hit the ice before it got going…'

'So we can't shoot at them — and they can't shoot at us. …Stalemate.'

'That's about it, Leo. We've got no choice — we attack over the ice…' He stared down at the shimmering 3D image: 'But what the Hell are we going to do about that?' he said, pointing at the camouflaged disc of the VTOL. 'It's armed with gatlings — and God knows what else. But it's got a cold propulsion system, like the jetwings, only on a much bigger scale. If we take it out, we could blow everything to kingdom come…'

They were interrupted by a knock on the door; a young USAF lieutenant strode in briskly:

'Sir,' he said, saluting to General Morgan, and handing him a grey data reader: 'preliminary report on the Russian jetwing, sir.'

Leo stared at the data reader, nonplussed: 'Do you know what it says, son?'

'Yes, sir.'

'Do you think you can give us a summary?

The young lieutenant seemed confused: 'Well…'

'Just in a few words?'

'Sir,' he began falteringly. 'It's pretty amazing — but also really primitive. The propulsion system is fuelled by thousands of almost microscopic cold fusion cells, all combining to create an enormous power source…'

'Would you describe it as "nano technology"?' Warren interrupted.

'That's right, sir.'

'Excuse us for a moment,' Warren said. 'Can you just wait outside?'

The lieutenant saluted, then turned and marched briskly out of the briefing room. Leo looked at Warren questioningly:

'Well?'

'There was a woman on their submarine. Stewart said she was an expert in nano technology. The laser, this propulsion system — it all has to be her. He said her name was Yekaterina…'

Leo stared down at the display: 'Yekaterina Michaelovna, to give her her full name. She's cropped up a few times in reports recently. A scientist, or at least she claims to be. As far as we can tell she's never studied anywhere. She has crazy ideas, then she gets the real scientists to make them work.'

'I've never heard of her.'

'I'm not surprised. She's kind of come out of nowhere. No record, no history, no known associates.'

'She was wearing a navy uniform. Kirkenes Marines.'

Leo grunted: 'Well, that's not very likely. She's surrounded herself with a gang of misfits, cutthroats and mercenaries, but no regular units. Last we heard they were operating out of Svalbard…'

'Well, they're here now.'

'Hmm,' Leo stared down at the image on the table — whatever he was thinking, he kept to himself. 'Let's get the lieutenant back in,' he said, changing the subject.

Leo ushered the lieutenant back into the room.

'So, what do we know about this propulsion system?' Warren asked.

'It's an idea we dismissed years ago…' the lieutenant replied.

'Why?'

'Well, it's incredibly unstable — and practically impossible to contain.'

'We saw that when one of them went up,' Leo commented drily.

'That's the thing,' the young officer continued. 'So, to counteract that the pilot is cocooned in a highly advanced survival pod…'

'What do you mean?' Warren interrupted. 'How advanced — what can it do?'

'Well, it completely protected you from the impact of an atomic blast, sir. And the radioactivity too: the jetwing was dangerously irradiated, but inside you were totally clean.'

Warren's mind raced: the cocoon had saved him — and if it'd saved him, there was a chance that Siv's had saved her too.

*

Day 24 : 0720hrs

Her shoulders hurt like Hell and she couldn't feel her hands. Siv opened her eyes: everything was spinning around. After a few seconds she realised that everything else was standing still — it was her that was spinning.

She looked up: she was in a narrow steel-walled room, not much more than a box. The ever present sound of ice floes groaning and shrieking against the hull told her she was back on some kind of ship.

She was hanging, suspended by a chain from a hook in the ceiling, her wrists were strapped to the chain. She tried to swing her legs up, to get herself off the hook, but they wouldn't budge. She glanced down: 'Oh, brilliant,' she muttered — they were tied to a steel ring on the floor.

'Ah, you're awake…' a voice behind her. A woman's voice.

A harsh, staccato step: heels on steel. Siv felt herself being spun around. Suddenly she was face-to-face with the woman in the lab coat.

'So, Warren's bodyguard is a girl… I must admit, I never expected that.' She pursed her lips — Siv couldn't help but notice that they were perfectly lined and coloured.

'What are you staring at?' the woman demanded, irritably.

'Your make-up — it's so perfect,' Siv replied. 'Me, I never have time…'

A smile twitched on one side of her mouth: 'Yes, I can see that… But don't worry, you won't need make-up to pull the boys — not any more…' She chuckled quietly to herself: 'My men haven't had a fuck-toy for months — not since they broke their last one.'

'Oh, thanks — that's just great,' Siv muttered. 'I should have killed you when I had the chance.'

'Yes, you should — but you didn't. Your mistake. But don't think I'm not grateful. I could have ordered my men to feed you alive to the orcas when we found you — that might've been fun. But this way you get to have sex with lots of different guys … Well, until you get too beaten-up and repulsive for them to want to fuck you any more — and then we'll probably feed you to the orcas anyway.'

The woman smiled: 'But on the plus side you don't have to worry about whether or not you'll get an STD — because I guarantee that you will; my boys have picked up all sorts of nasty little diseases over the years. And you don't need to bother about getting pregnant either, because you won't live long enough to even show…'

She waved and blew her a kiss, then spun Siv around again to face the blank steel wall.

'Have fun…' she whispered, and closed the door.

The light went out. Siv was left alone in the darkness.

*

Kane Basin, Greenland

Day 24 : 0827hrs

The airman rapped on Warren's helmet and yelled over the deafening noise of the aircraft engines: 'When we jettison you, two things are gonna happen. The pod will start to inflate straight away. A couple of seconds later your parachute will open…'

Warren nodded, shifting uncomfortably, encased in clear plastic and staring down through the plane's escape hatch at the grey nothingness below.

'… We're dropping you from a low altitude, so the parachute won't be a big help,' he continued, checking the altimeter and doing a quick mental calculation. 'But your pod should be fully inflated — that'll protect you from the impact.'

'What do you mean "should"?'

'We're dropping you from three hundred feet — you'll hit the ice in about ten seconds. The pod takes ten seconds to fully inflate. You'll be fine.'

'What if I land on water?'

'It's got enough air to last an hour. You can re-aspirate it, but you risk taking in water.'

'Better than suffocating, though.'

'Guess so…' the airman replied, all his attention fixed on his control console. 'We're getting close…'

'You're sure it'll take the impact.'

'Hell no, sir. Nobody's had to use one yet — and far as I know they've never been tested on ice.'

'Oh, right…'

'Over the target in three … two … one.'

Warren felt himself being flipped down a chute and out into the void. Immediately the clear plastic pod started to inflate around him. He stared back up at the aircraft as he fell away from it. Suddenly he was jerked back violently by his parachute — and the plane disappeared from sight.

The airman's voice came over Warren's communicator: 'Can you still hear me, sir?'

'Yes.'

'OK. You're strapped into the cradle. I want you to hold it tight and bunch yourself up into a ball. Done that?'

'Yep.'

'Disconnect your parachute as soon as you land. Got that?'

'Yep.'

'OK. Impact in five … four…'

Warren watched in horrified fascination as the insubstantial walls of his bubble vacillated around him.

'Three … two …'

Suddenly, it snapped into shape.

'… One.'

The bubble flattened right in front of him — almost touching his face. He lurched forward violently, then sprang back as it bounced — again and again — each time with less and less violence.

'Can you still hear me, sir?'

'Yes!' Warren cried, spinning head-over-heels as his bubble rolled around like a beachball.

'You haven't disconnected your parachute yet. If you don't do that you'll be dragged away from the target.'

'Oh, right.'

He punched the release button. The rolling slowed, and the bubble came to rest — with Warren left hanging upside-down, his head still spinning.

'Very good, sir. You're thirty-seven yards from the target. Please stay in the pod until someone comes to get you out. Goodbye, sir.'

Moments later he felt himself being turned upright — then back over, and over again. Hands pushed into the bubble, stretching into the skin, as they rolled him along. Warren thought he could hear laughter.

A long hunting knife pierced the plastic membrane and ripped sharply downwards. At once the bubble started to deflate, and flurries of snow rushed in. Many hands ripped at the plastic, widening the gash and Warren felt himself being lifted out of the cradle.

A voice came over his communicator: 'Good morning, Commander. Nice of you to join us.'

'Thanks,' he replied. 'Nice to be here.'

He flipped his visor to night vision. Four figures in Arctic survival gear guided him to a small raised mound, straight ahead. Two of them drew back a snow-covered camouflage net to reveal a submarine conning tower, lying low in the ice.

A hatch door opened and Dan Monroe beckoned to him.

'Come on Warren!' he hollered. 'We can't hang around here all day waiting for you!'

*

USS Tecumseh, Kane Basin, Greenland

Day 24 : 0850 hrs

'Well that was a neat trick,' Monroe said, climbing up into his chair. 'We only normally get mail delivered that way.'

'You mean that wasn't a survival pod?'

'Not to my knowledge,' he said, then frowned as a message flashed up on his console:

'Hmm, looks like we've got a race on our hands…'

Warren looked at him quizzically.

Monroe read the message out loud: 'It seems that two Borei-class submarines left the Murmansk Oblast yesterday morning. Ten hours ago they passed to the south of Svalbard. They're going full speed, making for the north coast of Greenland — and they're not bothered about concealment. Station Nord registered two contacts under the ice a couple of hours ago. …It looks like they're coming straight for us.'

'Any air activity?'

'Ah, we've got a couple of Timberwolves prowling around, but there always are,' Monroe replied, dismissively. 'Otherwise, nothing unusual.'

'How long until we get to the target?' Warren asked.

'Two hours, no more.'

'And how long 'til their subs get there?'

'Three to five, depends on the currents through the Nares Strait,' he replied, staring at the console in front of him. 'You know, the *Tecumseh* and the *Madison* are basically just glorified freighters. We carry torpedoes and countermeasures, sure — but we're no match for a fully-operational attack submarine, let alone two. I'm going to call for reinforcements. If we're lucky they'll arrive about the same time as the Russians…'

'And if we're not?'

'We've got to make sure there's nothing left worth fighting for when they get here. So you'd better get your job done quickly — otherwise we could find ourselves drawn into a full-on, knock-down shooting war…'

*

Day 24 : 1145hrs

Shut-up in a steel box in the darkness, Siv fought to keep back the waves of claustrophobia rising up in her.

'Focus, girl. You've got to focus,' she whispered to herself, clenching her fists, again and again, pumping blood back into her hands and arms. 'Concentrate on getting out of here…' She pulled herself up — as far as the ropes on her feet would allow — and slowly lowered herself down again. 'Got to be ready,' she muttered to herself, repeating each exercise again and again. 'I've got to be… got to be…

The door opened behind her. For a moment she saw her shadow on the steel wall — then it was engulfed by a looming darkness.

She felt heavy breathing on the nape of her neck.

The door closed quietly, furtively.

A body pressed against her body — a face next to her face, breathing in, smelling her. Clammy, trembling hands under her tunic, roughly dragging up her teeshirt, pushing up her brassière, roaming over her breasts, pinching her nipples.

Siv forced down the sense of revulsion and moaned softly.

A voice muttered, in broken English: 'You like?'

'Mmm…'

He pinched her nipples harder this time. Siv groaned out loud.

'You don't fight with me?'

She shook her head — she could feel his rough stubble brushing against her cheek.

'You're going to fuck me, if I like it or not — I might as well enjoy it.'

'You like sex?'

'Mmm…'

She felt his body next to hers as he shuffled around to face her, felt him fiddling with her belt buckle, unzipping her fly, pulling down her pants…

He stopped. He seemed confused.

'Is there something wrong?'

'Your legs — they don't open…'

'They're tied together. …Come on!' she implored. 'I'm waiting!'

She felt him drop to his knees, scrabbling with the rope.

'Oh, yes — that's right, that's *right!*' Siv breathed, excitedly.

Her legs were free, she felt the Russian stripping her pants off her ankles and fumbling with his own belt.

'Not yet,' Siv purred. 'Here…' she said softly, 'Take your time — use your tongue…'

He moaned appreciatively as Siv wrapped her thighs around his head, drawing him toward her.

'Get up,' she whispered, 'You don't have to kneel…'

Using the muscles in her arms and stomach, she slowly drew him up, giggling with pleasure, until he was standing, her legs still around his head, gripping him ever tighter.

Siv arched her back, as if his clumsy attempts were driving her to the point of ecstasy. She reached up and grabbed the hook — and gently slipped the chain off.

'Thank you…' she whispered — then twisted her body sharply, spinning around, his head clamped tight between her legs, feeling his neck snap.

'…Thank you…' she whispered as she lowered his inert body gently to the floor. '…Thank you…' as she dropped lightly down on top of him.

She unstrapped her wrists, then dressed quickly and opened the door a few centimetres. A strip of light fell across her victim's face. She glanced down at him. While he was molesting her, she'd imagined him to be some filthy old satyr like Bård. Instead, the light illuminated the delicate features of a beautiful young man — not much more than a boy.

*

USS Tecumseh, Kennedy Channel, Greenland
Day 24 : 1200 hrs

A sailor swung round the hatchway from the surveillance room: 'They know we're here, sir. Pinged us about ten seconds ago.'

'Did you get a distance to target?' Monroe asked.

'Their buoy's about six hundred yards away — but we can't get a handle on the sub itself. It's gotta be tucked up tight in the ice, like a tick in a wrinkle, sir.'

'OK — ready countermeasures.' He turned to Warren: 'This is where we find out if they can shoot at us…'

'Say, Kevin,' he called over to his navigator: I reckon we're close enough — have you got a nice bit of thin ice up there? I think it's time we disappeared off their sonar.'

'Sure have, sir,' Kevin Sung grinned as he shone a pointer up at a hovering display, showing the characteristics of the ice sheet above them. 'A couple of nice narrow berths with plenty of features all round them — right above us now.'

'No point in waiting around,' Monroe said, turning to his exec. 'Lock onto Kevin's coordinates and signal the *Madison*. We're going up.'

*

Siv shut the door behind her. A "do not disturb" sign fluttered from the handle. She glanced at it disdainfully: obviously the Russians liked a bit of privacy while they were raping their captives…

Suddenly an alarm pierced the air. A deep, strident, mechanical voice barked orders over the address system — orders that Siv didn't understand. How could they have discovered her so quickly? Was there a camera in the metal box? All around her she could hear voices shouting, boots clattering on metal decks, getting closer. She looked around for some place to hide, but there was nowhere, just the tiny metal box behind her — and she wasn't going back in there, no way.

*

USS Tecumseh, Kennedy Channel, Greenland
Day 24 : 1207 hrs

Warren ducked his head as he stepped through the hatchway. All around the cargo bay marines in white Arctic camouflage were staring up at a blank display screen, waiting. He picked out an assault rifle from the rack next to the hatchway. It felt heavy and bulky as he slung it over his shoulder — he'd got used to a slimmer, more elegant weapon over the last few days.

The screen flashed into life — the forbidding, weatherbeaten face of Colonel Zak Law appeared.

'Can you guys over on the *Tecumseh* hear me?'

The marines in the cargo bay bellowed in unison: 'Sir — yes, sir!'

Law nodded. 'OK. We're gonna be breaking through the ice in a few minutes, so we don't have much time. The target is a Russian sub. It's about six hundred yards due east of the *Tecumseh* and four hundred south of us on the *Madison*. Our job is to engage the enemy and destroy the target. The only way we can do that is to get up close and plant demolition charges to scuttle it. That means a co-ordinated frontal assault. We go as soon as air defence systems are deployed. Captain Murgia will take command of the attack from the *Tecumseh*, I'll lead from the *Madison*…'

Law held his hand up to his earpiece:

'Looks like the ice above us is thicker, so *Tecumseh* you'll be breaking through first.'

An excited murmur went around the cargo bay.

'OK, OK,' Law said, holding his hand up for silence: 'You all know Commander Warren. I'm gonna hand over to him for a breakdown of what we can expect when we get up there.

A micro drone zipped across the cargo bay and hovered just in front of Warren. His face flashed up on the screen:

'The target's protected by a Redut system,' Warren began. 'There's at least two arrays, maybe more. As you know, the Redut's primarily a surface-to-air weapon, but it can be repurposed to acquire targets on the ground — so our first priority is to get inside their acquisition zone. We'll get get cover from our Phalanx launchers — but we need to get across that ice quickly to be safe from missile attack. Once we get inside that, the target is protected by a ring of motion-activated machine guns…'

There was a general guffaw of laughter around him.

'… I know it sounds bad — but it's a standard defence perimeter and we've dealt with this sort of thing before. It's likely they'll have men out on the ice — so watch out for them. Finally, and this is very important — the Enemy has a vertical take-off craft. It looks like a flying saucer. If you see it coming — go for cover. It's armed with gatlings. Under no circumstances should you attempt to engage it — I'll repeat that, do not engage it. We're pretty sure it's powered by an unstable fusion reactor. If that goes up it'll take all of us with it.'

'Any other aircraft?' one of the marines asked.

'As you know, until we deploy the Phalanx arrays we're sitting ducks. After that — and bearing in mind their Redut system won't discriminate, I wouldn't fly a Timberwolf within a hundred miles of here…'

The micro drone zipped away. Zak Law's face flashed back up on the screen.

'So, the key to this is speed. One: get across the ice as quick as you can, don't stop for anything. Two: get through their perimeter defences. Three: engage and neutralise any hostiles you encounter. Finally, destroy the target. We have just one hour to do it, gentlemen. As ever, I don't want anyone taking any unnecessary risks with their lives, or with the lives of their comrades. Go in fast, go in hard — come back safe.'

'Sir — yes, sir!' the marines bellowed in reply.

They were silenced by a hollow grating and moaning noise that reverberated around the bay, as the Tecumseh broke through the sea ice. The marines dashed to their snowmobiles as the cargo bay doors above them started to open. Sheets of ice cracked and slithered down the dull metal doors and hundreds of gallons of phosphorescent green Arctic seawater poured over them.

The marines ignored the drenching. They watched intently as the sub's 21-pod Phalanx missile platforms raised above the hold doors and swung into position. Sailors stripped off the safety seals on the back of each pod, their numbed fingers working quickly — every second they were out of action, the *Tecumseh* was defenceless against air attack.

One of them punched the fail-safe: the air defence systems were active.

The cargo hold echoed with a deafening din as the marines started up their snowmobiles, their engines snarling as they revved them up.

Elliot Murgia's voice came over the communicator:

'Target straight ahead. Platoon commanders — on my word…'

Hatches opened along the starboard side of the hull. Massive steel gangplanks crashed down onto the ice.

'…In file by platoon, let's move out!'

Warren swung his snowmobile into the first wave, rattling across the gangplank, then surging out onto the ice. After them came two-man machines dragging sleds with heavy Dominator anti-armour guided weapons. Last out were the engineers' sno-cats, laden with the demolition charges.

Outside, a sombre yellow smudge spread across the southern sky, bathing the landscape all around them in a dirty ochre half-light. Warren sped up and fell in behind Murgia. Off to his left the conning tower of the *USS Madison* broke through the ice, rearing up above the featureless landscape like a medieval fortress.

His communicator crackled into life, it was Monroe: 'Guys, I've got a revised ETA for you. Looks like our friends could be in the locale in forty minutes, maybe less.'

*

Siv steeled herself, ready, waiting for them to come for her — but no-one came. Something was happening, the alarm was for something else — but what? Were they under attack? What if they were? If the sub was sunk she'd go down with it — and that'd be stupid, real stupid. She had to find a way out. The Enemy was everywhere, though. She'd never get out, she was too conspicuous in her NATO fatigues — too damned obvious.

But, she remembered, the Russian sailor she'd just killed was probably about the same size as she was.

*

Murgia waved him forward. Warren rode up alongside him.

'Where's the target?' the marine yelled over his communicator. 'I don't see it!'

'This is Law — we're locked onto the coordinates — I don't see the conning tower.'

Warren peered out to the east. He could see the cluster of shacks — but there was no sign of the submarine. Warren flipped his visor to infra red. There were targets straight ahead: small heat sources, scurrying around. Everything else was cold.

'It's out there,' Warren yelled back. 'They must have lowered the themselves down into the ice. They're getting ready to make a breakout. All they have to do is wait 'til the other two turn up and they can just submerge completely and go with them.'

'That's not going to happen, Warren,' Law barked. 'Not on my watch.'

Another voice came over his communicator: 'Weapons control, sir. We've acquired a target.'

'What have you got?' Law demanded.

'Three heat sources close together, half-high, low on the horizon. Looks like personnel on a conning tower. Permission to fire?'

'Granted,' Law barked.

Seconds later a RIM-116 missile screamed overhead from the *Tecumseh*. Its infra red imaging located the heat source, then its passive seeker took over, running along a terminal guidance radar beam — straight to its target. Warren watched as it arced over them, spinning like a rifle bullet.

There was a brilliant white flash — the sound of the explosion followed a second later.

A deadly firework display of missiles streamed out from the Russian base, twisting in mid air as they acquired their targets — and screaming straight for the attackers. The sky above them turned into a boiling cauldron of fire as the Phalanx arrays on the *Tecumseh* and the *Madison* deployed automatically to intercept them.

The barrage fell amongst them: explosion after explosion sent snowmobiles skittering and slewing across the ice. Warren was thrown violently forward as a missile hit a two-man snowmobile behind him, vaporising it instantly in a massive sheet of flame.

Missiles that missed their mark slammed into the ice field, breaking it up — turning the ice sheet into an archipelago of bobbing islands. Another blast sent Warren careering across the ice, struggling to control his machine.

A dozen voices came over his communicator at once:

'Shit — that was the Cap!'

'Oh — did you see that?'

'This is Warren!' he yelled: 'What's happened?'

'Captain Murgia's gone, sir. Ice opened up in front of him…'

'… then closed right up again…'

'Alright, I'll take command now.'

'Roger that, Commander.'

'Follow me!' Warren yelled. 'We've got to get out of this kill zone!'

He looked over his shoulder — they were with him. 'Keep moving!' he yelled, urging them onward. Men who had been thrown off their snowmobiles ran on, stumbling and struggling — until they could scramble up onto the back of another snowmobile. Still the missiles fell amongst them, creating vast rents and craters in the ice that swallowed man and machine in one. Warren egged them on — they had to get inside the target acquisition area — they had to get closer.

In the half-light he could make out the enemy submarine rising up above the cluster of shacks, plumes of black smoke belching from its conning tower.

Ahead, the ice field was littered with frozen corpses of polar bears.

'Stop!' Warren yelled, slewing his snowmobile, screaming and skittering to a halt. 'We're at the perimeter!'

The motion-triggered guns crackled into life, spattering the ice all around them. A snowmobile reared up, jettisoning its two-man crew, sending them sprawling across the ice, and speeding on toward the perimeter. Battered and blazing it exploded in a pall of yellow flames and dense black smoke.

In the dull light Warren could make out the shapes of men in black running, crouched over, deploying behind the perimeter guns, taking aim — waiting to pick off any attackers that survived the deadly crossfire.

'Fan out!' he cried. 'Fan out and take cover!'

Monroe came over the communicator: 'Thirty minutes and counting, guys.'

A missile plunged through the ice, exploding in the waters beneath. The ice was rent asunder, throwing up great blocks that fell among Warren's men. His communicator was drowned with screams and cries for help.

A marine banged him on the shoulder: 'We're still in the target zone!' he yelled.

Warren nodded. The perimeter and the kill zone overlapped — nowhere was safe. Looking around he could only see about twenty men — too few to rush the perimeter. They had to get through the defences, though — and they had to do it now.

'Bring up a Dominator!' he yelled.

Silence.

'Is there a Dominator team out there?'

His communicator crackled into life: 'Yo! Coming up right behind you, sir.'

A battered snowmobile lurched to a halt beside him.

'Sure am glad to see you, sir…'

'Get down!' Warren yelled, throwing himself at the troopers and dragging them to the ice, as a missile spiralled over them — the heat from its rockets scorching them as it passed.

'Shit…' the American muttered. 'That would've taken my head off…'

The marines scrambled back to the sled. Together they struggled to set up their Dominator, hampered by their clumsy Arctic gear. Finally in frustration, they threw off their heavy mittens and set up the missile using their lightweight under-gloves.

*

Siv opened the door and peered out. The coast was clear. The Russian boy's uniform fitted pretty well — his *telnyashka* striped shirt was a bit tight, so she'd had to discard her brassière. But, all in all, she figured she looked the part — just so long as nobody looked too close at her.

She jammed on his *pilotka* cap and stepped out onto the corridor.

Looking all around, Siv tried to get her bearings. She was up by the crew's quarters above the galley. Of course, she thought, that made sense — they'd want their fuck toy nearby in case one of them felt a bit horny in the night…

She sprinted along the corridor and leapt down the stairway to the galley, three steps at time. Suddenly the whole submarine was rocked by a massive explosion. Siv was thrown hard against a bulkhead. Falling head over heels down the stairway she landed sprawling on the galley deck.

A sailor running by stooped to help her up. Just at that moment the sub's systems switched to low power — instantly bathing everything in blood-red light.

The sailor muttered something unintelligible.

'*Spasibo,*' Siv muttered back, staring down. It was the only Russian she knew. It seemed to satisfy him, though. He carried on across the galley and was gone.

She could hear the rumbling of explosions outside, all Hell seemed to be breaking out — it was time to get out of here, she thought — and get out quick.

*

Warren scrambled back to the Dominator and tapped on the nearest marine's helmet,

'What's your name?' he asked.

'Rogers, sir.'

'OK, Rogers — you see those camouflaged cabins?'

'That where you want it?' the marine said.

'Just in front of them,' Warren replied. 'I want to blow a hole in the perimeter defences.'

The other marine was working on a computer screen. Rogers tapped him on the shoulder and pointed across to the target on the screen.

'That's where the man wants it.'

The other marine nodded:

'Targeting's all blown to hell, but I reckon I can hit it.'

'He'll get it, sir,' Rodgers cried back to Warren. 'He'd better do — we're the only Dominator team that's made it through!'.

Rogers took aim and launched the missile — it roared out of its cradle and screeched toward the target. The other marine's attention was fixed on a touch-screen, making fine adjustments to its track.

Warren watched as it sailed over the perimeter and slammed harmlessly into the cabin behind.

For a long moment nothing happened — then the whole cabin burst apart, sending missiles spiralling in all directions. One of them arced high into the sky, hanging there for a long instant — then, toppling from the peak of its trajectory, it fell screaming down on the submarine, bursting into a dazzling sheet of white light.

The fighting stopped — there was silence all around the battlefield. Everyone stared in amazement as the stern of the Russian submarine started to surge up through the ice.

*

Siv was flattened and thrown back by the pressure wave of an explosion. It came from the back end of the submarine — where the reactor was. Moments later a screaming alarm pierced her ears. What the Hell was that?

Sailors scrambled past her, shouting and yelling — all making for the front — frantically trying to get away from the stern. What was going on?

She could see the hatch she'd come in by straight ahead, only a few metres away — and no-one seemed to be taking any notice of her…

The submarine groaned — Siv felt a sickening lurch in the pit of her stomach — what was happening now? She grabbed the hatch wheel and span it — and flung the door open.

'Oh shit!' she yelled. Her door opened onto a sheer drop — down onto the roofs of the cabins below. The cabins were all on fire.

Suddenly there was an explosion inside the submarine — the force of the blast catapulted Siv out of the hatchway. She fell, tumbling through a cabin roof — and plummeted into a blazing inferno below.

*

Monroe came over the communicator: 'Revised ETA: twenty minutes and closing — their reactors must be red hot.'

The Russian base was burning from end to end. But they still didn't know if the perimeter defences had been knocked out by the blast. Warren knew there was only one way to find out. He jumped on his snowmobile, started it up and opened up the throttle full — its kevlar track skittered for a moment, then got a grip on the ice and propelled him at full speed, straight for the enemy perimeter.

'This is stupid…' Warren muttered, gritting his teeth. It was probably the most reckless thing he'd ever done. He cursed himself for doing it. But they had to break through, they just had to. He tucked his body low behind the windshield — not that that would be any good against a machine gun, he thought — and braced himself for the impact of a hail of bullets.

The snowmobile bucked under him as he rode headlong at the blazing enemy base. He was close now, he could feel the intense heat of the fires.

Suddenly he was through — the perimeter was behind him. He pulled up sharply and turned in his saddle — waving the "all clear" to the marines, who rose up from the ice and followed him.

*

Fire — shit — fire everywhere! How the Hell was she going to get out?

Siv recognised the blazing ring of fire straight ahead — it was the corridor she'd come in by. Behind, her escape was cut off by the dull grey, slick hull of the submarine — black seawater sloshed up from underneath. To her right were the two Redut launchers — bad place to go, she thought — real bad.

There was only one way left. She put her head down and ran straight for the ring of fire.

Bursting through the door into the drying room she made straight for the garbage hatch. Everything around it was on fire, but there was no place else to go. Dodging blazing beams and smouldering lumps of insulation falling all around her, she mad a lunge for the garbage chute, swung the lid open and dived in.

Shit it was hot! The steel walls of the chute were blistering hot — worse than her uncle's sauna! She scrambled out the bottom, straight into a pile of warm, unconsumed garbage, mixed with snowmelt. It smelt disgusting, but she didn't care — she was out.

As she scrambled away from the flaming cabins she was suddenly hit by the Arctic cold, freezing her and dragging the breath from her lungs. She couldn't go back, though — and she knew that trying to keep warm by standing next to a bonfire packed with missiles, with bullets flying everywhere was a real stupid idea.

But she had to find somewhere warm quick — before she froze to death.

*

'Look, sir…' one of the marines pointed to the bow of the submarine: '… They're abandoning ship!'

Tiny figures were sliding down the sides and holding up their hands as they hit the ice. Warren flipped his visor to binocular view to see if he could see Siv among them — but there was no sign of her.

Zak Law's voice came over the communicator:

'Looks like they've had enough. Second platoon escort them to the *Madison* — at the double to keep them from freezing. Engineers, you're clear to deploy demolition charges. All other units support the engineers — and keep on the lookout for any last pockets of resistance. You have ten minutes. Law out.'

'I'm going aboard, Zak,' Warren said.

'What the Hell for?'

'There's a chance that Siv Jagland could be on there.'

'OK, Warren, it's your funeral. But I'm not waiting around. I'm still going to blow that sub in ten minutes.'

'Got that, Zak,' he replied — Law wasn't known for changing his mind.

Warren dashed to the submarine, his boots creaking and crunching as he struggled through the weakening ice. Pushing past a bedraggled group of sailors, shivering in the Arctic wind as they waited to be moved off, he scrambled up onto the hull, forcing his gauntlets into hand-holds, his spiked boots scraping on ice-scored titanium. Bewildered sailors issued from escape hatches all along the hull. Warren made for the nearest one, at the base of the conning tower.

Inside, the emergency lighting was failing, flickering between dull red and darkness. Warren flipped to image intensifier and peered into the gloom. Straight ahead of him was the golden cylinder, tapering as it rose up to the top of the conning tower.

'This is Warren. I'm going over to record. Can you send a backup to Leo — just in case I don't make it out of here?'

'Roger that,' Monroe replied. 'And you've got nine minutes — I'll keep you updated, we don't want to lose you.'

'Thanks for that, Dan.'

He clambered down a steel stairway. Below him, a bank of computer consoles blazed, their self-destruct sequences triggered by the order to abandon ship. Slumped over one of them was the body of a man, flames licking up the sleeve of his white lab coat. Blood was still spurting from a gunshot wound in the side of his head.

'Are you getting this?'

'Sure are,' Monroe replied. 'Kind of weird.'

'We don't have anyone else in the sub,' Zak Law added. 'You're the only one.'

'You don't have any time for this,' Monroe reminded him. 'You're down to eight minutes.'

Heaving open a hatchway door, he found himself back on the corridor where they'd had the shoot-out less than twelve hours before.

He tried to imagine where they could be keeping Siv — if she was on the sub at all. What if she was in the same cell they'd kept him in? It was the only thing he could think of. He set off down the passageway, his boots clattering on the steel deck.

As he passed the jetwing bay he noticed the door was lying on the landing deck from where they'd forced it off its hinges. In the middle of the launchpad a single jetwing remained. Standing upright, illuminated from above by the open doors overhead, it stood motionless, its domed helmet leaning forward. But it wasn't coupled-up, and its cocoon was closed — it was ready to take off.

Warren walked up to it, his assault rifle at the ready. He tapped on the visor. It flipped open.

'Hello, Yekaterina...'

She smiled, wickedly: 'Ah, now you know my name. That is sweet. But how did you know it was me?'

'The man at the computer console — I assume that was your handiwork?'

Yekatarina wrinkled her nose: 'Pavel. Poor Pavel. His orders were to kill me rather than let me fall into enemy hands — even nice ones like yours. But the foolish man made the mistake of telling me about it. So I knew that if I were to survive, the first thing I had to do was kill him.'

'Poor Pavel,' Warren replied, raising his assault rifle. 'Now get out.'

'I'm afraid I can't do that, Commander Warren. It's far too cold out there. Besides, I have a rendezvous with some of my fellow-countrymen…' She glanced up through the open bay doors: '…out there.'

'You'll have to cancel.'

'Oh, that would be so rude,' she pouted. 'Anyway, I don't need to do that — because you are going to let me go.'

'I don't think so.'

'But I do. And you're going to tell all your friends outside to let me go too.'

'Really?' Warren replied, sceptically: 'Why would I do that?'

'Firstly, because if anyone fires on me there's a good chance — a very good chance — that this thing will just explode. And you know what that looks like, don't you Commander?'

Warren didn't reply.

'Secondly,' she said, smiling wickedly, 'You wouldn't really want to kill me — not when I could be carrying your unborn child…'

'Don't be ridiculous…' he muttered.

'Oh, please, commander — it's really quite natural. You know — when a man and a woman have sex?

Warren was stunned — how could that be true?

In his moment of hesitation, Yekaterina blew him a kiss, snapped her visor shut — and sent the jetwing soaring into the sky.

'Don't fire!' he yelled over his communicator. 'Let the jetwing go! This is Warren! Let it go!'

'Roger that, Warren,' Zak Law said over the communicator. 'But you'd better get yourself out here right now — 'cause we've got ourselves a helluva problem.'

*

Warren scrambled up a stairway back out onto the hull.

The giant looming disk of the enemy VTOL hovered overhead, a halo of crackling blue lightning radiating all around it.

'What do we do, sir?' a marine asked. 'Our orders are not to fire on it.'

'That order stands,' Warren replied. 'If it goes up we're all dead. Everyone get under cover — get out of its line of sight!'

'You've got three minutes, Warren,' Monroe reminded him.

So, this was her rendezvous, Warren thought. Yekaterina was going to get clean away. And, if she wanted she could kill them all now — and there was nothing they could do to stop her. Better that a few men died out here on the ice than losing both submarines and their crews.

The VTOL rose menacingly above them. Warren stared at it hanging in the sky — and as he did it seemed that it started to wobble uncertainly. Suddenly it lurched to one side, gradually losing altitude, until it was only a few feet above the ice.

The blue lightning faltered and went out. The craft slid backwards, crashing through the ice, embedding itself, poised precariously — sticking up like a giant child's toy. Then, slowly it started to sink. Marines swarmed toward it, clambering on the bumping, rocking flocs all around the crash site as the VTOL slipped through the ice, slowly disappearing into the depths of the sea.

Just as it was about to disappear completely, an ejector seat shot out, splintering through the cockpit and sliding, skittering and spinning across the ice, totally engulfed by its billowing orange and white parachute.

As it came to rest a few feet from the submarine, Warren heard a woman's voice:

'Oh, shit…'

He knew that voice. It was the one he wanted to hear more than any other. He slid down the side of the submarine and fell crashing into a pile of broken ice. Scrambling and stumbling, he reached the ejector seat just as Siv managed to scrabble through the swathes of parachute silk.

'Well, that wasn't exactly as I planned it…' she said, staring up at him, still buckled into the ejector seat and wearing a Russian sailor's uniform.

'You mean you had a plan?' he asked, helping her to her feet.

'Sure I did!' she replied, indignantly. 'I had to find somewhere warm and out of the way, so I thought that'd be a good place,' she said, nodding toward the hole in the ice where the VTOL had sunk. 'There were three Russians on board already. At first they thought I was one of them.' She laughed: 'By the time they realised I wasn't, I'd locked myself into the cockpit. I took one look at the controls — they were the same as a jetwing. So I thought "Well, Siv — here's your chance to do something to help our guys out there…" '

She glanced at Warren guiltily: 'Turns out I didn't have any more luck with that than I had with the jetwing…'

'God, Siv,' he whispered, taking her in his arms and holding her tight. 'I'm glad to see you safe.'

'Not as glad as I am…'

Law came over the communicator: 'Warren — are you out?'

'I'm just by the sub, Zak.'

'Well you've got one minute to get the Hell out of there!'

'Let's go!' he cried, grabbing Siv's hand and dragging her to his abandoned snowmobile. Siv clung on tight to Warren's back as he opened the throttle wide and sent the snowmobile snarling and skittering across the ice.

'What's happening?' Siv yelled.

Warren's reply was drowned out by a deafening explosion that sent their snowmobile bucking into the air. The ice beneath them lurched — then cracked and shattered under the force of the shockwave.

It was breaking up all around them.

'Shit,' she cried. 'They're trying to kill us!'

The Kevlar tracks rattled and skittered — the engine screamed as the ice floe beneath them sank under their weight. Warren wrestled with the handlebars, weaving to the left and right — throwing up green sheets of seawater — as he struggled to get purchase.

His eyes widened with horror as a great hole opened up ahead of them. They weren't going to make it. They weren't…

A second, much larger explosion threw them forward, launching them from their snowmobile and propelling them, rolling and slithering across the ice.

Warren came to rest, staring up at the stars.

'Siv!' he yelled. 'Where are you? Are you OK?'

'I'm underneath you,' she said, punching him in the back.

He rolled over and released her. Together they struggled to their feet and watched as the submarine sank, sliding stern-down into the dark waters of the Arctic.

'Wow,' he said, taking off his helmet and ruffling up his hair. 'That was … pretty exciting.'

'…it was,' Siv replied, exhausted — the adrenaline draining from her bloodstream — she felt like her knees were going to buckle under her.

'I think from now on I'll stick to strategy…'

'Uh-huh?' Her mind felt so numbed, it was a struggle to get any words out.

'I guess you'll be glad to get back to the *Etterretnings*.'

The word stunned Siv back to her senses — it was like he'd slapped her in the face.

'Oh, no, Warren. I'm not going back to *Jåttå* — not after this — no way.'

'You don't have to,' he replied, peering down at the chronometer on his visor. 'I applied for your transfer to the Northern Rangers before we left Stavanger. You just had to complete your twenty days in the Arctic without logistic support — which you did ... about thirty minutes ago.'

'Wha...' Siv replied, dumbly. She couldn't believe what she was hearing.

'That's right, Sergeant Jagland. When we get back you're joining the *Jegerkompani,* as their new specialist in surveillance and electronic warfare.'

'Fuck, Warren — I could kiss you.'

'I'm alright with that.'

Siv threw herself into his arms, jumping up and wrapping her legs around him — and kissing him long and hard on the mouth.

Then, suddenly, she pushed herself away:

'Look,' she said. 'This is all very romantic. But can we go someplace else – I'm freezing my ass off here.'

*

Excerpt from SOMMERKRIG — the second Warren/Jagland Arctic adventure

Siv Jagland could barely contain her excitement as she gazed down from the AW101 helicopter, travelling low and fast, skimming across the narrow waters of the Porsangerfjorden. The pilot jabbed his finger straight ahead toward a massive grey mountain that dominated the skyline:

'That's Čalbmelanrašša,' his voice chirped over her headphones. 'That's where we're heading.'

Her heart missed a beat. She could hardly believe this was happening. After more than three years of waiting, cooped up in the bowels of Mount Jåttå, staring at surveillance screens in the darkness, she was finally fulfilling her lifelong ambition. She'd been transferred to the *Jegerkompani* — the Northern Rangers, the Norwegian Army's élite Arctic warriors.

The pilot pointed down to where the wooded hills met the shoreline: 'The base is strung out, all the way up the valley. They moved there after the Setermoen bombing.'

Siv remembered the incident well, even though she'd only been a teenager at the time. The big base at Setermoen was the home of Brigade Nord, the army group that defended the northern half of the country. The *Jegerkompani* had been shipped in as part of a cost-cutting exercise. Unfortunately, another economy measure had been to outsource security at the base to the lowest bidder.

The bombers had targeted the ranger barracks. Six devices exploded simultaneously while the rangers were sleeping. More than a hundred men and women had been killed, and as many more were so badly injured they would never serve again. The press said it was a terrorist attack, but the perpetrators were never found. Investigators went through the wreckage of each building with a fine-tooth comb, but they didn't find anything: no detonators, no components, no casings — nothing.

At the time there was a lot of talk about disbanding the unit and deploying the survivors to marine and paratroop companies. *Jegerkompani* had never been popular with the politicians and defence chiefs in Oslo. The

Russians were always haranguing them about some outrage or another the rangers were supposed to have committed along the frontier. Wouldn't it be easier, they suggested, if the *Jegerkompani* just went away?

Then, one night, they did just that.

The survivors filtered back to Porsanger. Their old base had been sold and redeveloped long ago, so they carried on up the east coast of the fjord and made a new stronghold for themselves in a deep, narrow valley in the shadow of the mountain, chopping down pine trees to make cabins, blasting caves into the rocks — and blocking off the the foot of the valley with a formidable stone bulwark, topped with a five-metre high stockade — like a viking fortress. And that's where they stayed.

Nowadays the political climate was very different. Norway no longer jumped every time the Russian bear snarled, and the *Jegerkompani* was in the front line of their "Winter War" — the hidden war, far from prying eyes and cameras — the war for possession of the Arctic.

But the rangers hadn't forgotten that night at Setermoen. They didn't trust the government or the army command anymore — they ran everything for themselves. Supplies and hopeful recruits appeared at the stockade and were taken up the valley on ranger transports. Failed recruits — which was most of them — came back down with the garbage. And from time to time, especially during the winter months, an honour guard made up of every man and woman on the base would solemnly bear the ashes of their fallen comrades through the gates of the stockade to pass on to their waiting families. The *Jegerkompani* didn't outsource anything — they even cremated their own…

The pilot's intercom interrupted Siv's train of thought:

'Sorry, Sergeant Jagland, I've just been ordered make a quick stop at Banak.' he said, cheerfully, banking his helicopter round to the south. 'Shouldn't be too long, and then we'll be back on our way.'

While they were hovering over the fjord, waiting for clearance to land, Siv gazed out over the airstrip. Banak army base shared its facilities with Lakselv North Cape civilian airport. It was a partnership that worked well for the army: the base wasn't large enough to operate the airstrip all on its own. On the fjord side, nearest them, three rescue helicopters were lined-up waiting for any emergency; next to them a small Antonov transport aircraft was being refuelled. All very quiet, very orderly — very Army.

The civilian airport was far busier. Planes from all round Scandinavia and the Baltic states used it, including Russians, en route to Tromsø and the new Arctic oilfields beyond. While they were hovering Siv counted six airliners, all different makes and liveries, taking-off and soaring into the clouds.

The pilot gave her a "thumbs-up" signal. They'd been cleared to land.

*

A soldier in combat fatigues was waiting by the helipad. Bent over double, he ran to the helicopter as soon as it touched the tarmac and swung the door open:

'You Jagland?' he barked. Siv noticed the wolf's head patch on his shoulder — *Jegerkompani*.

'Yeah, that's me.'

'Get your kit. You're coming with us,' he yelled over the din of the rotor blades and tore off toward the transport aircraft.

Siv grabbed her kitbag, waved to the pilot and ran after the ranger.

Six men were crowded into the back of the cramped little Antonov. An older woman, with a major's star and bars above her wolf's head patch, sat at the front. The only remaining seat was next to her — an old Heckler & Koch MSG90 marksman rifle was slung unceremoniously over the back.

'Siv Jagland?' she said, brusquely. 'I'm Tuva Torgersen. We only use first names, so you call me Tuva, OK? The firearm's yours — check it and clean it thoroughly. If you need to piss there's a hatch in the floor at the back. Right, that's the welcome talk over. Sit down and buckle up.' She tapped on the pilot's shoulder: 'Let's go.'

***

Also by Ed Bowie:

SOMMERKRIG

CARNIVAL of HATE

TOTALITY

TOTALITY: The Lost Eclipses

MANDELMAN

NATURAL PREDATORS OF MAN

For younger readers:

ORC WORLD

In preparation:

PITERAQ — the third Warren/Jagland Arctic Adventure

ACT of MALICE

PURSUIT of EVIL

Printed in Great Britain
by Amazon